SOUL OF THE DRAGON FAE

Book One

KAY ARWEN

BALBOA.PRESS

A DIVISION OF HAY HOUSE

Balboa Press books may be ordered through booksellers or by contacting:

Balboa Press
A Division of Hay House
1663 Liberty Drive
Bloomington, IN 47403
www.balboapress.co.uk
UK TFN: 0800 0148647 (Toll Free inside the UK)
UK Local: (02) 0369 56325 (+44 20 3695 6325 from outside the UK)

Original artwork by Kay Arwen
Illustration by Kay Arwen
Cover design by Kay Arwen

Print information available on the last page.

ISBN: 978-1-9822-8959-1 (sc)
ISBN: 978-1-9822-8957-7 (hc)
ISBN: 978-1-9822-8958-4 (e)

Library of Congress Control Number: 2025901804

Balboa Press rev. date: 02/04/2025

This book is dedicated to Angelo and Lilo …
and to fellow free spirits everywhere …
Shine!

PART ONE

IANNA

CHAPTER 1

Isle of Skye, Scotland: Eighteenth Century

It was early dawn. The beach was deserted save for a lone heron standing like a sentry in the rocky shallows. At a sudden flash of movement in the water, the startled bird took to the sky, and seconds later the slender form of Ianna, a twenty-year-old Atlantian, broke the surface. She waded on to the black sand, the first light sparkling like jewels on her silver-scaled legs. Twisting water from her long auburn hair with blue webbed hands, she stared with bright turquoise eyes at the glen sweeping down to the shore from the black foreboding mountains beyond.

It must be here somewhere.

She took a laboured breath, the blue tone of her skin paling as Aweyna came to a standstill next to her. Her closest friend bore the same distinctive Atlantian traits, only her eyes were the usual deep-sea blue and her hair, the colour of golden seaweed.

Ianna indicated the needle-like pinnacles piercing the distant clouds. 'Over there.'

Aweyna pulled a face. 'I doubt the Druid would have hidden it on *his* doorstep.'

They slowly crossed the beach to its estuary, now white-skinned and human-like, save for the scales up to their waists. Then they took a track that led upstream through a pine forest. Here the air carried the heady scent of pine, and Ianna relished it, the aroma offering her some relief from its thickness. She surveyed the luscious green surroundings in delight and paused to examine the delicate pattern of a curled fern.

1

Someone's coming. Humans.

Their bare feet made little sound, but they were nearly upon them. Gesturing for Aweyna to follow, Ianna left the path and ducked into the undergrowth. Moments later two Scottish Highlanders, dressed in kilted plaids, strode past on their way to the shore. The Atlantians watched from their cover until the men disappeared and then continued through the forest in silence.

Eventually they came to where the trees gave way to the open moor at the base of the Cuillin mountains. Ianna scanned the glen from the treeline. Grasses, heather, and large clusters of dandelions and moon daisies stood undisturbed, save for the goldfinches that flew from the trees looking for seeds.

All clear.

They crossed the tufted grass to a wide burn, which fell down the valley in a series of pools and waterfalls. Ianna stood at the top of one waterfall and gazed down at the ice-teal water contained in the oval pool below.

I sense he was here, but Aweyna is right. Would he really have left a clue so close?

She gave a sharp rasping cough and, suddenly overcome with dizziness, stumbled across to a rock to sit down.

Aweyna rushed to her side. 'Want to go back?'

She shook her head and stared across the glen to the spot that haunted her dreams. 'It was over there …' She clutched at her chest as a sharp pain exploded in her lungs.

Aweyna drew her attention to a cluster of white flowers growing nearby. 'Look. Moon daisies. Breathe in the energy of the flowers. It will help.'

Mother's favourites.

Aweyna gathered some of the flowers and handed them to her. Yet before she could smell the scent, she began gasping for air like a fish out of water.

'Let's come another time,' Aweyna urged. Kneeling at Ianna's side, she placed her hands on Ianna's ribcage and sent healing energy into her lungs. 'Your brother will never forgive me if anything happens to you.'

'Which is why Gwynadon doesn't know we are here.' Ianna took a few deliberate breaths over the flowers and steadied her breathing. 'We must look now. I need to know.'

Following the burn to its source, they climbed to where an enormous avalanche of rocks had fallen, concealing the arched doorway that was hewn into the mountain. *They stole the light from the sun and the warmth from the air.* Ianna recalled the screaming figures carved onto the doors and shivered, an action that was not missed by Aweyna.

'Ianna!'

'Coming.'

Ianna reverently placed the moon daisies at the foot of the rockfall and then joined Aweyna in scanning the surrounding slabs for any clue as to the crystals' hiding place, but to no avail. Eventually she flopped onto a boulder, the lack of oxygen in her body now making her dizzy and nauseous.

The battle raged around the doorway, its gaping mouth leading into an abyss of darkness, men's eyes turning black as they succumbed to his power. Her own eyes glazed with tears.

'It wasn't your fault,' Aweyna said softly.

'Ever since I can remember, I've been told I'm the Dragon Fae destined to unite the shards and seal the doorway. Yet when the Druid gave me the crystals, I failed. Because of me, Mother died on the battlefield and Father ended up in there.' She threw a glance at moon daisies by the rocks.

'For the love of Neptune, you were fourteen! Your father died in honour, killing the beast that held the doorway open.'

'But trapping himself inside … If I had done my part, he wouldn't have had to.' She put her hand to her head as a sharp pain shot through it and glancing at the sky, caught sight of an unusually large crow high above them. She frowned at the dark shadow she could see around it and staggered to her feet. 'We have stayed too long.'

Back on the shore the sun was now an orange ball burning on the horizon. Ianna gazed at the orange and red reflections that shimmered across the water's mirror-like surface. 'We don't have light like that in Atlantia.'

Aweyna waded out, disturbing the illusion. 'No, but at least you can breathe!'

She made to follow but glancing down caught her reflection. The scales were gone from her legs and her hair was tied off her face by way of a bunch at the back of her head, making her white skin even more apparent. *Human. I look human.* She examined her body and, grateful to see her silver scales still intact, waded out to dive without giving it further thought.

CHAPTER 2

OXFORD: MODERN DAY

IT WAS EARLY DAWN. THE first light shimmered on the surface of the water, turning the river into a pink and orange ribbon. The kingfisher sitting on an overhanging branch turned a beady eye to the shallows, watching for the unsuspecting minnows to come back into sight. Seconds later the shoal shot past, disturbed by a larger creature coming to the surface. Startled by their speed, the kingfisher took to the sky, a flash of electric blue.

Kaia, a tall, slender twenty-year-old with long auburn hair held in a ponytail by way of a now wet crocheted scrunchie, watched the bird fly into the trees. Her unusual bright turquoise eyes were fixed on not only the bird's plumage but also the yellow and green light that emanated from it by way of its aura. She smiled, kicked her legs, then let her body glide to the riverbank. Here she paused, ensuring she was still unobserved. Then scrambling onto the rocks, she quickly retrieved her running gear. Getting dressed was difficult. The skin-hugging fabric stuck to her wet skin, but after much wriggling the blue Lycra tights gave in and were back in place. She turned back to the water and took a deep breath, consciously absorbing the expansive peace the scene offered. Then picking up a fallen leaf, she kissed it, and set it sail in thanks. Finally, after putting on her running shoes, she unfastened the leads of her two cockapoo dogs tied to the willow tree and reluctantly began jogging along the river path in the direction of her house.

Twenty minutes later Kaia ran up the narrow drive of a terraced town house, passing a faded camper van. An image of her deceased parents flashed into her mind, triggering the familiar feelings of anxiety and regret. She grimaced and retrieving the key from the upturned flowerpot next to the step, quietly opened the front door. However, the attempt at silence was fruitless. As soon as their leads were disconnected, the dogs scampered through the narrow hallway and in their exuberance knocked over a bike wheel that had been leaning against the wall. The wheel fell onto the tiles with a clatter that echoed through the early stillness.

Enough to wake the dead. Kaia involuntarily stiffened, but there was no immediate repercussion, so replacing the wheel she followed the dogs into the kitchen, where she filled the kettle. It had just finished boiling when the door opened and her partner, Rick, a twenty-three-year-old model with large dark-brown eyes, chisel faced and well-built, strode into the room, wearing road cycling gear and surrounded by a sludgy looking orange light by way of an aura. The dogs scurried under the table and squeezed against the wall, no doubt seeing muddy orange too.

'What time d'you call this?' Rick looked at her, pan-faced.

She glanced at the kitchen clock, currently displaying seven, and then looked back at him as though to say he could read the time for himself.

His face relaxed. He took a step nearer and putting his arms around her waist, planted a kiss on her mouth. 'Chillax. I'm just messing. What are you wearing for the gig tonight?'

A sudden knot in her stomach made it churn. Pulling away, she began making toast and coffee. 'Not sure. Maybe my black dress. I know I've worn it before but it's the dressiest thing I've got.'

'It's fancy dress.'

She turned abruptly, still holding the teaspoon she had been using to stir her drink, in time to see a flash of green light by Rick's face. 'Fancy dress? When did you find that out?'

'It's always been fancy dress – a costume ball. I told you.'

The green light turned darker. *Deceit.* He hadn't told her. She would have remembered. Going out with his model friends was stressful enough at the best of times. If he had mentioned that a costume was required, she would have ensured she had a great one lined up. She returned to stirring the cup, her head swimming.

'Babe, I'm going to pick up my costume later. I'll see what they've got left in your size.'

'Thanks.'

Rick strutted into the hallway, where she could hear him reconnecting the bike wheel to his bike. Seconds later, he left, closing the front door with a slam.

Realising she had been holding her breath, Kaia audibly let it go. Then opening an old biscuit tin, she took out two pieces of home-made chocolate tiffin. She put the cakes onto her favourite cracked-glazed blue plate, then transferred her not-so-healthy breakfast onto the pine table.

She must have been mistaken. Rick must have mentioned it. No doubt she had been so stressed with work, it had not sunk in. Putting on the purple hoodie hanging over the back of the chair, she folded her legs onto the blue seat-cushion, opened her laptop and clicked on a recent file.

'... In conclusion, for centuries people believed the world was flat, but we now know that perception is wrong. Yet humankind still struggles to shift constructs of how things are perceived. Time, or more specifically, the perception of a timeline with a designated past, present and future, could simply be a concept we cling to, just like our ancestors clung to the notion of a flat world. Quantum physics is proving the fluidity of time and possible time travel, so how can the reification of time be so rigid, or as straightforward, as a linear line?'

More like arcs, circles ... orbs ... She took a sip of coffee, opened a new file and began flicking through images she had sourced online. One, taken from the bow of a boat, showed a slender figure with silver fish scales on its legs, swimming through the waves.

Water fae. Mermaids have legs and not always a fish tail.

She moved on, scanning images of unusual figures dressed in unusual attire, caught on camera in equally unusual places.

If these are real, they prove time and space are more flexible than we acknowledge.

She flicked the screen back to her finished article. She had hoped writing the esoteric column of 'New Woman' would give her the opportunity to investigate new avenues to more traditional topics, but so far that had not proven the case. She had on occasion tentatively put forward proposals, but Layna, the magazine's editor, rigid in her agenda, had shot her down with whiplike rebuke. Instead of researching what she considered to be groundbreaking content, Kaia found herself writing articles that fed into current reifications, the latest brief, on past-life recall, being no exception. She hovered her fingers over the keyboard.

Submit this, and I'm in the firing line.

She closed the file.

The computer screen momentarily went black, showing the reflection of a young woman with no make-up and a slightly worn expression. She grimaced, looked away, and ate a piece of tiffin. When she glanced back, her reflection had changed. Her eyes were the same but now regarded her from a blue-skinned face, and her hair, although still auburn and long, now hung wet and loose over her shoulders.

Water fae.

She checked her hair was still in its scrunchie. Her reflection did the same, only the hand that touched her head had webbing between its fingers.

I've had too much coffee … or sugar …

She pushed the plate of chocolate tiffin across the table and distracted by buzzing, glanced to where a bluebottle was hitting against the window in a frenzy. She let the fly out, watching the light around it change from bright red to pale blue as it buzzed past the overgrown bushes, the washing line, and the wooden garden fence. *The humdrum of suburbia. Landlocked. Gridlocked. Just like me.* She closed the window and picked up one of her crystals from the window ledge, aware of energy swirling within it. *There is even more to a rock.*

She returned to her computer, opened a new blank page, and was staring at the blank screen when she was distracted again, this time by a news feed announcing further riots in central Oxford. *People are dissatisfied … things are shifting.*

Opening her email account she typed a message, attached the article she had finished, and paused her finger over the send button as an image of a gladiator arena flickered across her mind. She steeled her expression, clicked, and watched the system register that her email had been sent. A knot of unease grew in her stomach. The feeling became more intense, and after a few moments she picked up her mobile and rang through to the magazine office, where she was connected to Bella, her friend and Layna's secretary.

'Hello, girl! Layna's not in the office. Can I take a message?'

'I've sent my submission.'

'I'll keep an eye out. I'm looking forward to reading it myself.' Bella sounded full of enthusiasm. 'I've always been fascinated by past-life stories. I'm even thinking of having a regression into my dark distant past. Maybe I was an African queen—or Cleopatra!'

The hot bolt of doubt exploded. She should have spoken to Bella before she sent the article. She groaned inwardly and forced a light-hearted tone. 'I think Cleopatra. JD treats you like a queen!'

'Unlike Rick,' came Bella's retort. 'The way he treats you—'

'We're going to one of his modelling agency's events tonight … I was calling to give Layna the heads-up. I put my own spin on the article.'

'You got a death wish girl?'

She could picture the look on Bella's face. 'I know it's a risk. If Layna doesn't go for it, I can still catch the deadline.'

'Will pass that on,' Bella replied with a sudden air of efficiency as someone else entered the office. 'Layna will be in touch.'

CHAPTER 3

⬩⬩⬩⬩⬩

Ianna and Aweyna left the pod of dolphin and swam deeper, entering a craggy ravine the sides of which rose higher to form tunnels around them. Eventually they arrived at the tunnel mouth which housed the way into Atlantia. Aweyna swam ahead, but a disturbance in the water brought Ianna to an abrupt halt. She turned as a familiar voice echoed through her mind like a crashing wave. The Guardian.

What did you find?

The ravine looked empty, but she was not to be fooled.

There was no sign of the crystal. Perhaps he took it to another island.

It's on the Isle of Skye. I sense it.

There was movement through the water, and she caught a glimpse of glistening blue scales as the Guardian moved away. She turned back to the tunnel, swam on and seconds later she was swimming through a vortex of blue light which became green water as she entered Atlantia. Rays from its crystalline sun illuminated pieces of broken statues set on huge pillars, echoes of the once great city.

Ianna rose to break the surface. She gazed across the green ocean to a white coral beach framed by the life-giving calla-lily forest, which regulated the biome and provided oxygen. The lilies grew tall, greater than any tree in the third dimension, and were topped by cream and gold blooms that gleamed like temple spires. She took deep breaths as their honeyed scent carried across the water and slowly the colour returned to her blue skin.

Peace …

A force field separated the realm of Atlantia from the third dimension and its surface world, but through it the blue ocean could be seen, appearing as the topmost part of the Atlantian sky with sea creatures passing by instead of clouds. She watched a shoal of bluefin tuna swim past, then darted to catch up with Aweyna who was already on the shore.

'I'll never tire of the scent of Atlantian lilies,' Aweyna murmured moments later as they walked through the forest.

'That's just as well. It's the only smell here!' Ianna let the energy of the lilies fill her and watched in amusement as Aweyna stared at her now translucent form.

'How do you do that?' Aweyna asked as she reappeared.

'I just breathe in the energy of things and merge with it.'

'Making you invisible. Being dragon-blessed gives you so many gifts.'

She flinched. 'The Guardian made me a Dragon Fae and blessed me with abilities, but what good are they? I couldn't make the Dragon's Heart whole, and I'm the only Atlantian who gets sick in the third dimension. Maybe the dragon made a mistake.'

'I doubt that.'

Arriving at the edge of the forest they retrieved the shimmering sea silks they had hidden among the lily roots. Each twisted the fabric around her body, crossed it over her chest and then let it drape elegantly across a shoulder in the traditional manner. Then, as they left the forest, the white-coral castle with its three towers supporting the crystalline sun, an enormous crystal sphere that gave light and held the force field in place, came into sight. In the daytime the crystal glowed almost white, but currently its light had a blue tinge; the day was fading. They passed the coral statues standing guard at the entrance of the castle courtyard, impressive warriors in battle regalia supporting crystal points that were now beginning to glow as the crystalline sun faded.

'Promise me you won't mention we went to the surface.'

'Of course not.'

Walking up the three steps to the castle entrance, an arch carved as two leaping dolphins, they entered the vast, white-columned hall with its sweeping mother-of-pearl staircase, which resembled rolling waves.

Gwynadon, the King of Atlantia, four years Ianna's senior, clad in shimmering green and gold scaled body armour, strode across the hallway to join them. He was a tall and strong figure, with wavy brown hair brushed back from a handsome regal face, scales to his waist and, as with all Atlantian males, also swirling down his arms and across his chest. He scooped Aweyna in his arms and kissed her firmly on the mouth.

Aweyna blushed a deeper shade of blue and leant away. 'Ianna is your sister, but there is still a time and place.'

Gwynadon grinned. 'I have been in the third dimension. Only a few hours in our time, but that equates to a few days in theirs. I think that gives me an excuse.'

'And did you find anything unusual?'

Atlantians were advocates for peace and freedom. As king, Gwynadon led scouting parties to the third dimension to watch over the sea creatures, but Ianna knew that he had another motive too. Gwynadon was on the alert for any sign of Scathchornail. The shadow colonel may be trapped in Shadow Side, but his influence was far-reaching.

'Nothing of circumstance. Broken nets cast into the sea had ensnared a pod of seals. Aside from that, the ocean was calm. Neptune's blessings are with us. Come.'

They crossed the hall to enter a large banquet hall. Its long, elegant tables carved from coral were laden with shell platters filled with an array of dishes primarily made from seaweeds and sea fauna sweetened with lily nectar. As they entered, the other Atlantians, who had been seated in rows along the tables, rose to acknowledge them.

Gwynadon raised his hand and smiled. 'Friends, be seated and let us celebrate another day of peace and prosperity.'

The meal began, and the sound of murmuring voices filled the room like the rise and fall of waves. Ianna, sitting beside her brother, gazed around the room at her fellow Atlantians. The women were tall and elegant, dressed in various colours of shimmering sea silk made by mussels and woven into byssus cloth. The men, all warriors like her brother, were dressed in faulds made from sea serpent scales, or byssus tunics. Sitting among them, the children were dressed similarly to the adults according to their gender. *Serenity.*

She watched as Alevin, a six-year-old boy, reached a slender arm across the table to take a sea parcel which he proceeded to put whole into his mouth, his eyes widening as he tried to chew whilst keeping his mouth closed. His mission accomplished, and not learning from his mistake, Alevin repeated the endeavour. *Innocence.*

Yet Scathchornail sought to destroy it all. He had opened Shadow Side's doorway by twisting the mind of the great beast whose magic had kept it closed, and her father had disappeared into swirling blackness as he forced the beast back into Shadow Side, a fight to the death. Moments later the earth had groaned and trembled as the doors slammed shut.

Her appetite gone, Ianna pushed her plate of food away, made her excuses, and left the room. She climbed the mother-of-pearl staircase to the first floor and walked along a series of arched corridors heading for her chamber. This was a large, airy room, its ceiling inlaid with crystal quartz, housing a chair and her bed, which was formed from a polished giant clam inlaid with abalone shell.

Once inside she untwisted her sea silk and gazed from the window. The crystalline sun had faded, and the castle courtyard was now lit by the two crystals at its entrance. Their light was soft and subdued, two moons casting silver light onto the force field above. She gazed upwards, watching huge shadows pass by overhead. *Whales.* There was so much life in the third dimension, so much richness. There was harshness, it was true, even cruelty. The natural world there was a fight for survival. Yet there was beauty within that harshness that Atlantia, despite its elegance and poise, just could not match.

CHAPTER 4

✦✦✦✦✦

Sick and tired of hearing about the riots, Kaia clicked off the radio and finished putting up her hair. She checked in the mirror and dissatisfied with the result, untied the plait then ruffled her hair through. It was seven o'clock. They were supposed to be leaving in half an hour, and Rick still wasn't back. His predictable behaviour was tiresome. He would return, there would be a tornado of him changing and grabbing a drink. Then, once ready, he would expect her to be waiting near the door.

Another day. Rinse, repeat ...

She stared critically in the long mirror. Although not exceptional, her dress looked good, but her rubber-soled ballet flats weren't exactly dressy shoes. She would have loved to wear elegant heels, but her feet were oddly square at the toes, and pointed heels were implements of torture. Barely enough to blend in with the models on a good day, in this outfit, at a fancy-dress event, she was going to stick out like a sore thumb. She imagined the minimalistic costumes the models would squeeze into. Her body wasn't bad. Rick's fellow models had often paid her compliments, saying her tall willowy figure was perfect for the catwalk. Yet each time Rick had dismissed their nice comments and had gone on to critique her assets under the guise of good humour. She had laughed his remarks off, but in truth they stung and sat like gremlins on her shoulders, continuously reminding her of her shortcomings.

The door downstairs opened, and the proverbial whirlwind flew up the stairs. 'You can't wear that rag.'

She said nothing as he began to strip off his slim-fit shirt and jeans, replacing them with an elaborate pirate costume. A flouncy shirt was left provocatively open to the flamboyant sash tied around his middle, and black pants—well fitted in all the right places—were pushed into very expensive looking leather boots that came over halfway up his calves. She doubted they had been part of the costume hire, and they explained why he was back so late.

'New boots?'

'Yep. What about it?' He gave her a sharp look, quickly disguised by a flamboyant scooping up of a large pirate hat complete with a bright green ostrich feather. He bowed and swooped the hat onto his head. 'I'll grab a drink. I got you a costume. It's on the kitchen table.'

He clearly could not manage to carry it upstairs. The weight of his own costume and ego must have been too great.

Glancing at the small carrier bag on the table in the kitchen, her heart sank. 'Where did you get it from?'

'The costume shop. You know, the one you really like. There was nothing decent left in the hire place. It's a big do. I guess people had made plans.'

You think. The shop he referred to was one of her favourites. It sold a bit of this and a bit of that, and she did enjoy rummaging through its randomness. It was not, however, the sort of place you shopped to get something decent for a big social event.

She opened the bag and took out a tacky bright yellow foamy sock.

'I am not going to go as a banana! I'll take my chances in my dress.'

His mouth paused over the rim of his wine glass. 'It's fun. It will make people laugh.'

Yeah, for the wrong reasons. 'I'm not wearing it. Thanks all the same, but I'll go as I am.'

Rick refilled his glass and then ordained to pour one for her. 'You're not coming without a costume.'

'Are you serious?'

'Costumes are required. No girl of mine is going to show up without a costume. Have a drink. It'll be fine. Everyone will love it.'

Feeling numb, she took off her dress, slipped the yellow monstrosity over her head, and looked through the hole that now framed her face. Rick let out a loud guffaw and spat the mouthful of wine back into the glass.

'Hilarious. Come on, we've gotta go.'

CHAPTER 5

✦✦✦✦✦

THE CRYSTALLINE SUN CAST ITS first light across the castle courtyard and onto Ianna's face. She was sitting in the arched window, the giant clam shell bed undisturbed. She had been awake for hours trying to unravel the conundrum of how to sustain being in the third dimension and how to unite the shards when she had them. It was only a matter of time before Shadow Side's colonel came up with another way of opening the doorway. She had to find the shard and seal it, preferably before he did.

There was movement amidst the shadows outside, and a young couple emerged, walking across the courtyard hand in hand. Coming to a standstill they turned to face each other and embraced. Gwynadon and Aweyna. She stood abruptly and, to distract herself from the ache in her heart, grabbed the sea silk from where she had draped it over her shell chair then left the room.

Moments later she entered the large castle kitchen where food for all Atlantians was prepared. Its shelves housed shells filled with sea vegetables, sea nuts, and lily nectar. An enormous shell basin was set into the floor at one end, continuously filling with bubbling water by way of a geothermal source, and a huge white table was set in the middle of the room, around which several Atlantians had gathered and were currently deftly folding seaweed leaves over a prepared filling of sweet sea nuts. At the far end of the room was a doorway, the only other exit from the castle.

'Morning's blessings.'

'Morning's blessings, Ianna.'

An older Atlantian, her white hair elegantly twisted into a large dome on top of her head, scooped finished parcels into a woven basket and dipped them into the hot water. For an instant the smell of salt filled the kitchen before being dissipated by the scent of Atlantian lilies wafting through the open window. The steaming complete, the Atlantian placed the basket on the table and indicated for Ianna to help herself.

'Thank you.' She took a warm parcel, exited the kitchen door, and walked round the to the castle courtyard.

'Morning's blessings, Ianna.'

She turned. Aweyna was looking radiant. 'Gwynadon has left already?'

'He said he has much to do and left to complete surveillance early.' Aweyna looked at the half-eaten parcel. 'You're not planning on going to the third dimension alone?'

'I'm only going to speak with the dragon.'

'Will that help? He never gives you a straight answer.'

Aweyna was not only beautiful but astute; no wonder Gwynadon had fallen in love with her. She was happy for them both yet dreaded them marrying; she would lose her only confidante.

She forced a smile. 'I will be back in time for class.'

Moments later she was through the vortex and in the ravine. She swam slowly, sending her awareness into the caverns and tunnels that led from it. *There.* The smallest disturbance within the water, easily mistaken for stray plankton, but she was not to be fooled. She was not the only being who could breathe in the energy of a place and appear invisible.

I know you are here. I order you to show yourself.

There was another movement, a flash of scales, and then the elegant head of an indigo blue sea dragon slowly appeared in a cave entrance. It regarded her for a moment with commanding golden eyes before its voice rumbled through her mind like a storm stirring the ocean.

You presume to command me?

I do and I will. Other Atlantians may be intimidated by you, but I am not.

The dragon chortled, and dark blue steam shot from its nostrils to waft through the water around her. *No, the Dragon Fae is not like other Atlantians. You never were and you never will be.*

Stretching its slender neck from the mouth of the cave the dragon circled its head around her and for a moment Ianna found herself lost in an enormous eye. The sea dragon was a magical creature. It had foretold

17

Scathchornail's invasion, of it being her destiny to unite the two shards of the Dragons Heart Crystal and then use it to seal the doorway. It was this very dragon that had blessed her with its magic, making her a Dragon Fae and linking her to dragon-kind. It knew almost everything, including her innermost thoughts.

You torment yourself. Even if you had succeeded, the outcome would have been the same.

How can I stay long enough on land to find the other shard? How do I reunite them?

The dragon raised its head and regarded her in surprise. *The answer to both questions is the same. You must ground your energy in the surface world.* Its eyes softened as it breathed warm magic around her in the form of purple mist. Slowly the mist formed shadowy figures. *Remember the last words your mother spoke.*

The sound of the surrounding battle paled to nothing. Her hand shook as she wiped her mother's face, sending healing and willing the blood to stop pouring from her mouth.

'It's too late for me … follow your heart …'

Her mother grasped at the ground and finding a flower broken from its stem brought it into her line of sight. A moon daisy. Her eyes froze over.

The vision faded. Over five Atlantian years had passed, yet her fourteen-year-old self still felt the pain. Brushing tears from her eyes, Ianna stared at the fading form of the sea dragon.

It would be nice if just for once you gave me an actionable answer.

You misunderstand Dragon Fae. I have.

CHAPTER 6

IANNA SWAM ASHORE, HER MIND turning over what the dragon had said. It only ever gave enough information for her to work out the next step for herself. It was more than frustrating.

A bell suddenly rang out from the castle causing her to hurry through the now deserted kitchen to the entrance hall. She climbed the sweeping mother-of-pearl staircase and the winding staircase of one of the coral towers to enter a circular chamber, its only feature an impressive, sculptured octopus that sat against the wall, with extended arms that held record-keeper crystals. Aweyna and the high priestess, an older Atlantian dressed in a full-length white robe and wearing a silver circlet on her long golden-brown hair, were waiting with a group of young Atlantian girls.

As she entered the high priestess selected a crystal point from one of the octopus's arms and ran her fingers along it. Immediately the crystal projected a symbol onto the white wall, where it shimmered and slowly rotated.

'The last of the five light codes. This one represents air.'

The young Atlantians drew the symbol in the air, attempting to create it with healing energy. Some succeeded, whilst others created deformed shapes which faded to nothing. Ianna and Aweyna circled the room helping the girls become proficient and eventually the chamber was filled with beautiful swirling symbols. Energy emanated from these and feelings of love and freedom washed through the chamber.

'The dragon said if I ground my energy in the third dimension, I won't get sick.' Ianna whispered, coming to a standstill next to the high priestess. 'What does that mean?'

'When you are grounded, you are at home in your body, and in your environment,' the high priestess said. 'Perhaps focus on the things that make you feel like you belong.'

The lesson over, Ianna sat with Aweyna on the window seat of one of the castle's arched windows and rested her head against the intricately carved waterfall that formed the side.

'It all weighs so heavily,' Aweyna said. 'I wish there was someone for you. Your burden might not feel so great if you had someone to share it with.' She paused. 'What about Lasulet?'

Follow my heart.

Ianna did not respond. Instead, gazing at the vista, she drew a light code and blew the symbol towards the force field as the familiar shoal of tuna swam past. In one synchronised movement each fish turned to look down at her.

'You are able to use light codes in so many ways.'

The fish swam away.

'Yet I cannot use them to keep from getting sick.'

'If grounding is the answer, what does make you feel at home there?'

'Sea creatures ... and the creatures on land. We have no wildlife here. Atlantia is stark by comparison. ... Where shall we look next?'

Aweyna looked blank. 'For it to just disappear without a trace ... it's so odd. The Druid must have left a clue somewhere, one perhaps only you will understand. He knew Scathchornail would send his minions searching. A single shard has great power that Scathchornail could learn to wield and, with a shard in his possession, your task would be impossible.'

'It is anyway! If only I hadn't dropped it.'

'At least you saw the Druid retrieve it and run from the battlefield ... and you have been able to study the one shard.'

'I still haven't learnt how to connect it to the second.'

'Maybe not, but you have unlocked the five light codes. Perhaps you can use them to reunite the shards, healing the Dragon's Heart Crystal.'

'Perhaps.'

Aweyna was distracted by a sudden noise from the great hall below. 'Gwynadon is back. Let's see what news he has.'

Gwynadon and a group of warriors were standing in the great hall.

Two of them supported a third whose golden hair was twisted into a small knot on top of his head. He had a deep wound in his side.

'Take Lasulet to the healing pyramid. We will be there shortly,' the high priestess said, entering the hall from a side corridor.

The two warriors saluted and left, taking the wounded warrior with them. Aweyna gave Ianna a sideways glance which she deliberately failed to notice.

'How did Lasulet get so badly injured?' the high priestess asked when the warriors were out of earshot.

Gwynadon flashed a boyish grin which lit his demeanour in an instant. 'We came across a whaling vessel following a mother and calf. We distracted it.'

'You know better than to interfere with the affairs of man.'

Gwynadon regarded the high priestess intently. 'I know our parallel realms are interconnected, and I know all lives are divine. I will stand for life, especially when innocent lives are threatened.' The high priestess inclined her head, and Gwynadon continued. 'I trust and value your advice, as did my father and mother, but humanity can be a liability.'

Aweyna stepped forward. 'Yet our worlds are intertwined, they are our brothers and sisters.' She greeted Gwynadon, and the tension dissipated. Yet another display of her worthiness to be queen. The high priestess withdrew, beckoning for Ianna to follow.

Stepping from the white steps they passed a group of Atlantian children playing in the courtyard. The older children were creating orbs of light by way of healing energy from their hands which the smaller children were chasing and popping like bubbles. Her mother had played the same game with her. …

Blocking where her mind was taking her, Ianna walked on, following the high priestess through the forest to the clearing where the healing pyramid, built from quartz crystal, sat in its lake of salt water. They crossed over a crystal bridge to enter the pyramid's outer chamber. Once inside, Ianna twisted her hair into a tight knot and pinned it into place with a green crystal that she retrieved from a shelf carved into the wall. She glanced at the only other item, a box carved to look like a closed clam, then followed the high priestess into the inner chamber, with walls that joined in a pyramidal apex above them. Lasulet was leaning against an enormous crystal point set on the floor and pointing up to the apex. He looked pale and gave her a worn smile.

Ianna drew a light code and sent it through the pyramid wall, causing the water in the lake to rise. The pyramid chamber amplified the sound, and as the high priestess drew the other light codes Ianna began to sing light language, the elemental song that the Guardian had taught her. The rise and fall of her notes floated around the chamber in harmony with the tones from the water, and the crystal responded, sending a beam of light to the pyramid apex. The light expanded to fill the pyramid and for an instant was blinding. When it contracted Ianna stopped singing, and the pyramid filled with a deep sense of stillness. Lasulet stood slowly, his wound now completely healed. He looked at Ianna intently, but she turned before he could speak.

Back in the outer chamber, she opened the clam box and took out the crystal it contained.

'It all seems impossible.' She watched as the crystal began to glow with soft lilac light then turned to the high priestess. 'Our fate is intertwined with the third dimension, and to save both our realms, I must somehow rejoin this with its sister.'

'I am certain you will work out how. You saw the light codes within it.'

The symbols that amplified the Atlantian gift of healing. If she had known of them before, perhaps she could have saved her mother. She placed the crystal back in its box and clicked it shut.

'Mother said to follow my heart. Would a relationship really solve the dilemma?' She asked as they crossed the crystal bridge.

'Perhaps she meant follow what inspires you.'

She threw the high Priestess a blank look as Gwynadon came striding to join them.

'What news of Lasulet?'

'He has left already,' the high Priestess answered. 'There are many things that light you up, Ianna. The sea creatures for one.'

'I know of something.' Gwynadon grinned. 'We met Pendragon, and he asked to be introduced.'

'The kelpie?'

Living predominantly in the sea in a form that resembled a horse with mermaids tail, kelpies could also survive on land by transfiguring into beautiful white horses. Sightings were rare. If they were seen, it was usually when racing to the shore, half galloping and half swimming through breaking waves. Pendragon was one of the ancients, with a reputation for curiosity and fun.

'Now that does inspire!'

Sometime later found Gwynadon and Ianna swimming from the ocean ravine towards the Isle of Skye. Pendragon had been waiting and came racing towards them, scattering a pod of alarmed seals.

Pendragon.

The regal kelpie slowed his pace and let his horse–shaped forehead rest against her own. Immediately Ianna felt magic fizzing through her. *You have my friendship.* He flicked away and began to swim around her like an oversized excited puppy. *Shall we race your brother?*

In a swift movement Ianna swam onto Pendragon's back and held onto his seaweed-like mane as he sped away. Glancing over her shoulder she gave Gwynadon a provocative wave. Her brother was strong, but there was not an ocean's hope of him catching up with a kelpie.

· ◆◆◆◆◆ ·

Meanwhile, on the island, a pack of wolves ran through the forest undergrowth and came to a standstill in a small clearing. The dark grey alpha raised his head to stare at the canopy through piercing, green-flecked eyes that mirrored the colour of the pine trees. He sniffed the air, reading scent, but there was no trace of their quarry.

Seconds later Owen, a broad and lean well-built figure, with the same piercing, green-flecked eyes, stood up from the forest floor, bare save for the traditional plaid kilt, a short sword in a leather sheath he wore at his waist, and his sgian dubh, a long intricately carved dagger, strapped to his calf. He ran his hands through his ruffled dark hair, brushing it back from his handsome face, then dusted the dried pine needles from the wolf's head tattooed across his muscular torso. Crossing the clearing he stepped onto a narrow track and made his way to the shore, his bare feet making no sound. Their quarry could have changed form and flown away, but his instinct screamed it was nearby. He was not overly concerned. If the blasted thing intended an ambush, it would get more than it bargained for.

Distracted by a movement in the water, Owen instinctively crouched low. He clutched the sgian dubh and scanned the shoreline. To his surprise, a kelpie raced for the shore with an Atlantian woman on its back. The kelpie leapt from the waves, changed into an impressive white stallion, and then began to gallop along the beach.

Owen was transfixed. The Atlantian clearly loved the pace of their game, outstretching her arms to either side of her body as though to embrace the wind. They got to the far end of the shore, turned, and raced back, coming to a sudden halt as another figure emerged from the water, an impressive Atlantian male.

'What took you so long?'

'How am I supposed—'

'Race you back!'

Owen chuckled as the kelpie and the Atlantian woman disappeared back into the waves, leaving the male behind for a second time. Moments later he dived after them, leaving the beach deserted.

Yet Owen's instincts told him he was not alone. Something else had been interested in the Atlantians. Catching a movement in the trees, he muttered a curse. His instinct had been right. With a triumphant caw, an enormous black crow emerged from the shadows and took to the sky.

CHAPTER 7

K AIA SLOWLY REVERSED THE VAN into a car park space, checking the wing mirrors to ensure she was in between the lines. Not that she would get a parking fine, the car park was solely for visitors to the magazine office, but everything had to be just so when it came to the magazine. An attitude comprehensively epitomized by Layna herself. Turning off the engine, she checked her face in the vanity mirror. *You can do this.*

She muttered her prepared argument, wiped a finger under her eye to remove stray mascara and steeled herself for the forthcoming meeting. Layna had rejected the article, and she was daring to appeal.

Crossing the car park, she waited for the large glass doors to slide open and then forced her feet to enter the immaculate lobby. The rubber soles of her ballet flats squeaked on the taupe tiled floor, causing the receptionist on the main desk to look up. Kaia cringed, waved apologetically and then stepping into the lift, pushed the button for the top floor. As it lurched, she muttered a prayer of deliverance, and when it came to a halt, she stepped into the glass-walled corridor before its doors had finished opening. Her heart now pounding with adrenaline, she headed for Layna's office, catching her reflection in a section of the wall as she passed.

Blue skin. Loose wet hair.

She paused and took a step backwards.

Ponytail and not so elegant make-up ... I would have looked better without it. Wishing she had worn trousers and not the blue tea dress and cardigan, she stuck her head round Layna's door.

Bella, immaculately made up, wearing a chic blue tailored suit and heels, looked up from the keyboard. 'Kaia! Happy birthday. Twenty-one!'

25

She flinched. Halfway through the day, and Bella was the first person to give her birthday wishes.

'Good luck.' Bella gave a smile of encouragement as she clicked a red-nailed finger on the intercom to the office beyond. 'Kaia's here.'

The reply was instant. 'Show her in.'

She entered an airy office, with white décor and a white desk. The only flash of colour came from a large fern in a green pot set in the corner near the one large window, which displayed a view across the city. Layna's petite form, also clothed in clinical white by way of a Dior suit, stood leaning over the desk sending an email. Her body language spoke volumes, as did her spiky red aura.

A Rottweiler, ready for a fight. She took a deep breath to steady her nerves. 'Morning, Layna.'

Layna tapped a French-polished nail on the send button, picked up two sheets of paper from a white tray, and then clicked to the front of her desk.

'Is there more for modern man?' She slapped the papers down with force. 'What is that?' she said in a voice that did not invite any explanation. 'I'm disappointed, Kaia. More than disappointed. My brief was specifically tailored to the zeitgeist.'

Kaia pulled her attention from the Jimmy Choo heels. 'Past-life regression opens up interesting questions of how we perceive time.' She clenched her fist, deliberately digging her nails into her palm. 'It is current to explore that. I think people are looking for more.'

Layna gave an impatient flick of her hand. 'If you won't write what I ask for, others will. Understood?' The shoes returned to the other side of the desk, and Layna's attention, back to her computer screen.

Call you, Bella mimed as Kaia squeaked past her desk moments later.

She returned to the lift, pushed the button to the ground floor, and flopped against the wall, brushing tears of frustration from her cheeks.

Outside the office building, Kaia made a beeline to a coffee shop and purchased a takeout caramel latte. Then she headed for the river on autopilot.

An hour later saw her sitting in the shallows. She turned her face to the sun enjoying the sense of light behind her closed eyes. Images of Layna's pinched face – and three bitchy Egyptian priestesses fawning over Rick – drifted across the screen of her mind. She imagined the water washing them away and replaced them with her godfather's kindly face. Jim was a history professor and had been her parents' closest friend. She had lived with him until she was eighteen, then a year and a half later she had met Rick. She still wasn't quite sure why she had given up her flat and moved in with him, but she had. Still, there was a way out. She had to take the bull by the horns and move on.

Distracted by a cold wet nose nuzzling against her shoulder, she turned to discover one dog had found a ball. She playfully threw it into the river. Then, while the dog swam back and forth playing water football, she gathered moon daisies which were growing in profusion on the bank.

CHAPTER 8

DARTMOOR: MODERN DAY

THE TWO MILITARY TRUCKS SPLASHED along the boggy track over the bleak moor. Coming to a standstill by a craggy granite tor, the officer in the lead vehicle tapped a security code into the keypad set on the dashboard. The air tremored as an energy shield retracted to reveal an enormous structure made from dark-grey flecked metal, topped with strange black satellite dishes, resembling upturned fungi with spiked stalks.

The vehicles swept on. The force field re-formed, concealing their presence, and the base, from prying eyes. On their approach a large hangar door slid open at the foot of the structure. The vehicles drove inside, the doors closed, and the entire room sank to the complex below.

Gracilior, stocky and lean, with short dark hair, stood in the vast, dimly lit octagonal hangar staring at the lift from black soulless eyes. Beneath the veneer of human skin, his Skinwalker self, writhed. He had not left the base since he arrived, which meant he had not fed, and he was agitated, ready to explode. The colonel had forbidden the absorption of human staff, and despite his bulk, Gracilior was not about to contradict the colonel's orders.

Unlike Regalis. He glared as the tall, lanky Regalis entered from a small side corridor, stretching his body to adjust to the flesh he had ingested. 'You're a fool. Your activities don't go unnoticed.'

Regalis shrugged nonchalantly. 'The entire base is underground. It would have made more sense to complete the lowest section first. If plans can't be made to accommodate and feed us, I don't see why I shouldn't look after myself. Besides, I'm an inspiration. I'm showing humans what their future looks like.'

The lift doors opened, and the vehicles pulled into the hangar. An officer began barking orders, his breath visible in the cold, damp chamber. Gracilior flinched and stared at the man with venom.

'Take him. You want to,' Regalis taunted with a smirk. 'Absorb. Feed.'

'The substation *is* complete, you idiot, and the first delivery of flesh is due tomorrow. I'll feed then.'

The men began to file past, heading for the maze of corridors leading deeper into the subbase. Gracilior stepped from the shadows to accost them.

'The latest shipment of panels is ready. The colonel wants you to collect them.'

The officer flinched and gave a salute, deliberately avoiding Gracilior's eyes. Gracilior clenched his fists, turned abruptly, and marched for the transmission chamber.

'Your form is bulky, but you have no balls,' Regalis taunted from behind. 'Are you really one of us?'

They walked through a series of dreary corridors to the largest hangar in the base: a vast chamber with a ceiling over seventy feet above, housing both equipment that serviced the transmission tower and the tower itself, a dark, grey-flecked metal column holding a spiked, grey-glass dome which connected to a metal structure on the ceiling and then to the satellite dishes above ground. A narrow platform circled the base of the dome, accessed by a thin ladder fastened to the column's side. As the two Skinwalkers watched, a technician descended the ladder and, once back on the ground, opened a panel to flick a series of levers. There was a loud crackle, and the dome above began to fill with a swirling black lightning which then faded to nothing.

'Report.'

The technician crossed to a large table-like screen and began to pull and swipe as images appeared. 'The tower is transmitting from the seed crystal and linking to the mobile network ...' He broke off, clearly reluctant to continue.

Gracilior narrowed his eyes. Weakness. Always weakness. He could smell the man's adrenaline and his sweat. Regalis shuffled behind him.

The man swallowed. 'Transmission is weak and there is no other way to enhance it. We need more power.'

Gracilior strode away. 'Keep your smart remarks to yourself, Regalis,' he said before Regalis had the chance to speak. He indicated a piece of equipment at the far side of the hangar. 'Check for Skinwalker energy signatures and have them collected. The colonel doesn't want to lose the element of surprise. Until the transmission affects the entire populace, he wants Skinwalkers kept a secret. They are to be brought to the base to work on the monolith's construction.'

He watched Regalis saunter away and scowled. Regalis was walking a thin line. Feeding on humans was one thing. Mocking him was another. He would regret it.

Arriving at the green sliding door of the communication chamber, he ran his hand down a panel on the wall. Inside the dark metal-lined room, he crossed to a hexagonal plinth and placed his hand on its interface to connect to Shadow Side. The air above the plinth shuddered as a hologram of the colonel appeared: a middle-aged, six-foot figure, drawn and pale, dressed in a dapper Victorian gentleman's suit, complete with leather gloves and top hat. Gracilior gave his report. The colonel did not speak, yet Gracilior could detect a static in the air which became thicker with each passing moment. He clenched his fists, fighting his urge to react to the vibration.

The hologram sneered and the energy subsided. 'The tower functions.' The colonel spoke in a clipped voice. 'Once we have the crystal shard, it will be sufficient.'

The hologram shifted and Gracilior saw an enormous obelisk of black crystal that looked to be made of the same swirling black lightning as in the tower dome.

· · ✦ ✦ ✦ ✦ · ·

In his castle in Shadow Side – a foreboding black structure set on the pinnacle of a black mountain overlooking a charred desolate landscape filled with creatures that moved but did not live – Scathchornail ended the communication. Stepping back from the hexagonal plinth, he stood in the shadows next to the seed crystal, the source of Skinwalkers. His eyes narrowed to slits as he considered what he had gleaned.

Skinwalkers were no better than humans when it came to hiding thoughts. Gracilior doubted not only the effectiveness of the tower, but also the capability of the monoliths designed to disrupt the earth's magnetic field. Yet that was of no concern. What was unacceptable was blatant disregard of orders. Still, Regalis was right on one count, Skinwalkers were scarce. He would curb him when he was of no further use.

Making his way back through the gloomy cellar – its walls and ceiling riddled with dark calcite that in places protruded like thin imprisoned fingers – he stopped where rows of ancient oak barrels were stacked on their sides against the wall, the top row connected to dark copper taps. He picked up a heavy crystal glass from a shelf hewn into the rock and filled the bottom with liquid. Then, holding the glass near his face, he swirled it appreciatively. The dark red liquid clung to the sides of the glass, an unusual viscosity and an unusual iron bouquet. His special claret.

Leaving the cellar, he ascended a black spiral staircase to the floor above and entered a stone room of the castle. There was no light. Beings of the shadows needed none. Crossing to a black mahogany table supporting one of his many chess sets, he studied the game in play. There were a set number of pieces, a finite number of moves. He ran his gloved hand through the air over the black bishop. Immediately the piece slid effortlessly across the board and took the square previously occupied by a white knight. He gave a satisfied smile as the white knight flew from the board. Then, turning his attention to the white force, he made the white queen move forward three spaces.

Good.

Soon she would be exactly where he wanted her to be.

CHAPTER 9

'I CAN'T DO IT!'

A large, tattered crow with white opaque eyes soared from the gaping hole in the mountain and swooped across the battlefield towards her.

'Run!'

Her legs were shaking, and her muscles, now leaden, refused to work. Grabbing her hand, Gwynadon dragged her away, milliseconds before black lightning struck the ground. Another bolt came and another. She stumbled, dropping a crystal shard. She was going to be hit … there was a cry of pain …

'No!'

Ianna sat bolt upright. Out the window, the crystalline sun had not begun to shine. The castle grounds were still and silent, but she would not get any more rest. Aweyna was right. If she had someone to hold her, to share her innermost thoughts, then things could perhaps be different.

She stared at the crystalline ceiling of her chamber, making shape and form from the inclusions. *A turtle, a whale … a kelpie. Pendragon.* It had been exhilarating swimming with him. His magic would work wonders on her spirits now. She swung her feet onto the floor and slipped silently through the shadowed castle.

Ianna scanned the island's shoreline as Pendragon leapt onto the beach transfiguring into a stallion. He reared and whinnied, enticing her to run.

Your answer to everything. Striding from the water, she leapt onto his back. *To the end of the beach, then to the cottage!*

She glanced at the sea birds swirling above them. Higher than the gulls, silhouetted against the sun, was a different kind of bird. It suddenly dropped from the sky, disappearing into the forest canopy. Ignoring the sense of unease gnawing at her stomach, Ianna focussed on the thrill of galloping through breaking waves, but her joy was short-lived.

A large black wolf raced from the treeline, murder in its white opaque eyes. Pendragon startled, turned sharply and Ianna lost her grip. Falling to the ground, she found herself facing glinting fangs as the wolf bore down. Pendragon reared, slammed his hoofs onto the demon's back and knocked it from its feet, giving her the chance she needed. She drew the air light code and set it spinning across the ground, creating a tornado of sand. Yet before it hit, the demon changed form and took to the sky.

Pendragon snorted in disgust. *A creature from the shadows has no place here.*

She leant against him, consciously soaking in his bubbling energy. *I didn't know demons could transfigure.*

You should not explore the cottage. It's too dangerous.

It's gone, and I want to see.

Pendragon led her along a small track from the shore to a tiny stone dwelling set in a pine clearing. Ianna gazed in delight at the tiny wooden door and straw roof. She had seen human dwellings from a distance, but not up close or inside. She crept nearer and gently pushed the door open.

It was a single room with one window next to the door, sealed by wooden shutters fastened by a rusted metal bolt. She worked the bolt free, and the shutters creaked open, allowing rays of light into the shadowed room. She examined the soot-lined fireplace, the basket of chopped wood standing next to it, and the two stone shelves built into the wall above, holding a candlestick and white candle. Picking up the candle, she ran her hands along it, sniffed the blackened wick and then the soot in the fireplace. Both had recently been used. She examined the flagstone floor. *Freshly swept.*

Her eyes fell on the willow broom and the deep red rug in the corner. She tentatively gathered the rug then held it against her face, relishing its texture and smell. Lanolin, the scent of a wolf, and a male. She inhaled deeply, a reassuring scent of strength and …

Ianna!

She had sensed it too. Someone was coming. Hurrying from the cottage she hid in the trees as Pendragon raced for the shore. Seconds later a human, carrying a large she-wolf, his open shirt held tight against his narrow waist by a plaid kilt and wearing a leather sheath and sword, stepped from the trees. She drank in his athletic body, the wolf's head tattooed across his chest, and his aura, which shone like the sun. Seeing the door and window open, the man froze, and she ducked low. She waited until she heard him enter. Then, leaving her hiding place, she crept to the window.

The man had laid the wolf on the rug in front of the fireplace. There was a gaping wound on its flank where it had been shot at close range. The man lit a fire and turned his attention back to the animal. Gently stroking his hand down the wolf's cheek and neck, he slid a long knife from a sheath at his leg. Talking softly, the man swiftly inserted the knife into the wound and deftly removed a large ball of lead. Then he tore a piece of cloth from his shirt and pressed down hard on the wound. The wolf did not even flinch. The light around it looked thin and faded. It was going to die.

Drawing a light code, Ianna sent it through the window. As it sank into the wolf's body, the man exclaimed in astonishment and turned sharply to face her. For a second that felt like an age, Ianna found herself staring into deep green eyes the colour of sunlight through pine. She ran.

'Wait!'

Stopping among the trees she turned to face the man, now standing at the door.

'Can you heal her?'

She nodded and walked back, her heart pounding. Squatting by the wolf she drew the five light codes, directed them into the wolf's body, and then placing her hands over the bullet wound, softly sang. The wolf let out a breath of contentment as its muscles relaxed. Trauma melted, and beneath her palms flesh and fur renewed. She stopped singing.

The wolf whined, nuzzled against her hand, and then sat to look at her adoringly.

'Thank you. From both of us.'

He extended a hand, and she tentatively placed hers against it. His skin was rough, warm … *and something else.* He snatched it away as though sensing her thoughts, and startled, she darted from the cottage for the shore.

The man and the wolf chased after her.

'Stop! I mean you no harm.'

She turned, a wave of energy, similar to Pendragon's magic, rushing through her body. The she-wolf came to sit at her side and began licking her hand as three other wolves appeared from the trees to stand by the man.

I understand but cannot speak your words.

I'm Owen.

She stared open-mouthed. *You can read my thoughts?*

Aye.

Owen took off his shirt and washed the wolf's blood from it in the shallows.

Share the fire. I'll be drying this and not be leaving till it's burnt out.

He returned to the cottage, his kilt swinging over muscled buttocks, his equally muscled back bearing the scars of battles. *A warrior.* Curiosity getting the better of reason, she followed him inside.

Here.

Folding the rug, he indicated for her to sit as the wolves lay down on the flagstones. Pulling her knees to her chest, she stared at the fire, fascinated by the flames flickering across the logs. The movement drew her in. Tiny figures danced within the flames, swirling red and orange light, beckoning to her. She saw a larger fire and people dancing, and then the figures shifted. She blinked and looked away. Owen was staring at her.

You see Fire Fae.

She nodded.

I didna know Atlantians did that.

I have not heard of men speaking with their minds or walking with wolves.

He grinned. *What's it like?*

Atlantia?

Aye. In the water.

Atlantia isn't in the water. Not once you're there. It's underwater but not in water … it's beautiful, serene. The she-wolf changed position and came to lay beside her. *But there are no animals or birds, not like here.*

35

I imagined it a bonnie place. He put another log on the fire and laid out his shirt on the floor to dry. *It's strange to think you don't feel the cold. The frost biting at your fingers, or the howling wind freezing your skin. Do you feel the heat of the sun? Or the warmth of the fire as it soaks through to your bones?*

I feel warmth, sometimes … You know much about Atlantians.

I've been around a while.

He ran his hands through his thick dark hair. She squirmed and directed her gaze back to the fire and then to the window, the trees, and the sky. She could smell pine, seaweed on the shore, salt, and drying sand.

She looked back at him spellbound. *What's it really like here?*

Och. This is a bonnie place too! Wild and wet, but bonnie even then. That's when the earth smells rich, and the forest comes alive. The fae dance. I run there … often. Then there are the mountains you can climb, where you can watch eagles fly and feel like you're touching heaven … but nothing beats sitting by a roaring fire and feeling its heat soaking into your body – he turned to face her and looked deeply into her eyes – *and into the body of the person who is sharing that fire with you.*

She returned his gaze, sinking into the green depths, sensing rawness, strength, loyalty, and *magic*.

He looked away, picked up a stick, and blacked its end in the fire. Then he made a mark on the flagstones. *Owen. That's how you write it.* He looked at her questioningly.

Ianna.

Owen wrote her name alongside his and then wrote another word.

'Wolf. You say it.'

She sounded the word slowly, then repeated other words as Owen pointed at different things within the room. At first it felt odd, but after a while her mouth and tongue got used to making the sounds.

'That's the beauty of having magic. It allows you to adapt and learn quickly. I can teach you more.'

He drew a series of symbols on the flagstones and sounded each one. Then, the fire now nearly out and his shirt dry, he put it back on. She watched his muscled hands pushing the bottom of it back under his kilt.

'All our words are formed from these letters. I can bring books here if you like. You could learn to speak and write Gaelic.'

CHAPTER 10

AWEYNA HANDED IANNA A BLUE sea silk and then passed her a closed shell. 'Happy birthday.'

It had been only a day since her visit to the island, but it felt like an age, and in surface world time it would have been. She pulled her thoughts into the moment and opened the shell. Inside was a hairpin decorated with a single blue pearl.

'It's beautiful. Thank you.'

Aweyna beamed. 'Perhaps Pendragon's magic did something, helped you ground your energy there, and that was why you could stay so long without getting sick.'

'Maybe.' Her mind instantly returned to the cottage, the fire, the wolves … and Owen. 'But I was not with Pendragon the entire time.' She broke off. 'There was a man with an injured wolf. I healed it.'

Aweyna looked shocked. 'Be careful, Ianna!'

She knew what Aweyna was implying, and she resented it. 'I was not going to stand and watch it die! One minute you would have me matched with Lasulet, the next you think I'm with a human! Speaking to someone doesn't mean you are falling in love with them!'

'I know! But you know what happens if we fall in love with humans.'

'We turn human, can stay in the third dimension, on the surface world, and then have all the time in the world to look for lost crystals,' she quipped, annoyed by Aweyna's mammoth leap and conclusion.

'We turn human and forget all about Atlantia and that crystal shards exist!' Aweyna snapped back. She took a breath and gathered her composure. 'I'm sorry. Today of all days is not one for disagreements. Come and see.'

They had all gathered in the banqueting hall, now decorated with strings of shells and tiny crystals. The tables had been moved to create an area for dancing and were laden with sea delicacies and ornate crystal vases of sea wine. Musicians were waiting and, as she and Aweyna entered, began to play soft music on instruments made from enormous white shells. The Atlantians parted, and Gwynadon, now dressed in a blue scaled robe, crossed the room to join them. He led Ianna to the dance floor, and for three dances he twirled her around the room before breaking away to dance with the high priestess.

Lasulet, who had been watching them from the side of the room, immediately stepped in. 'May I?'

Taking his hand, Ianna danced two more dances and then excused herself to join Aweyna.

'You look good together.'

'Lasulet is brave and loyal to Gwynadon, but he is not the one for me.' She filled a glass with sea wine.

'Is anyone?'

She threw Aweyna a stern look, demanding she change the subject.

Aweyna took the hint. 'You love wildlife. You healed and made a friend in the wolf. Perhaps those things grounded you?'

'Wishful thinking. We both know it won't be that simple.'

'Why not?'

Gwynadon approached, interrupting their conversation 'May I have the honour of my future queen?' He offered Aweyna his hand, his eyes shining.

They swirled away across the dance floor, fluid and flowing, unable to take their eyes from each other. *So much in love.* Ianna was suddenly aware of the other couples, dancing in a similar way, in a way she had never experienced. She was an outsider. *A being from another world.*

Finishing her sea wine, she fortified herself with a smile, floated around the room as was expected, and was only truly happy when the party was finally over.

CHAPTER 11

❖◆❖

SOMETIME LATER FOUND IANNA SWIMMING towards the island, trying to keep up with Pendragon. She came to a standstill in the water. *I haven't the energy to swim so fast.*

Then rest. He darted into the forest of kelp below.

She swam slowly over the swaying seaweed, keeping a watchful eye. No doubt he intended to shoot out and make her jump, but she was not going to let him. The kelp began to move against the sea current, giving away Pendragon's approach. Dropping into the seaweed herself, she waited.

He passed her hiding place. Moments later he swam past again, trying to see which way she had gone. When the end of his tail was within reach, she snatched hold. Pendragon let out a cry of surprise and shot through the seaweed with her hanging on. Whooshing to the shore, he transfigured into a stallion and unceremoniously dropped her onto the sand. He reared, feigning annoyance as she lay on the sand laughing.

Sometime later she walked to the cottage and let herself in. It was swept clean like before, only now it contained a wooden chair and a small table holding a pile of books, a small pot of squid ink, a long feather with its quill cut to a point, and a pot containing white flowers. *Moon daisies.*

She stared at the white flowers with their bright yellow centres. Of all the ones he could have picked.

'I knew you would be here. I felt it in my blood!'

Owen stepped into the room, followed by the four wolves, his open linen shirt hanging loosely over his plaid kilt and the short sword in its leather sheath at his waist. He picked up a leatherbound book from the

39

table, untied the cord from around its middle, and showed her the pages. She stared at the exposed blank page, trying to understand his enthusiasm.

'You can practice.'

He dipped the quill in the ink and drew the same letters as before, saying them aloud. Then he passed her the feather, indicating for her to sit down and do the same. She copied the letters and then looked enquiringly at the books.

'Drift your eyes over the words. Look for patterns and say what you see.' Owen picked up a small green book. '*Trip's History of Beasts and Birds.* I thought it would appeal to you. It's written for children. Each page gives a description of a different animal. It's a bit simple but a good place to start. Where there is a dot, take a breath. I know for a fact you will learn quickly. Like this.'

Placing the open book on the table, Owen leant over her shoulder running his finger underneath the words as he read them. Ianna followed along, then focussed on the muscled hand and strong bare arm – and the smells of musk, pine trees, the freshness of foliage dampened by rain ...

'Now you.'

She turned her attention back to the page, at first overwhelmed by the groups of letters. Owen returned his finger to the first line and spoke it again. She slowly repeated what he said then suddenly saw the letters differently. They came alive, flashing their meaning as her eyes lingered on them. After a few minutes she managed to complete the page.

'I knew it!' Owen was exuberant. 'It's just a matter of practice. Writing may take more effort, but reading will teach—'

'Me write.'

She spoke slowly, fascinated by hearing herself speak. The resonance of her voice was the same, but she sounded ... *human.*

'It's not so bad being human,' Owen said softly. 'They age quickly, but the men and women I have known would not have changed a thing. They relished the colour of their lives, embracing both laughter and moments of tears.'

You have magic. 'Not human.'

Me or you?

She held his gaze, but at that moment one of the wolves which had been lying by the door, roused. It gave a low whine then ran from the cottage, closely followed by the others.

'The light is fading. They need to eat.' Owen moved to the door. 'The villagers are having a fire and autumn ceilidh tonight. Why don't you come?'

'Ceilidh?'

'A highland dance, with bagpipes and fiddles. The music will be loud! No one will hear if you speak or not!'

It was madness to even consider accepting. Not only would she be agreeing to mix with humans, but she was committing to staying on the surface longer. Yet she hadn't felt ill yet.

'The village is near the shore.'

Had he sensed her concern or read her mind? She glanced at her scaled legs.

'That's no bother.' Owen passed her the red rug. 'If you tie it like a dress, you'll fit in well enough. Come. It will be fun.'

He won her round. She twisted the rug around her body in a similar way to her sea silk. It wasn't long enough to drape over her shoulder so instead she brought it round her neck and tucked it in at the front to fasten it. *I can hardly swim in this.*

'Bonnie.' Owen studied her outfit approvingly. 'You won't have to swim. I'll row.'

CHAPTER 12

OWEN LED HER THROUGH THE trees to a different section of shore where a beautiful wooden rowing boat, with an elaborately scrolled bow and stern, and two highly polished wooden bench seats, had been pulled up onto the sand. He pushed the boat into the water and then held it steady whilst she clambered in.

An unusual boat.

'Aye. It's designed for seafaring and can cut through big waves. I made it myself.'

He passed her a woollen jacket that had been laid across a bench, retrieved polished oak oars from the bottom of the boat, and then began to row. Progress was slow at first, but once past the breaking waves, the boat gained momentum. Ianna was entranced. Twilight was setting in, seabirds were flying low across the water looking for a place to rest, the northern star was now showing in the sky, and the colours of the disappearing shore were becoming subdued and dreamlike.

'Want to try?'

Taking hold of the oars, she tried to copy what Owen had done, but it was not so easy as it had looked. The pull of the waves was strong, getting the oars into the water at the same time, a challenge, and after a few minutes of going round in circles she accepted Owen's offer of help.

Straddling behind her, Owen placed his hands over hers and pulled on the oars with her. Ignoring the closeness of his body, Ianna deliberately focussed on the rhythm of the motion, the way the oars twisted before hitting the water, and how far back to pull, yet when Owen finally moved away, she felt a pang of disappointment.

The boat swept towards the shore, and soon they were mooring it alongside a well-used wooden jetty. The sound of bagpipes suddenly cut through the stillness.

Call me by a human name so I fit in.

Owen thought for a moment. 'What about Meg? Meg is a strong name.'

Following a narrow lane, they entered a small field at the rear of cottages where a large fire was burning brightly against the darkening sky. The cottages were larger than the one by the shore, but still small and squat, the fire flickering shadows across their whitewashed walls. The people, the men dressed in plaid kilts like Owen's and the women in dresses not so dissimilar to her rug, were either dancing or standing next to a table containing drinking vessels and a small wooden barrel which they were taking liquid from by way of a metal pipe.

'Owen!'

The people spoke and laughed, welcoming both Owen and her to their gathering. She listened to their talk, smiling and nodding when addressed and in a short time had learnt much about their dynamics. The people did not have the same element of the wild as Owen, but they were like the land they lived on, rugged and resilient. They were good people. An elderly lady, her grey hair twisted into a bun at the back of her head, was sitting on an upturned wooden box near to the fire wrapped in a thick tartan rug.

Owen addressed her: 'Morag, this is Meg.'

Morag looked up. Her eyes were unusually bright. The lady might be old, but she was sharp and astute, not unlike the high priestess. Ianna felt an immediate affinity with her.

'Hello lassie. Have you come far?'

She nodded focussing on words. 'From over the sea.'

Morag's eyes danced, gazing at her face as though reading what she hadn't spoken. Then she looked at Owen knowingly. He nodded but said nothing.

'Play your fiddle, Laylan!'

The man who had called out did so again, and others followed suit, stirring a middle-aged man with ragged ginger hair to produce an instrument from underneath the table. He began to play, moving his fingers across the strings at such speed they were almost a blur. All but the older villagers responded. Jigging and kicking their legs to the rhythm, they danced around the fire in a line like a sea serpent celebrating the night. Those not dancing clapped or thumped the ground with their feet. The light from the fire, glowed orange across her face and across the bodies of the villagers. Laughter and music echoed across the sky. Ianna had never felt more alive.

Eventually Laylan stopped playing. Heckled to continue, he raised his hand to the group in general. 'Give a man the chance to drink!' Crossing to the table, he poured liquid from the barrel into a drinking vessel and then gulped it down.

What is it?

'Ale.' Owen poured some for her to try. 'Malt from grain, brewed with water to make wort, then fermented with yeast.'

She took a sip, screwing up her face at the bitterness, and doing her best not to spit it out.

Owen grinned. 'It's an acquired taste.'

He was distracted by a young man running over from the fire, gesturing in the direction of the cottages. The field fell silent, and all merriment left Owen's face as he gave the three approaching figures a hard stare, hovering his hand over the hilt of the sword hanging at his side.

'Easy, Owen,' Laylan said quietly. 'We knew they were comin'.'

'They've no right to collect at this hour. They should work in the day like normal folk and treat people with more respect. Not only that they've ridden. They've got no respect for their horses either.'

The newcomers, dressed in leather riding boots and woollen trousers and jackets, strode up the field. 'Taxes.'

'All ready. I'll take 'ee to them.' The man who had spoken walked down to meet the tax collectors, deliberately diverting them from the group.

Laylan gulped down another drink. Then, picking up his fiddle, he called out across the field. 'Who's for another dance? What about "Split the Willow"?'

He began to play, even more furiously than before. The villagers cheered, formed groups and began to spin, determined not to allow the brusque tax collection to dampen their spirits.

Owen pulled Ianna to one side. 'How would you feel about rowing the boat back on your own?'

I have no fear of the water, but it may take me a while.

Owen grinned, his teeth flashing white, looking almost canine. 'Then I'll walk you to the jetty.'

Sensing his urgency, she followed as he slipped from the ceilidh. They walked in silence, Owen seemingly lost in thought. On the jetty he cast the boat off, watched until she got into the rhythm of rowing, and then ran from the shore.

CHAPTER 13

HOURS HAD PASSED, HER ONLY company a lone owl hooting from the trees. Ianna had sat reading aloud until the candle burnt out and then had taught herself to light a fire. Once it was glowing brightly, she had discarded her rug dress, laid on it on the floor, and read on.

Something had opened inside her mind, and she could now sound words fluently. She had finished the book about animals, and was nearly through one about flora, when the door burst open. Owen entered carrying a dark brown leather saddle bag. He looked dishevelled, covered in bits of dry fern and stinking of sweat. He had been running and fast.

He dropped the bag onto the table with a loud chink. Then, joining her by the fire, he took off his shirt and lay down on the floor next to her. She remained silent.

'It will soon be dawn.'

She nodded, and placed another log onto the glowing embers.

'You're a brave woman. Not just for rowing the boat back, but for going to the village in the first place.'

There was a seriousness in his voice she had not heard from him before. This was not a man talking, but a warrior.

'You have magic. I know that, but you are special for other reasons. Royalty?'

She nodded.

'And a free spirit.'

There was a long period of silence. Eventually Ianna spoke, stumbling as she chose words. She told him of her life in Atlantia, her search for the crystal shard, and the demon that had attacked her on the shore. Owen

46

listened without comment, showing no surprise until she told how she usually got sick on land.

'You haven't felt ill once?'

She shook her head.

'Yet you've been here all night.'

She stared at him, her mind making connections. 'You know about Scathchornail.'

'Aye. I've heard of him well enough, and the demons that sniff around doing his dirty work.' He stretched. 'Come here, whenever you like, use it as a base for your search. No one uses the place save for me. You won't be disturbed. I must get to the village before the day sets in. Delivery from Sir John.' He clambered to his feet.

'Sir John?'

'Aye. The wretch who claims the taxes.'

She made the connection with the injured wolf and the bag currently on the table. 'Is this something you do regularly?'

He gave a wry smile. 'I do stand for honesty and integrity, but also fairness. The villagers have barely anything, and this year has been particularly harsh. I just do my bit to restore balance; that's all.' He picked up the bag and moved towards the door.

CHAPTER 14

⧫ ✦ ✦ ✦ ⧫

K AIA TURNED OFF THE KITCHEN tap, placed the kettle on its stand to boil, and then opened the cupboard to reach for the tin of ground coffee. She scooped two heaped spoons into the small cafetière, relishing the intense fragrance. The green vase of moon daisies was on the window ledge next to her crystals, and outside the sun was deciding to come back out after the recent rain shower. Sunlight was catching on raindrops hanging from the washing line, making them shimmer like jewels. *Mindfulness. The beauty of the moment. Could be an article.* Layna's face popped into her head like a great white shark. *Maybe not.* She grimaced and turned her attention back to the kettle as the switch clicked off.

Placing the lid on the cafetière, she caught sight of a large black crow taking off from the washing line, causing rain droplets to splatter onto the ground. It had not been there moments before. She watched the bird fly from sight and then turned her attention to her laptop on the table when her inbox pinged.

She had asked Jim if he would dig into historical records for anything that could verify her interviewees' past-life recalls. Seeing he had agreed, she dragged and dropped photographs onto a memory stick, glancing apprehensively at the kitchen clock. She had three quarters of an hour before Rick got back. She clicked back to the interviews she had transcribed. She would begin the article with the man who had recalled being murdered. His past-life regression had been so detailed that he had passed the recalled information onto the police. His account proved to be of an unsolved murder and, what was more, was so detailed that the murderer, still alive, was subsequently caught and convicted for the crime.

Dramatic.

By contrast, she would cover the couple who recalled soul love. They had both experienced regressions to a lifetime where they vowed to meet again. The feeling had been so intense they had spent years searching for one another. In this lifetime, they were both male, yet they had recognised each other instantly and were now married, totally in love. Her parents had looked at each other in the same way. ... She stared into space, fiddling with her fingers. *Soul love. Fat chance. Guys are either complete idiots, control freaks, or taken.*

One of her dogs padded to the kitchen door, only to skulk back under the table as the front door burst open and then slammed shut with a force that seemed to shake the entire house. She glanced at the clock accusingly and threw a concerned look in the direction of her dog, willing it to stay quiet. If Rick was early, his casting had not gone well.

Rick entered the kitchen, scowled at her laptop, reached for the cafetière, and emptied it into a mug. She pulled a face.

'What's your problem?'

It would be impossible to write. 'I'll work in the van.' She gathered her things.

'You're her puppet. The way you dance to her tune.' He kicked out in irritation as the dogs scurried past him, their tails between their legs.

Kaia held the van door for the dogs to jump in, slid it shut, and then flopped back against the multicoloured crocheted throw covering the chair. Her parents had been adventurous free spirits who would go wherever their hearts led them. The van had been their pride and joy, a shabby chic sanctuary, haphazardly decorated with trinkets collected on their travels. It could serve as a bedroom, living room, and in this instance her office. Rick hated it and had often told her to sell. Yet she had stuck to her guns. The van was a link to her parents and one day would be her ticket to freedom.

Annoyed by the tears on her cheeks, she wiped them away with force. Then opening her laptop, she tapped on Bella's Zoom link.

'How is it going, girl?' Bella waved from the screen dressed in yoga gear. 'I'm having a joyous day. Layna has just called me into the office. At the weekend too!'

'She runs the office like a military campaign. She should be in the forces. She could end the riots single-handed.'

Bella chuckled, but her face fell. 'Van again. For God's sake. I'm not going to ask what he got for your birthday.'

'I think you can guess.' *Don't feel sorry for yourself.*

'The guy makes Layna look like a pussycat.'

'Layna would make a great cat.' An image of Layna preening immaculate whiskers and tail flickered through her mind as Bella's partner, who played in an amateur football team, appeared on the screen in a jogging top. Kaia waved. 'Hi, JD!'

'Kaia, how's it going?' JD kissed Bella's neck. 'No cooking tonight. We can grab a takeout when you get back.'

Bella's aura was flashing crimson. *She looks radiant.* Kaia forced herself not to appear despondent as JD waved goodbye.

'You're his goddess.'

'I'm an incarnation of Kali. He must treat me right, or I'll have parts of him for breakfast he doesn't want to lose!'

'I wish I was Kali.'

'She is in there, girl!' Bella pointed at her from the screen. 'You're more powerful than you think!'

At that moment there was a knock on the van door. Through the window she saw her next-door neighbour, a single mother of twenty-eight, dressed in a floral dress and green cardigan, standing in the drive, looking stressed.

'It's Sue. I'll catch you later.'

'Sorry to bother you,' Sue said apologetically as Kaia stepped from the van. 'I was on my way up to the house and heard you talking. Jake's bad again. Would you come? When it's convenient of course.'

'Now's fine. I'll grab some crystals and be right there.'

Sue hurried away, leaving Kaia to return to the house. At the door, she discovered her moon daisies unceremoniously strewn across the step. Determined not to let the provocation work, she gathered the flowers together, scooted into the kitchen, selected the crystals she needed from the windowsill, and hurried back out.

Sue placed the Moon Daisies into a slender red vase and admired them. Kaia smiled. Their effect had been magical. Some of the tension had left Sue's face and her aura was considerably lighter.

'Come on through.'

She followed Sue into a dimly lit lounge. Dark green curtains with a swirling leaf pattern were drawn across the bay window, and Jake, a young man of fifteen, was lying on a faded green leather couch. He looked jaded, as did his aura, which was dull and weak.

Kaia pulled up a small, green-upholstered stool and sat down next to him. 'Sorry you're feeling rough.'

Jake responded with little animation. Placing her crystals around his head, she began to send energy, instinctively singing strange words which had no meaning but still broke up the energy that felt solid and sticky. She continued to work until Jake's aura was a vibrant cocoon of light. The effect was miraculous.

'Magic. Thanks.' Jake flashed a grin and sat up reaching for his mobile.

'No worries. What brought it on this time?'

'His phone,' Sue replied, opening the curtains. 'His headaches always start after he's been on it. That can't be a coincidence.'

Jake rolled his eyes.

'Some of your friends have started getting headaches too,' Sue said, underscoring her point. 'Although it could just be that our phones are faulty. Sometimes their home screens freeze and go all black and swirly; that can't be right.'

Back in her van, Kaia tentatively opened the home screen of her own phone, but it looked normal.

CHAPTER 15

KAIA HAD ARRIVED AT THE campus early and, to fill time, had taken the dogs for a run through the oak woods. Pounding along the dirt trail, she leapt exposed tree roots and then sprinted the last few yards to the car park. There were no cars on the move, so signalling for the dogs to follow, she jogged over to the van.

Three students, of a similar age to her, passed by. Two had been on their phones but suddenly began to jostle and taunt the other, becoming increasingly aggressive.

'Leave off. Don't be such shits.'

The young man who had spoken tried to pull away, which seemed to inflame his companions. Wrestling him to the ground, they began pulling at his jacket. Kaia cringed and opened the van door to get away. There was the sound of ripping fabric.

'You wanker!'

She turned. The student was now being pinned to the ground by one antagonist whilst the other was pulling a laptop out of a rucksack. She saw red.

'Leave the guy alone!'

They turned. 'Or what?'

Their eyes were completely black, as though their pupils had expanded to fill their entire sockets. *Holy shit.* Shock extinguished the fire of her own outburst. They took a step nearer.

A car pulled into the car park, and a thickset fellow let out a large Alsatian. The two students scurried away, and the one on the ground got to his feet.

'Sorry about your jacket.'

'Yeah, but it'll be cheaper to replace than to buy a new laptop. Thanks.'

He walked away, leaving her to cross the pristinely mown park to an impressive wrought iron gate. She passed through it and crossed the cobbled forecourt of an austere stone building.

The interior of the building was equally impressive. Dark oak panels lined the walls, and a grand oak staircase swept up from a striking black and white tiled entrance hall, past a stained-glass window of scholars holding scrolls. The air was cool and had a musty smell which added to the illusion of being in an ancient library or museum. The perfect place for the history faculty.

She walked along a narrow, creaky-floored corridor and knocked on one of the many doors leading from it. There was a brief pause; then Jim's face appeared from the disorganised chaos that made up the inside of the room, a look he mirrored with his scraggy greying hair and unshaven face.

'Kaia!' he exclaimed, his grey eyes sparkling in delight. 'You're early!'

She kissed him on the cheek. 'Is now a good time?'

'Always for you.'

She entered the oak-panelled room with its two enormous floor-to-ceiling oak bookcases and three slim leaded windows separated by stone mullions. The entire place was crammed with papers and artefacts that Jim had gathered on his extensive travels.

'I've no more classes until this afternoon,' Jim said, crossing to a rickety wooden chair and lifting the pile of papers stacked on it. 'Take a seat.'

He placed the papers on top of another pile that had been balancing precariously near the edge of his oak desk. The papers began to slide, and Kaia grabbed them just before they spilled all over the floor.

'One day I'll get my filing system sorted!' Jim pulled a self-critical face and began to shuffle through other heaps of paper stacked on his desk. 'Just give me a sec, and I'll find those pictures. How's things?' he asked without looking up.

'Same as.'

'Too bad.' He stopped what he was doing, lifted an exhumed small parcel wrapped in brown paper, and pointed to a photo standing in pride of place next to his treasured seventeenth-century history books. It showed a younger version of himself next to a happy-looking couple. 'Your parents didn't play to rules,' he said with strong affection. 'They wouldn't want to see you being dragged down. He sucks you dry. If there's such a thing as an energy vampire, he is one!'

Many a true word spoken in jest. Yet she wasn't about to admit it. If Jim opened her up about Rick, she didn't trust herself not to cry. She forced a laugh to deflect his concern.

Jim studied her face, seeing through her mask. 'I promised your mum and dad I'd look out for you. You're twenty-one. You'll get full access to your inheritance. You can go. Do whatever you want to do. Here. Happy belated.'

She bit her lip, tears threatening to fall. She opened the parcel and took out a silver cuff bangle which had the scene of a river engraved on it with tiny, embossed fish swimming in it. 'It's lush. Thank you.'

Jim now looked emotional too. 'I know it's tough to talk about, but you don't need to stay trapped … in anything. Why not take a break? Rediscover who Kaia is?'

She nodded and swallowed, the constriction in her throat rapidly becoming a hot stone. Jim gave her a hug and then went back to rummaging through the papers on his desk.

'Here they are!' he exclaimed triumphantly, pulling out some photocopies. 'I take it you brought the files?'

She took the memory stick from her rucksack. He uploaded the files to his computer and began to compare the images with the photographs he had found.

'I'll be … look at their faces!' He moved to one side so she could see over his shoulder. 'If that doesn't verify the recall, I don't know what would.'

She studied the photograph of the missing person and the picture she had taken of the man who recalled being murdered. The bone structure, nose and eyes were the same. It was like looking at an actor playing a different role. Underneath surface differences you could tell it was the same person.

'That's incredible!'

She studied other pictures, including some of the couple who recalled being in love. The photographs Jim had discovered were faded, and the man and woman were a lot younger than the modern-day men, but there was no mistaking the similarities.

'D'you think it's possible to find soul love?'

'I'm probably not the right person to ask,' Jim replied wistfully. 'I could see you with someone though … if you left Dick.'

She gave him a stern look that turned into a grin, mirroring the one that appeared on her godfather's face.

'Just saying,' Jim added, his eyes now sparkling in merriment.

He turned his attention back to the pictures, leaving her to explore the contents of the room. She was drawn to an old painting, depicting an enormous oddly shaped rock sticking out at a peculiar angle from a mountain overlooking the sea. The rock had majesty, like a sentient being overseeing its domain. She could smell the sea air. She was on the pebbled shore. A man was walking towards her dressed in an eighteenth-century kilt.

Kaia.

'Did you say something?' She turned to see Jim staring at her from his desk.

'Nope. Seen a ghost?'

'I'm not sure.' She indicated the painting. 'Where's that?'

'Isle of Skye. Storr Rock.' He pushed the chair back from his desk, pulled a book from one of his bookcases, and passed it to her. *Wild Guide to the Scottish Highlands*.

'Your parents loved Skye. We went there a lot. Magical place. You should go and check it out.'

'There's work.' She flicked through the pages. *Another vision relating to Scotland, and now Jim hands me this.* She paused on a page showing an illustration of a woman with webbed hands and feet, swimming next to what looked like a large seahorse. She read the footnote. *Water Fae. Kelpies.*

'Not to mention Rick,' Jim said. 'You have to take that step across the threshold, then destiny can meet you on the road.'

She shut the book with a snap. 'You haven't told me what amazing breakthrough for historical academia you are currently working on.'

Jim raised an eyebrow. 'Another outstanding paper that doesn't stand a hope in hell of being published.' He chuckled. 'Still, one can but try.'

'What's it about?'

'You inspired me to do some digging of my own into people's recollections.' Jim explained. 'People don't just recall past lives in linear time. Some recalled lives in other realms.'

'I originally wrote the past-life article from the stance of linear time and space being a misconception.'

Jim pulled a face. 'I'm guessing Layna was suitably impressed?'

'She threw it out.'

'Tough. No doubt with as much grace as my peers, when they read my papers. One day they will stop going round and round debating the same old stuff and embrace historical advancement.'

'Sounds an oxymoron.' Her phone pinged, and seeing a message from Bella, she scanned the first line. 'Bell's not well. She's left work early. I'll pop round on my way home.' She typed her response as Jim downloaded the pictures onto his computer and took out the memory stick. 'Could I borrow the book?' she asked, putting the stick back in her bag.

'Sure. Consider what I have said. Use it. The sky is the limit. You deserve to be happy.'

She kissed him on the cheek and went back to the van, considerably more buoyant.

· + + + + + ·

Half an hour later, she tapped on Bella's front door. 'How are you doing?' she asked as Bella's worn face appeared.

'Awful.'

Kaia followed Bella through to the kitchen. Bella lifted the kettle from its stand and looked at her questioningly. She shook her head to decline a drink, at which Bella flopped onto the couch in the corner. Jake had looked the same.

'Have you been on your phone a lot lately?'

'No more than normal. Why?'

She related Sue connecting Jake's headaches to his phone and then told her about the incident in the car park. 'Their eyes were solid black.'

'Was it their auras?' Bella waved her hand listlessly. 'I haven't a clue, I don't see things like you do. How's the article going? Layna's gunning for you.'

'Jim's given me some great pictures … He gave me a travel guide to Scotland.'

'Then you should go.' Bella let out a groan and put her hand to her head. 'I could use some of your magic.'

CHAPTER 16

ᛁᛁ ANNA HAD PAID SEVERAL VISITS to the cottage now and had worked through several stacks of books. Owen had explained that he was great friends with a man called Alexander MacDonald, a clan leader who lived at the other end of the island. Alexander had a library, and it was thanks to his beneficiary that Owen was able to bring her so many. Owen, it seemed, split his time between living at Alexander's, in the cottage, and in the forest with the wolves.

She understood he was a free spirit and contained magic, which somewhat explained his affiliation with wolves and why he was reluctant to settle in one place. Yet what she found odd was him disclosing that he lived at the cottage. He had no belongings here, no bed, and although the cottage had facilities for making a good fire, there were none for making food and until her own visit, no furniture, books, or anything that made the room a home.

Finishing the page, she closed the book and pushed it across the table. They were windows into the surface world, and she had absorbed much information about it now. Atlantians lived for a very long time by human standards, and as such she had lived through much of the history the books described, but reading about it through human words was like discovering it anew. The more she read, the more she understood human perspective and – reading between the lines – their psychological passions and their prejudices. It was fascinating, and the more she learnt, the more ingrained she felt. She had asked Owen if Alexander had any books on the Druids, hence the current book. She had known Druids had an affinity with crystals and could commune with rocks and trees, but that was all. She now had a clearer understanding of Druid practice, yet had not unearthed any clue as to where one might choose to hide a crystal shard.

The day was now drawing in, and she had been here since dawn. Closing the shutters she left the cottage and headed back for the shore.

———————— ·+◆◆◆+· ————————

Sometime later she joined Aweyna in the castle kitchen. It was busy. Food had been prepared for the evening meal and Atlantians were in the process of taking platters into the banqueting hall. Alevin clearly wanted to help. Unnoticed by the others, he slid a platter, much too large for him to carry and piled high with seaweed parcels, to the edge of the table. Before she could intervene, Alevin picked up the platter, turned, knocked into another Atlantian, and lost his grip. Seaweed parcels slid across the floor, some splashing into the bubbling hot water of the shell basin.

Everyone turned and Alevin, clearly embarrassed, began scooping the parcels up.

'Alevin, no!'

Her warning was too late. Noticing the seaweed parcels in the shell basin Alevin plunged in his hand to retrieve them. He squealed and withdrew his arm, staring in shock as the skin around his scales began to blister. Ianna and Aweyna rushed to his side, squatted on the floor, and began sending healing energy, Ianna softly singing. Almost immediately the blisters shrank. All that was needed was a light code to complete the process. Ianna moved her fingers through the air to create one, but nothing happened. She had her back to the room, and no one had noticed, save for Aweyna, who looked concerned. Somewhat bemused, Ianna tried again but still no light code appeared. She sat back, stunned, barely aware of Aweyna sending a symbol into Alevin's arm.

CHAPTER 17

Ianna somehow got through their meal, feigning a calm demeanour when inside she was in turmoil. No matter which way she looked at the situation, she always came to the same conclusion. There was only one thing that explained her inability to create a light code, and it was a disaster.

'I was watching you,' said Aweyna. 'You didn't eat a thing, and what happened with Alevin? Are you ill?'

Ianna pulled her behind one of the white columns at the edge of the great hall and glanced around nervously. 'No.' There was no easy way to say it. 'I think I am turning human.'

'You're what?' The colour drained from Aweyna's face. 'You can't be. You haven't fallen in love.'

Ianna's legs suddenly felt like jellyfish. She leant against the pillar for support. 'I have done what the dragon said. I have spent time in the third dimension and have grounded my energy in the surface world. I haven't fallen in love with *a* human, but I have fallen in love with the place, with *humans.*'

'Holy seas.' Aweyna studied her face intently and then visibly relaxed. 'You don't look any different. Perhaps if it's not with a person, it isn't the same. Maybe a healing in the pyramid will realign your energies.'

There was the sound of voices as a group of Atlantians entered the far end of the hall. Gwynadon was among them.

'You must tell him.' Aweyna stepped from behind the pillar.

'There you are!' Gwynadon said as Aweyna crossed the hall to join him. 'We've been looking for you. Where's Ianna?'

'She is wanting to speak with you and the high priestess,' Aweyna said, displaying her usual diplomacy and tact.

Aweyna left the hall with Gwynadon, climbing the staircase to look for the high priestess. Ianna waited for the others to leave and then climbed the stairs after them, her feet heavier with every step.

'No matter how wise one is, the future is never clear, and the path, seldom straight,' the high priestess said when she finally found them. Concern showed on her face, but she kept her voice calm. 'Perhaps being human *is* part of your path Ianna, but you are not prepared. If you stay away from the third dimension, I am certain we can stop the change and give you more time to plan.'

Gwynadon was too emotional to speak. He stared as though she were the alien she felt she was, and she wished the ground would swallow her.

Ianna spoke slowly, doing her best to keep her voice steady. 'When I am human, you can remind me who I am, who I was?'

'No! We cannot! You won't understand our language, and even if you did, we still would not. It could turn the human mind mad. It could destroy you!'

She drew back, alarmed by the high priestess's sharp tone. 'Then a human cannot remind me either?'

The high priestess shook her head. 'The only way you can safely overcome the amnesia is to work through it yourself, giving the human mind the space to adjust, but even then, the chance of you remembering everything is next to non-existent.'

'I cannot accept you are destined to forget,' Gwynadon blurted out. 'You will be weak. An easy target.'

'I am not weak!' The tension caused her to snap. 'If this is my path, I must walk it. My soul will know. My intuition will remind me somehow.'

'But how many lifetimes will that take?' Aweyna pointed out. 'Scathchornail will hunt you down. He will destroy the third dimension and then Atlantia.'

'Long before you remember who you are,' Gwynadon added.

There was an awkward silence. She felt sick to the core.

'I understand and feel for you, Ianna, I really do,' the high priestess said eventually. 'But as high priestess of Atlantia, I advise you to cut all ties with the third dimension until we have thought this through more fully.'

'As your brother and king, I command it,' Gwynadon stated.

She stared at his face, taking in every detail. How could it be that she was going to forget the faces of those she had known all her life? Even her brother? She could see her pain mirrored in his eyes.

It was too much to bear. She turned and kept her poise, walking to her chamber with her head held high. Yet once the door was shut, she crumpled to the floor, sobbing as though she was never going to stop.

CHAPTER 18

K AIA HAD FINALLY FINISHED THE article. Now all she had to do was proofread. She could have a juice break, do a read-through, and get the article across before deadline.

She loved fresh juices but didn't often make them because cleaning the machine was such a faff. However, finishing the article was worth celebrating. She pulled a handful of carrots and an apple from the fridge and set up the juicer. Then she had the satisfaction of watching it transform the fruit and vegetables into a glass of frothy, vibrant orange liquid.

She cleaned the machine and put it away, wanting to savour her drink. It was Rick's machine, and she didn't want to give him any ammo. Since his encounter with the Egyptian priestesses, his controlling behaviour had become more overt. He hadn't said where he had disappeared to that night, nor had he apologised for having left her standing at the bar looking like a banana. *Literally*. She shuddered recollecting the looks she had received as she stood alone, the flamboyant pirate having dropped her like a hot brick.

The door slammed, and said pirate, now wearing skintight road cycling gear, marched in carrying his bike. He leant it against the washing machine, drank her juice, then began to dismantle gears, carelessly sliding dirty oily cogs onto the table with no regard for her open laptop.

'I'd made that for me. You could've shared.'

He gave her a thunderous look. 'Can't a guy get a drink?'

She did not bother to respond. Scooping up her computer, she left for her van and had no sooner set up a makeshift office when her phone pinged the arrival of a voice mail. It was from Layna.

'The magazine is clearly not a priority,' Layna's voice scolded. 'This is your last warning. Deadline. Two hours.'

Something inside her snapped. She squeezed the screen to return the call, waited for the answer phone to finish, then spoke.

'It's Kaia. I won't be sending the article, or any other. I quit.'

She hung up.

Fuck.

Her head swirled. She wanted to throw up. She had just dropped the position she had worked so hard to get. Letting out a groan, she tapped a FaceTime request, and seconds later Jim's face appeared on her screen.

'Ah, van. Tell me you're not parked on the drive.' She nodded. 'Pity.'

'I've quit.'

'The mag?' He assessed her face. 'Good for you. It wasn't what you'd hoped. You'll find else, something that makes your heart sing.'

There was a sudden banging on the van door. Mouthing a 'Sorry,' she slid the door open. Rick was on the drive looking hot and flustered.

'These are in the way. They stink.'

She snapped her fingers, and her two dogs leapt into the van to huddle as far from the open door as they could get. Rick staggered away muttering a curse.

'For Christ's sake, Kaia,' Jim said from the screen. 'Get away, go and explore Scotland for a bit.'

Muttering an apology, she ended the call. To stop herself from going down a rabbit hole of self-pity, she reached for the travel guide Jim had given her. She flicked through the pages. *Maps, cafés, walk routes …* Her mind began to wander, taking her far away from the drive …

A man and woman in eighteenth-century dress walked along a loch shore, the woman's long auburn hair blowing in the sea breeze. Holding hands, they walked through pine trees, to a tiny stone cottage set back from the shore.

The image shifted. Black mist crept over the water. Weaving through the trees, the mist stretched into clawed fingers that tore at the couple, ripping them apart. The mist thickened, and the woman began to run, not seeing the wolf skulking through the trees, its opaque eyes locked on her …

'No!'

Kaia came to with a start, unsure if she had called out, or the woman in her vision. Either way, her heart was pounding.

She closed the guidebook. How many signposts did she need? Scotland was calling her. Jim was right. Quitting work gave her freedom to explore. *Rick.*

She sighed and leant back against the seat. *The wolf.* The wolf had not looked real. It symbolised Rick. He disempowered her. He had disempowered her for too long.

She marched from the van to the kitchen. Music was blaring from the lounge, and the kitchen floor was now covered in smears of rust remover. The empty bottle of rust remover had been thrown into the sink, along with the rag Rick had used to wipe the floor.

You've got to be kidding.

She picked up her running top between her finger and thumb, then dropped it in disgust.

Rick was in the lounge, slumped in the armchair, seemingly asleep. Crossing to the coffee table, she turned off the Bluetooth speaker and noticing his phone's home screen, picked it up. It was displaying swirling black static. Her vision blurred. In her mind's eye she saw the profile of a slim Victorian man who in one sharp movement turned to stare at her. For an instant she saw every detail of his face, the piercing eyes, the fine-boned nose, the sallow cheeks, the hair scraped against his head topped by the expensive hat that smelt of damp … and death …

She dropped the phone in shock, and Rick came round with a start. 'What the hell are you doing?' He pulled himself to his feet.

'I—'

Rick's eyes were flicking from brown to solid black. She backed away and dodged as he lunged. He hit the wall, let out a cry of rage, and made to grab her, but she leapt for the door.

'I'm leaving!'

A snarl came from behind her as she raced from the house.

She drove, missing red lights and cutting off cars at junctions. The sounding car horns making her flight response even greater. It was only when outside the city and in open countryside that awareness of her surroundings returned. She pulled into a lay-by under some horse chestnut trees and crawled into the back of the van. Then she FaceTimed Bella to tell her what had happened.

His eyes. She fought to keep her voice steady. 'It was like he was possessed.'

An expression of disdain flashed across Bella's face. 'He's always been an animal. Want me to come and get you?'

'I've got what I need in the van. I'm going to Scotland.'

'Just take it easy. I'll call in the morning, but I'm here if you need me.'

She signed off, suddenly feeling exhausted. The lay-by might not be ideal, but tonight it was home. She pulled her sleeping bag out of its stuff-sac and poured dried dog food into a bowl. Then, as the dogs crunched on their biscuits, she snuggled in, her head swimming.

CHAPTER 19

UNABLE TO SLEEP, IANNA SAT staring out into the shadowed courtyard, turning over everything in her mind. All she had done was follow the Guardians' advice. Had she known the full implication, she would not have been so quick to stay on land. Or would she?

She thought of running along the shore with Pendragon, her time in the cottage, and the laughter and joviality of the villagers around the fire. She was kidding herself. Even if she had known what would happen, she would have made the same decisions.

Then there was Owen. A series of images flickered across her mind: his face when he laughed, his sparkling eyes, the deep resonance to his voice, his body ... She took a breath as her heart skipped a beat. She knew she had fallen in love with the land, but had she also fallen in love with ... No. Owen was a kindred spirit; that was all.

She turned her thoughts back to her conversation with the high priestess. She had been right. If she could control the change, she would be able to make plans. Perhaps the Guardian knew how she could do that. She had plenty of time before dawn broke. She could see what advice the sea dragon had and then discuss it with the others at first light. Silently she left her chamber and made her way to the shore.

⁂

Is there nothing I can do?

The sea dragon had sensed her distress and had appeared as soon as she entered the ravine. *This is a current you cannot swim against.* He let out a puff of steam that washed around her, infusing her with strength and courage. *Fate deals the hand. You choose how to play it.*

The steam dissipated, vanishing to nothing. She could act like Dragon Fae or like the steam, and time was not on her side. The only plan of action she had was to draw the five light codes in the book that Owen had given her. It wasn't much, but it was something. She did not know how to write a reminder of what light codes were, or of her need to find the shard, but at least the symbols would not be lost to her. She could still be back before daybreak, and as soon as it was light, she would take Aweyna's advice and go to the pyramid for an energy alignment.

She swam for the shore. It was the middle of the night here too. The stars were out, but a ferocious wind was howling, stirring the water into intimidating waves that raced for the shore. She swam with them but, misjudging where they broke, found herself churned into the sand before being spat onto the beach. She stood, her legs shaking, and shivered.

Pushing alarm to the back of her mind, she walked the path to the cottage. Owen and the wolves were inside lying by the fire, his sword in its sheath on the table.

He looked up and reading the expression on her face, leapt to his feet. 'What is the matter?' Taking her arm, he led her to the fire. 'You feel cold.' He stared at her questioningly.

Her teeth began to chatter, preventing her from speaking.

'Don't try to talk. Think.'

I'm turning human. She related what had happened and her plan to record the light codes. *If this is feeling cold, it's not much fun.*

Owen grinned. 'The fun about being cold is getting warm afterwards.' Wrapping the red rug around her, he began to vigorously rub her back and arms.

Now I know how a wet dog feels.

She was suddenly more aware of the fire's heat on her face, as though someone had turned up its intensity. *Owen, I don't think I've much time left …*

'Then write them down. Quickly.'

He passed her the book and quill. With her hands still shaking, she wrote the five symbols in the middle of the book and passed it back to him.

They heal, and I think they could be used to reunite the two shards somehow. They represent elements, that one is air ... Holy seas.

Owen paused writing and looked up sharply. 'What?'

The other shard. It's still in Atlantia! I must get it before it's too late!

'Ianna!'

Ignoring him, she raced to the shore. The waves looked angry, smashing high, seemingly determined to keep her from the water, but she had no choice.

'Ianna! Look out!'

She turned. A demon in wolf form had slunk onto the beach and was creeping towards her. Its surprise attack blown, it narrowed its eyes and snarled viciously, extending its claws to daggers.

'Get in the water!'

Owen protectively ran for the demon, blocking its attack. As it leapt, he lunged and crashed against the demon's shoulder, pushing it away with force. The demon fell to the ground but instantly got back on its feet, white eyes burning with anger.

Owen drew his sgian dubh from the sheath at his calf and held the blade in front of him. 'Go!'

She turned to the sea as the sound of baying came from the direction of the trees. *Owen's wolves.* She threw herself into the oncoming wave.

+ + ✦ ✦ ✦ + +

The demon knew it was outnumbered. As the wolves circled it transformed into a large black crow and took to the sky in a whirlwind of sand and shadow.

Owen turned to face the sea.

'Ianna!'

He raced into the water, diving through oncoming waves to see beyond them. Her body was floating face down in the water. Waves broke over him, determined to drown them both as he grabbed hold and pulled her body ashore. Back on the sand he pumped his hands over her heart, willing her to take a breath, and muttered his relief when she eventually convulsed and vomited.

Carrying Ianna into the cottage Owen wrapped her in the rug. Then he cradled her by the fire as the wolves came to lie around them. She began to tremble, her body yearning for heat, and then finally her eyes opened.

She focussed on his face and then glanced around the room as though recollecting what had happened. Eventually she spoke. 'Owen?'

He nodded.

'The demon?'

'Got away. It didn't fancy its chances against the wolves.'

The wolf she had healed shuffled nearer, wagging its tail, and Ianna began stroking its head absent-mindedly.

'I'll get the book. You should finish telling me about the light codes.'

She knitted her brow. 'Light codes?'

Collecting the book from the table he turned to the page of symbols. As she shuffled her body to see, the rug fell, revealing smooth legs. She studied the page intently before giving him a blank look.

'They're Atlantian … under the sea. Where you're from.'

She began to spasm, her body juddering and eyes flickering wildly. Dropping the book, he loosened the rug, powerless to do more until the seizure ceased. Once her body stilled, he laid her on her side and then stoked the fire, surveying the interior of the cottage critically.

Eventually she stirred, stared at the roaring flames and after a while she slowly sat upright.

'Do you remember your name?'

Her eyes turned to him.

'Meg.'

Part Two

MEG

CHAPTER 1

◆ ◆ ◆ ◆ ◆

K AIA WOKE UP SHIVERING. FOR a split second she lay staring at the ceiling, trying to recollect where she was. Then an electric bolt of reality hit. *I've no longer got a job or a home.* Letting out a groan, she rolled onto her side and looked down at the dogs, who were curled up by the folding bed. One thumped its tail happily against the floor and shuffled nearer.

Scotland had always seemed a world away, yet it was only a ten-hour drive. She could cover the distance in two days with a stopover. She studied the relevant pages, planning where to break her journey and which route to take through the Highlands to the Skye Bridge. Then she turned to another page depicting the entire island. It was easy to see why Jim referred to it as magical; it looked like it had wings. It would not be out of place in a children's story, full of pirates and dragons. She traced the island with her fingertips, pausing over the southernmost point. The topography of the mountains, the beaches …

The page blurred, and for a time she could smell the sea and hear the waves rolling onto the shore. There was a white horse galloping towards her, and behind the horse was the man she had seen before, the Highlander, dressed in an eighteenth-century plaid kilt. He was rugged and handsome, with sparkling green eyes that danced like sunlight glistening on the sea. Her heart leapt.

The dog licked her hand, bringing her attention abruptly back inside the van. She folded the bed back into a seat, tidied up, and then set off on her journey.

Later that afternoon she pulled into a campsite for her stopover. It was busy with campers hitching vans onto electricity hook-ups and setting out tables and chairs. These modern camper vans dwarfed hers, yet the simplicity of her van often paid dividends, and today was no exception. All the gravel spaces for camper vans were booked, but as hers did not need a hook-up, the site manager said she could park in the area designated for tents.

Needing supplies for her evening meal, she first stopped by the campsite shop. It was the sort of place that appealed, having an area containing a selection of outdoor clothes, another of camping essentials, maps, postcards, and finally food. She scooted a miniature trolley through the aisles, gathering a few extra T-shirts and two pairs of black leggings. Then, spying a teal blue hoodie with a leaping dolphin embroidered in blue and green on the back, she checked the price tag. Fifty pounds. She put it back, turned away, and then, changing her mind, put it in the trolley with the other items.

Food. She pushed the trolley past the sugary carbonated drinks and no-sugar options, lurid liquids in shiny plastic bottles, and stopped by the fresh fruit juices. Then she turned to the aisle containing chocolate, passing a lady and a cute-looking toddler with blond curly hair and a man in jeans and a bomber jacket speaking on his mobile phone.

A prickling sense of unease trickled down her neck. The man's aura was starting to take on the look of thick syrup.

So was the child's, with dramatic effect. 'I want!'

'No,' the mother replied in a steady voice. 'We're not buying sweets.'

The toddler grabbed several packets of sweets from the shelves, hurled them onto the floor, then threw herself alongside the strewn sweet packets trying to scrabble them together,

'*I want!*'

She began to swim along the floor in a rage as her mother steadfastly began putting the packets back on the shelf.

Kaia scooted to grab croissants, bread, cheese, and nuts and then went to the counter to pay. Other campers streamed in. They grabbed baskets and swooped down the aisles like a plague of locusts, stocking for a siege.

Outside in the car park things were equally chaotic.

'I haven't got all day!'

She regarded the angry lady signalling to take her parking space, deciding it would be prudent not to highlight an alternative spot nearby. 'You might want to back up a bit. I'll need room to swing out.'

'I'm not moving,' came the retort. 'You should not park a van in the car park. It is a *car park*! Don't you know anything?'

Ignoring the provocation, Kaia climbed into the driver's seat as the woman slammed her car horn. She grimaced and reversed from the car park. Then she drove to find a quiet spot for the night.

Parking next to the hedge in the corner of the field, she converted the inside of the van into a bedroom, pulled out an organically grown apple from her bag of shopping, and set off to walk the dogs.

When she returned, a man wearing a faded blue T-shirt, his longish hair scraped into a ponytail, was standing next to the van. He would have been attractive if he smiled, but as it was, his aggressive scowl made his face as dark and dour as his aura.

'You can't stop here, doll.'

Barbie. 'Why not?'

'You've gotta move it. This here is a tent spot. This ain't a tent.'

No shit, Sherlock. She did not respond, which did not do much for his demeanour.

'Bet you said you had a tent, to get in cheap!'

She flinched at his aggressive tone, but she was done with letting men intimidate her. 'See it as a metal tent. It might help.'

The man glared, muttered something about her being too smart for her own good, and stormed away in the direction of the site office to register a complaint. At that moment his phone rang from his back pocket. He answered it, and then pandemonium broke out. Banging on the door of the nearest camper van, Ponytail started an argument with a tattooed man who answered. The two hurled obscenities, then the situation escalated as other campers joined in. Finally, a young girl started screaming she wanted to go home.

Kaia drove back to the office.

'I won't be needing the spot after all.'

The site manager was sitting behind the counter, staring at the screen of his own mobile, his aura also dark and muddy.

'Don't worry about a refund.'

For the next few hours, Kaia drove north, going over what she had witnessed. *Mobiles transmit a signal. A signal that brings the worst out of people. ... Who is behind it, and why?* It was a conundrum she was determined to unravel.

She drove from Glasgow, crossed the Erskine Bridge, and suddenly found herself alongside Loch Lomond. For the next few hours, she drove through delicious sweeping glens past mountaintops lost in a darkening sky, every bend in the road bringing another vista that took her breath away. By the time she crossed the Skye Bridge, it was too dark to see vistas, yet not only could she picture them in her mind, but she also had the overwhelming feeling of having arrived home.

CHAPTER 2

O WEN HAD INSTALLED A WOODEN screen with a curtain for a door that now separated the living area from Meg's bed. He had also made her a wooden washstand and an oak chest. The other villagers had also been generous, donating blankets, a large pot for cooking, a vase which was currently on the table filled with moon daisies; two dresses that Morag, skilled in needlework, had altered to fit; and an array of pots which were now in situ on the shelves above the fire, filled with seaweeds Meg had gathered and dried.

Although Meg could not remember how she had learnt, it turned out she had an uncanny knowledge of seaweed. She had initially made a remedy for Morag to help with her arthritic fingers, as a thank you for altering the dresses. Morag had been delighted and had told Elsie. Elsie in turn had asked if she knew how to help soothe her bairn's gums as he was teething, and so it had gone on. Not that Meg minded. It kept her busy and gave her mind something to focus on.

The remedy she had recently made was now cool. She carefully poured it from the jug into a tiny bottle, sealed it, put it into her pocket and then walked to the shore. The clouds were hanging dark and heavy, yet the rain held off as she rowed across the loch, and it was only as she was letting the boat glide alongside the jetty that it began to drizzle. The men had set the day to put a new thatch on Elsie's cottage, and she hoped they had got most of it done.

After making fast the boat, she stepped ashore and smoothed down her tartan dress. She tied a grey crocheted shawl tighter round her shoulders and made her way along the lane to Morag's cottage. A black shadow

77

crossed the ground at her feet, cast by a black crow flying low over the hawthorn hedge. It landed and began plucking bright red berries from the branches. Its presence taunted, but any remnants of memory sank into the recesses of her mind. The bird flew away, disappearing into the trees at the other side of the field.

Morag's house was larger than her own, a squat black stone house, which looked to be melting into the ground it sat on. Its neatly thatched roof was laced with stones to stop the gusting winds from blowing the straw loose.

She found Morag huddled in her usual spot by her peat fire, a green and grey tartan rug over her knees, the chair near to the fire but positioned so she could also see out the window. Haggis, a stout Scottish wildcat with a snubbed face and torn ear from his feral fighting days, was curled on her lap as she worked on her latest piece of embroidery.

Meg crossed to the fire, placed on fresh peat and told Morag about the crow. 'It made me imagine a shadow in my head, one that feasts on my memories.'

'Give yourself time.' Morag said smiling as the heat from the fire intensified. 'Memories are like wildcats. Chase them, and they run. Ignore them, and they'll come to you.'

Haggis, disturbed by them speaking, yawned and began batting loose threads with one paw.

'Och you are a nuisance. Settle ye down.' Morag pulled some grey and blue tangled threads from her work basket with swollen arthritic fingers. The movement triggered Haggis to launch himself into the basket. Morag jumped, and the naughty cat stuck his head from the basket with thread hanging over his ear.

'What are you stitching?'

Morag's eyes sparkled. 'That would be telling. Your cottage needs a bit of something. I'd get it finished soon enough if I had a little less help from him.' She pointed at the cat as he leapt back onto her lap.

Haggis had no sooner settled when Meribeth, Morag's niece, a freckle-faced, fun-loving sixteen-year-old, with long, thick, curled ginger hair, burst in carrying a plate laden with oatcakes.

'I don't know how you do it, lassie,' Morag said, her wizened, kindly face lighting up as she took a cake and nibbled at it. 'You must have magic in those fingers of yours.'

'It's just an oatcake. Although I did add a few blackberries and an elderberry or two.'

'Like I said, magic.' Morag chuckled and breaking off a few crumbs offered them to Haggis, who sniffed at them suspiciously. 'How about a story? Your favourite?'

Drawing up the second wooden chair, Meribeth set the plate of oatcakes onto the battered oak table next to the bottled remedy and then settled herself next to her aunt. Meg knew well enough which story it would be. She turned her attention back to the fire as Haggis closed his eyes and began to purr as though wanting to hear the story too.

'The morning sun rose in the east, sending shimmering gold and pink across the aqua blue loch,' Morag began in a soft, spellbinding voice. 'Oystercatchers paraded along the shoreline, searching for their morning fare amid the seaweed, which clothed the rocks in deep swaths of green and gold. Ianna swam faster, trying to catch Pendragon, who was racing ahead. She might be merfolk, but she was still no match for the kelpie, who twisted and turned in the water, his mane flowing around him like the seaweed itself. Indeed, when he swam low, it was hard for Ianna to distinguish his form amid the forest of seaweed swirling in the current of the water.

'"Hiding is cheating!" Ianna called out as she tried to spot him. "What chance have I got of ever catching you, if you are catching your breath?"

'As if to answer her question, Pendragon shot out from the seaweed and brushed past her at lightning speed, racing for the surface and the shore. "Let's see if you can catch me on land instead!"'

Meribeth smiled in delight. 'Ianna did not stand a chance! Even on land Pendragon could outpace her. Who can catch a kelpie when they have turned into a horse?'

Morag chuckled, her grey eyes sparkling in the firelight. 'Who indeed? A fine white stallion at that. Now shall I finish the story, or shall you tell it?'

'You,' Meribeth replied. 'To think kelpies are here, in the lochs. I would love to see one.'

Meg stiffened involuntarily and caught Morag's eye. Morag regarded her shrewdly.

'I'd love to see one too.'

'If anyone will see a kelpie, it will be you … or Bran,' Meribeth said. 'You two are always on the water. I think I shall ask Bran if I can go fishing with him. Then I may see one.' She turned back to Morag. 'Go on, aunt. The kelpie became a horse …'

Morag returned to her story. 'Ianna swam towards the shore, but Pendragon was already leaving the water and beginning to change. His green frondlike face and neck became the head of a beautiful stallion that matched in colour the white crested waves, and his body morphed into the four-legged body of a white horse. He reared, tossing his head teasingly as Ianna waded onto the beach. Then as she ran towards him, he trotted just beyond her reach, picking up his feet slowly and deliberately, as if mocking her attempt to catch him. Neither of them felt the chill of the spring dawn, and neither did they feel the sharpness of the rocks beneath their feet. For the fae of the sea are immune to such things. They ran across the shoreline as light-footed as the air and the water itself.

'"Enough! You win!" Ianna said eventually.

'Pendragon slowed and turning, nuzzled his head against her shoulders. "Let's run together."

'Ianna pulled herself onto his back; then Pendragon galloped along the shoreline, faster and faster, running in the shallows where the waves were breaking. Ianna laughed as the wind blew her hair out behind her, but fae or not, she still had duties to perform, and when they got to the end of the beach, Pendragon galloped back into the sea. As his legs became submerged, they turned back to being a green sea frond covered tail, and for an instant the man who had been watching saw the woman riding, not a stallion, but a green kelpie. Then a wave crashed over them, and they disappeared.

'The man watching had first seen them many moons prior when he happened upon them by chance. He should not have gone back to the beach to look for them again, but he could not help himself, for he had fallen in love with Ianna at first sight. Soon afterwards he started to leave her presents on the shore, a bunch of wildflowers and a string of white shells that he had collected and made into a necklace. Then one day Ianna waited on the beach to see who had been leaving her presents. They met, and as soon as Ianna looked into his eyes, she loved him as much as he did her—'

'They got married and lived happily ever after!' Meribeth leapt up from where she had been sitting and kissed Morag on the cheek, disturbing Haggis, who leapt to the floor and sauntered nearer to the fire with his tail held high. 'I do love that story.'

'How can I finish the tale properly, if you finish it for me?' Morag teased.

Meribeth shrugged and tossed her loose brown hair. 'I'd rather not hear the rest. Ianna falling in love is a good ending, but her leaving her water world and forgetting all about Pendragon … that makes me sad.'

'Aye, lassie,' Morag said, nodding in agreement. 'It is sad, but in life you have to follow your heart and let love lead.'

Meg shuddered, picked up the iron poker, and began stoking the fire vigorously.

'Are you all right, Meg?'

'Just cold,' Meg replied, 'and the cold does nothing to ease my mind. This thick fog inside my head refuses to move.'

'The wind is picking up,' Morag noted as a gust of wind blew around the cottage and sent a cold draft down the chimney, blowing the flames of the fire sideways. 'A vasanti wind, a wind that brings change. Perhaps that will help.'

Meg smiled ruefully. 'It will take more than the wind to blow it away.' She brushed down her dress, tied her shawl tighter around her shoulders, and held Morag's gaze for a moment before turning her attention back to the fire.

The flames were now roaring. Meg was aware of her body yearning to relax in their warmth, but something seemed to prevent it. Perhaps it was Morag's story. The story of Ianna always troubled her, but she could never grasp why. *Damned amnesia.* The flames flickered, drawing her in. The salamanders, the fae of the fire, were weaving their magic.

The salamanders were replaced by a dark, creeping mist that engulfed everything. She was lost … She saw Owen's sgian dubh and sword, the engraved leaves on its hilt … Silhouetted figures appeared, evil and cruel. There was a roar. A dragon sent a burst of fire shooting from its mouth—and then the dragon's fire became the real fire. The salamanders stopped the vision and danced their usual dance over the half-burnt peat.

Meg turned to face the room. 'The flames speak of ill tidings.'

Morag looked concerned but did not respond.

'Will you be needing anything else?' Meribeth said, reaching for her shawl. 'I've been longer than I said. I'd best be getting back.'

Morag waited until Meribeth had closed the cottage door and then turned her attention back to Meg. 'Don't ye go bothering yourself about your memory anymore. You are part of the village, that's what matters.' She gestured towards a bottle of whisky on the dresser, and Meg passed it to her. 'Have a wee dram. It'll calm your nerves.' Morag poured the golden liquid into two small glasses. 'I wonder how the men are getting on with the roof?'

'They'd best be near enough finished else the wind will blow it away.' She took a sip of the whiskey, instantly feeling its warmth spreading across her chest. 'I'll go and see.'

Morag smiled. 'Aye. I'm glad you're staying here tonight. That's a strong wind; the loch won't be friendly. I shouldn't settle thinking you were rowing it.'

CHAPTER 3

OWEN CUT THE LAST SHEATH of straw to shape and deftly laced it down. 'All yours, Laylan!' he called out, throwing the last section of rope to the Highlander on the ground.

'This blasted wind is not helping,' Laylan called back, his ragged ginger hair blowing across his rugged face. 'What a day to thatch!'

Owen agilely ran along the top of the ridge of the black house to haul another section of rope, complete with its hanging stones, over the thatch. 'At least it's not raining. The turf has stayed dry.' He secured the rope and then scurried down the roof. Oblivious to the height and precarious footing, he swung over the edge and landed on the grit and pebbles without making a sound.

'Just glad he's on our side,' remarked another man as he unrolled the sleeves of his shirt and put back on his brown wool jacket. 'Wouldn't want to meet him on a dark night, if he wasn't.'

Meg helped the others tidy up. Scooping up the last of the cut straw, she threw it into the waiting cart as Laylan began coiling the remaining rope around his thickset arm.

'Lithe can breathe easy tonight,' Owen said as he joined them. 'His house will stay dry, even if the wind brings in a beast of a storm.' He looked across at Lithe, who was staring anxiously past them. 'Is it not to your liking?'

Lithe gestured toward the lane, his face ashen.

The tax collectors had returned. The group stood like statues as the three men pulled their horses to halt. 'Taxes.'

Owen looked the man directly in the face. 'We've paid.'

The burly man who had spoken gave him a look of scorn and dismounted. 'Taxes were not received, and payment is overdue.'

'I say we've paid—'

'Taxes are due, and we've come to collect.' The man pushed past Owen towards the house. 'If you can afford a roof, you can afford to pay. Whose house is this?'

Owen stepped nearer. 'Mine.'

The man gave a grunt and turned back to face Owen. He took off his riding jacket, rolled up his sleeves, and then punched him on the cheek. 'You'll pay, dog, else we'll take—'

He didn't finish. Owen lunged, shouldering him in the chest. They grappled and fell to the ground. Seconds later, Owen landed a punch on the man's face, knocking him out cold.

In an instant Owen was back on his feet with his sword drawn as the other tax collectors dismounted. The two men knew they were outmatched and hesitated, hands over the hilts of their own swords.

'We've paid.' Owen's eyes were flashing dangerously. 'But if yer wanting more, I'll gladly gi' it to 'ee.'

Drawing their swords the men attacked simultaneously, yet they were no match for Owen. He disarmed one immediately and seconds later stood with the tip of his sword at the throat of the other.

The men dusted themselves off and got back on their horses in silence as the villagers lifted the third man, still unconscious, across the saddle of his own horse. They rode away, and Owen sheathed his sword.

Lithe broke the silence. 'It's a bonnie roof, but I'll not be long under it.'

Laylan slung the coiled rope in the cart and began gathering the tools. 'Take heart, man.'

'You've paid, and Sir John knows it. I'll visit Sir John and say as such,' Owen said, rubbing the back of his hand across his forehead.

'But tonight, we celebrate a roof well done,' Laylan stated, putting his arm across Lithe's shoulders. 'Annie will have the fire on. Will you come, Meg?'

<hr>

Inside Laylan's snug cottage the howling wind seemed miles away. The room was roasting, and the fire, now a pile of bright orange embers, cast a warm glow on their faces. Annie, a middle-aged redhead, was sitting on Laylan's lap. She had a wicked sense of humour and had been making fun.

Laylan pretended to be shocked and clutched at her thigh. 'Och, you've got a harsh tongue, woman! I dinna know why I put up with ye.' He kissed her roughly on the mouth and then turned to them. 'Another song! Your turn, Owen!'

Owen had been staring at the glowing embers, seemingly miles away. Hearing his name mentioned, he came to and locked eyes with hers. Intense, hungry. She held his gaze, feeling a yearning in her body. Then he stirred and started to sing. A slow haunting melody, made more so by the deep resonance of his voice.

Owen sang in a language she didn't understand, but the words carried her to the raging sea and a ship with wind in its sail. Finishing the verse, Owen sang it again, this time in their Gaelic tongue.

'The great wind roars, waves they roll.
Carrying us afar across the ocean blue
We must away, to the dark shore
To the mountain with its doors of fire.
The great wolf will howl our homecoming call.
Return triumphant, shields renewed.
Light the fire, and fill the horn,
Gather fish and new acorns.
We will sing and tell our tale,
Our longships steady with unfurled sails.'

They sat in silence long after the last note had finally faded away. Owen was an enigma. Not much older than her and yet he knew so much; skilled in craftsmanship to a degree that should take lifetimes to accomplish, and so wise when it came to understanding the dynamics of men. She vaguely recollected him saying that he had been around a long time, and she wondered exactly how long that was.

CHAPTER 4

LEAVING MORAG'S EARLY THE NEXT morning, Meg found Lithe and Owen, dressed in woollen riding jackets, tacking up their horses at the edge of a field near the shore. The wind was spooking the horses, and they skittered, pulling on the reins which were currently securing them to the wooden gate.

'Lithe has been filling me in on the joys of sleepless nights,' Owen jested, raising his voice to be heard over the wind.

Lithe's eyes looked red and sore. 'What a bairn wants a bairn will have.'

'Aye ... Whoa there.'

Lithe ran his hand down the horse's neck and pulled its forelock through its bridle as Owen untethered and mounted his own horse. Owen kept the horse reined in until Lithe was also mounted and then let the reins longer. His horse immediately set off along the track, with Lithe's close behind.

Meg continued to the jetty, where she untethered the boat and set off across the loch. The shore was soon far behind, but out on the open water the wind felt stronger and was making waves larger. She pulled on the oars as hard as she could, struggling to keep the boat steady as rain started to fall. Driven by the wind, the raindrops struck her face like stones. She began to get disorientated. All she could see were waves, which were getting bigger by the second.

Oh, for the love of God.

An enormous wave came racing towards the bow, seemingly determined to sink it. Yet at the last second, the wave changed direction to travel with her, carrying the boat along. For the briefest moment she could have sworn the wave crest took the form of a horse's head. *A kelpie.*

There was no time to think. She had to focus. Propelled by the wave, the boat was now racing towards the shore with such speed, she had to pull back hard on the oars to keep it from crashing on the rocks.

Once ashore, she secured the boat to its mooring. Then picking up a white shell from among the pebbles, she kissed it and threw it into the loch. It was a ritual she undertook after every safe passage and today, soaked to the skin, with water dripping from her face, she was grateful to be back on land.

The gesture was not enough. Reaching to her neck, she untied her string of white shells and gently placed them at the water's edge, whispering her thanks. Then, wiping water from her face, she pulled her sodden shawl tightly over her shoulders and hurried through the driving rain to her cottage set back in the trees.

⋅⟡⟡⟡⋅

Sometime later, Owen and Lithe crossed the Minch in a boat to land on the mainland a few miles from the baronet's estate. The wind was picking up, but the clouds had not broken. Arriving in a cobbled yard, they fastened their horses to a rail situated near the stables, then made their way to the main entrance of the foreboding grey building. Lithe had long since fallen silent and was looking increasingly anxious.

'Let me do the talking.' Owen muttered, giving him a reassuring look.

Inside they were ushered into a large room filled with extravagant décor. The plush purple curtains, gilded furniture and crystal chandelier would have been more suited to the king's court than a country manor house. Yet Sir John had an inflated ego and considered himself kingly, proven by the exceedingly large portrait of himself standing in the exact same pose as a recent portrait of His Royal Highness that hung over the intricately carved fireplace. Sir John was standing by the fireside dressed in plum and rust velvet attire, with a three-quarter-length satin jacket laden with gold embroidery, which looked to have been cut several sizes too small for his opulent, rotund figure.

Lithe hovered by the door as Owen delivered their message. 'The upshot is this: the land does not bear a good crop,' Owen concluded. 'What little has grown this season they need for themselves.'

Sir John gave Owen a glare from his piggish eyes and turned his back to stare at the huge fire burning in the hearth. 'Damn the cold, damn the island, and damn you.' He picked up a large poker and began stabbing viciously at the burning logs, visibly wishing they were Owen. 'You are not a clan leader, and you are certainly not a baronet. What you are … is above your station. Highlanders are forbidden to wear plaids. Yet here you are.' He waved his hand behind him, indicating their apparel. 'I could have you both flogged. Now get out of my sight.'

Sir John swung round brandishing the poker, now gleaming red with heat. Owen instinctively hovered one hand over the hilt of his sword, but no blow came, so he removed his hand from the blade, drew out a leather pouch, and placed it onto an ornate table. 'This will cover the outstanding debt.'

Sir John's eyes lingered greedily. 'There's not enough in there to cover what is due.'

'I can assure you there is.'

'I say different,' Sir John said shrewdly. 'The delay incurs a penalty.' He took an embroidered silk handkerchief from his pocket and nonchalantly wiped it across his bulbous nose.

'You do not have that authority.'

'Do not challenge me!' Sir John's eyes narrowed dangerously.

Owen swallowed his anger. He had encountered many miserable assignees like the man before him, power-hungry wretches with no thought for anyone but themselves. He made to pick up the pouch from the table, but Sir John pounced on it.

'A down payment of the outstanding debt,' he parroted with a sneer. 'If the full amount is not repaid by the end of the month. I shall issue indentures.'

'My bairn!' Lithe's eyes were wide in shock.

'Can go with you,' Sir John said, waving his hand whilst still holding the handkerchief. 'I will have what I am due. Three years working land in Nova Scotia will do you good.'

'Come, Lithe,' Owen muttered through gritted teeth. 'We're wasting our time here.' He stared at Sir John, his voice like steel. 'There will be no indentures. Every man has a right to his freedom.'

'They are not free,' Sir John spat, as Owen turned and marched to the door. 'They belong to the land. They belong to me!' His voice rose to a shriek. 'Taxes have increased. I will have what is due.' He paused, expecting a response. 'I will get a decent price per head!' he shouted as Owen slammed the door.

Lithe was silent until they arrived back at their horses. Then: 'My God. Indentures.'

Owen swung himself into his saddle. 'The man is as narrow-minded as he is dim-witted. He can't thumbscrew the village.' He gave Lithe an encouraging look. 'If he serves indentures, there'll be none to work his precious land. I've seen men like him come and go, men who take from the mouths of others. You must stand up to their sort, or they trample you into the mud.' He flicked the reins, and his horse began to walk. 'Take heart. You'll see another summer here.'

CHAPTER 5

MEG HAD SPENT THE AFTERNOON foraging for seaweed. She put another log onto the fire and turned the kelp and dulse she had set to dry, unperturbed by their pungent aroma. Lighting the half-burnt candle, she placed the candlestick onto the table next to the moon daisies, her favourite flowers.

A sudden noise came from the roof. She stiffened. *It's just a roosting bird.* She cursed herself for being edgy and folding her shawl, placed it at the foot of her bed. The noise sounded again. Louder this time, and suspiciously like scrabbling claws. *Not a bird.* She scurried to the door, slid the bolt into its fastening, and then darted to the window, to check its shutter bolts, as whatever had been on the roof leapt to the ground.

Her heart now pounding, she seized the broom and took up a stance by the door, ready to strike. She was aware of the creature circling the building and imagined it looking at the door, the shutters ... the chimney. *The chimney!*

She dropped the broom and ran to stack on more wood, causing smoke to billow and an angry snarl to come from outside. Meg retrieved the broom, then positioning the chair by the door sat down, in preparation for a long night.

Though she thought to evade sleep, the creature outside was long gone when Meg woke the next morning, stiff from leaning awkwardly against the broom.

She opened the door and cautiously looked out. Everything was calm and serene. Through the trees she could see the sun rising across the loch and oystercatchers striding back and forth in the shallows.

She stepped outside wondering if she had imagined her visitor.

She had not. The thatch looked to have been slashed with a scythe, and there were deep prints where the creature had leapt to the ground, like wolf prints, but with claws twice as long as the footpad. She followed the trail around the cottage and then through the trees to the shore.

'Meg!'

She looked up to see Bran, a stocky young fisherman, waving from his rowing boat.

She returned the wave. 'Have you seen anything around the loch? I've had an unwelcome visitor.'

Bran rowed closer. 'Tax collectors? They don't know the cottage's lived in.'

'No.' She told him what had happened.

Bran screwed up his weathered face. 'The fishermen I met earlier said a lassie from their village went missing yesterday. Her body was found in the night. She'd had her throat slit.' She felt the blood drain from her face. 'I'm on my way back.' Bran continued. 'When Owen hears about the girl, he'll go out with the wolves to track down whatever did it. I'll tell him it was here too.'

She watched Bran row in the direction of the village. Owen was always at the forefront of everything: taxes, visiting Sir John, and now tracking down whatever had killed the girl. He didn't even have an established home here, and yet they all looked to him as leader of the clan, even the wolves. She knitted her brows, thinking of the tattoo across Owen's chest, the way his teeth had glinted in the fire of the ceilidh, his agility and fierce, protective nature when it came to the villagers. ...

She stared across the pink and orange water. He did say he'd been around a long time. It was more than a flippant remark. The song he had sung echoed through her head. It was an old song, and he had sung it as though recalling faces, as though he had been with the men on the ship sailing to the mountain.

Her head began to swim. She needed to clear her mind. If Owen had been on a longship, then he had been alive for centuries, and that couldn't be right. Without further thought, she discarded her outer clothes, waded into the water, and dived.

She could see clearly underwater. Owen had said it was unusual and suggested she focus on the ability, saying it might trigger memories. Yet so far, it had not. Spying a bonnie patch of sea lettuce and making a mental note to come back for it, she swam deeper, pushing through sea kelp to surface farther out across the loch.

Back on the shore a dark shape flickered through the shadows of the trees. Silently gliding to a rocky outcrop, which the high tide had temporarily made into a tiny island, Meg crawled onto the rocks to get a better look.

That's a strange wolf.

She watched the creature track her scent across the beach to her clothes. It raised its head, looking out across the water as though understanding where she had gone. She ducked low, waited for a few moments, and then peeped back out from the rocks. The beach was now empty. Yet instinct warned her it was hiding nearby. She would have to swim ashore someplace else.

She was slipping back into the water when she caught sight of a faint symbol, not unlike the ones in her diary. It had been carved a long time ago; its edges were eroded and in places obscured by barnacles that had taken up residence. She instinctively knew there was a message in it for her. Perhaps even a clue to her understanding the symbols she had drawn. Yet now was not the time to figure it out. If she was lucky, she would meet Bran somewhere on the loch. If unlucky, she was going to have a long swim to the village.

CHAPTER 6

$\clubsuit \spadesuit \spadesuit \spadesuit \spadesuit$

'YOU WERE LUCKY NOT TO catch your death.'

Meg gave an involuntary shiver and finished the bowl of vegetable broth Morag had insisted on her having. She was sitting by the fire in Morag's kitchen, wearing one of Morag's old dresses, her own underclothes hanging by the fire to dry. Haggis was also enjoying the warmth and was currently sitting in Morag's work basket with his eyes almost shut, pretending to be asleep.

'I'm a strong swimmer, and that worked magic.'

'Aye. You're at home in the water, lassie, but I wasn't talking of your swim. What you saw … bears the marks of a demon.' Morag's hand trembled as she lifted her spoon to her mouth.

Meg did not want to stress her more than she already had. 'Perhaps I was mistaken.'

'Tut! I know your game, lassie, and I'm not a weak-minded woman who'll faint at the news of a demon,' Morag said feistily. 'It isn't the first to come sniffing around these parts and maybe won't be the last.'

She indicated the black pot hanging over the fire. Meg helped herself to another ladle of broth and returned to her chair, removing a disgruntled Haggis who had moved like lightning into her vacated seat.

'Wolves don't climb onto house roofs looking for a way in,' Morag stated.

At that moment the door burst open. 'I've just seen Bran.' Owen's eyes flashed in anger. 'He told me about the killin' and said you were on the shore half drowned.'

Haggis arched his back, hissed. and slunk back to the workbasket.

93

'I hoped to catch Bran on the loch.' She watched bemused as Haggis buried himself in the threads and then glared at Owen over the edge of the basket. She related events from the previous night.

Owen looked increasingly grave. He unsheathed his sgian dubh and pushed it across the table. 'You carry it. You can't kill demons with it, but you can defend yourself should one attack.'

She stiffened. 'Then you think it was a demon too?'

'Aye.'

She picked up the unusual foot-long blade connected to its intricately carved metal hilt that looked to be made from twisting vines, topped by a dark green stone. *How old is this?*

'Do you think the demon showing up has something to do with the baronet?'

'Sir John is on a dark road with little thought for anyone other than himself.'

'Yet you don't think he's linked to the demon.'

'No.' Owen spoke with conviction. 'Sir John is many things but has neither the wit nor the way withal to summon demons. Just keep the blade close.' He turned to face the fire as though battling thoughts.

She finished her second bowl of broth in silence as Haggis, ending his vigilance, wrapped his tail around his face to go to sleep.

'Sir John's a fool,' Owen said eventually. 'None here can afford what he asks. Some of us are riding to Alexander MacDonald's to make our voices known. Sir John's weak-livered. He may reconsider the taxes if the villages stand united. Come with us.'

His eyes burned into her. It felt a command, not a question. She nodded her consent without saying a word.

CHAPTER 7

A FEW HOURS LATER FOUND OWEN, Lithe, Laylan, and Meg heading out of village for the south of the island. Meg knew Owen spent time at Alexander's lodge and wondered what the place was like—no doubt a far cry from the tiny cottage by the shore.

They rode hard, through a forest, across the side of the escarpment, and then out onto the open moor. Several hours later they clattered across a cobbled yard adjacent to an impressive sandstone building. Owen leapt from his horse and approached the stable hand, a gangly fresh-faced youth with straw-like hair, who was carrying fresh hay into empty stables.

'Have you any spare, Jess?'

The young man indicated an area in the stable block. Owen led his horse inside and slid off the saddle. The he picked up a handful of straw and began to rub the sweat from his horse's back.

'I can brush 'em down and make sure they're all fed and watered,' Jess said, holding out a grubby hand to take the reins. 'It's no bother.'

After leaving their horses with Jess, they crossed the yard and walked through a stone archway to the main entrance. The thick oak door was open, allowing passage to a large wooden-panelled hallway with a dark wooden staircase at the far end and oak doors on either side. There were baskets, shotguns, and various leather boots lined against the wall near the entrance. A bear of a man with a red-whiskered face, dressed in highland kilt and green wool jacket, was crossing the room carrying a basket of wood that looked to contain an entire tree. He immediately accosted them.

'Owen!' Putting down the basket, he gave Owen a rough hug and slapped him on the back of his shoulder. 'It's been a while. What's brought you back?'

Owen introduced Meg to Alexanders' brother, Angus, and told him the reason for their visit.

'Och, that's hefty handed.' Angus's face turned solemn. 'Alexander will have a thing or two to say. He's due back from hunting. Come on in.'

Angus ushered them into a large wooden panelled room, with a roaring fire burning in its huge place and offered them a dram from a glass decanter set on a large oak dresser. They had not been there long when the sound of chatting came from the hall, and a group of men bustled into the room, among them Sir Alexander. He made a formidable figure, thickset, with greying hair brushed back from a weathered face, dressed in woven wool hunting trews, a traditional woollen bonnet with a pheasant feather pinned to its front, and at his waist, a leather sheath containing a well-used sword. His grey eyes shone with intelligence and warmth, but as Owen related the reason for their visit, the atmosphere in the room changed, and Sir Alexander's face darkened.

'I'll not stand for indentures. I will send word to Sir John today.'

The other men moved closer to the fire and began chatting among themselves, leaving Owen to introduce Meg. Alexander kissed the back of her hand.

'The clans could rally.' Owen spoke in a low tone. 'If faced with a unified voice, the baronet would be forced to back down.'

Alexander regarded him shrewdly. 'You should be a politician, Owen.' He lowered his voice to a whisper. 'You know me well enough. I'll stand for Highlanders and kinsmen, even if that means standing against the Crown.' He gave Owen a knowing look and then slapped him on the back. 'Stay. Return tomorrow. We had good hunting!'

The energy of the house turned to camaraderie as game was set to roast. Whilst it cooked the men went out to the rear of the lodge to play shinty. Meg stood at the side of the field with two young women, wives of two of the players. They laughed and jeered as their men grappled with shinty sticks, using them in a fashion more akin to weaponry than sport.

'What's the point of the game?' Meg asked as one man swiped the other from his feet, then barged into a third, who retaliated by landing a blow across his shoulder. The man bent double, in line with yet another, who leaping over him, raced over the grass, and whacked the ball, which then flew into the air in their direction.

One of her companions let out a squeal and ducked. 'There's none!'

The game escalated. Owen ran to the ball, whacking it back along the grass, diverted a tackle from an opponent, and then whacked the ball again, landing it near the man still on the ground. Ignoring the ball completely, the man stood and then tackled the man who had hit him.

'I saw my missin' heifer. She was runnin' with yours.'

'She was wandering by the burn, lad, looking for a new home.'

They began to fight with their sticks, teeth bared, unaware of the game ceasing and everyone watching. Owen stepped in and tried to pull them apart, receiving a blow to the stomach for his trouble.

At that moment Alexander strode across the grass to swing a bucket of cold water over both men. They glared and cursed but stopped brawling.

'Settle yer differences and save yer fire for when it's needed.'

Alexander's face broke into laughter. Offering his arm, he pulled both to their feet, and the game recommenced, with as much zest and enthusiasm as before.

Later that evening, the roast eaten and drinks having flowed, the house became a haven of safety and allegiance. Meg particularly relished the sense of so many under one roof, the feeling of being in unison, ready to face whatever was to come from the world outside. She watched Owen laughing with two of Alexander's men, so comfortable and at ease. The thought made her flinch. She was not part of these dynamics, not really.

'You look lost.'

Owen was at her side, his eyes dancing. She was suddenly aware of his proximity, of his open shirt revealing a well-toned chest and tattoo. 'I think I've been found.'

'Aye. Won't be the first time I found ye, will it?'

There was a movement in the doorway, and Alexander's mother, an elegant, elderly lady dressed in a long green tartan dress with white hair plaited onto the top of her head, crossed to join them.

'Freya.' Owen took Freya's hand in his own and kissed the back of it.

Freya swiftly turned his hand over to examine his palm. 'You are not long staying on these shores. The men look to you for brotherhood.'

Owen abruptly pulled his hand away. 'In Odin's name, I didna ask for that.'

'You know me well enough. I speak as I see.' She turned to face her. 'You must be Meg.' She held out her hand.

Meg hesitantly placed her hand in Freya's, who began to study its palm. She pursed her lips and then glanced at Owen with raised eyebrows. 'Strong and wise.' She let her hand go. 'You have been enjoying our books, I hear.'

She nodded. 'I have learnt much.'

'Then come and pick some for yourself.'

Freya led them from the room to a dark oak door that opened into a large library. Meg gazed round in delight at the shelves stacked with leather, or clothbound, books.

'I am not fond of reading myself, but Alexander reads in here in winter when the nights draw in early.' Freya indicated the dark oak table and a board with strange figures standing on it. 'Although I am partial to the occasional game of chess.'

'Chess?'

'Aye. It's an ancient game.' Freya moved across to the board of squat carved figures sitting in squares and passed one to her. 'That piece is the white queen. What do you sense when you hold it?'

Meg examined the exquisitely carved lady sitting on a throne, looking deep in thought. 'Nothing.' She made to pass the figure back. 'Wait ... I can smell flowers, like honey, and a white room ...' There was a flash of light in her mind, she caught a glimpse of a shimmering symbol, and then nothing.

Freya gave her a knowing look. 'It's a game of strategy but also of the age-old battle of light and dark. The dark seeking dominance and the light, expansion.'

Owen had been examining the chess pieces. 'Bone. I canna believe it. The last time I saw a set like this ...' His voice broke off.

'It has been in our family for generations. One of my father's greatest treasures.'

'Aye. The last set I saw was made from walrus ivory.'

'I can only imagine.' Freya fell silent, then waved her hand at the books on the shelves. 'Pick some.'

Freya turned back to Owen. 'The one you would lead has another path to tread. A path you will share, but not for many moons.'

Meg circled the room. The fusty smell from the books was somehow reassuring. They almost had a persona, pockets of knowledge and insight. She pulled a leatherbound one from its shelf. *Navigation Accounts* of William Dampier and George Anderson. She flicked through the pages describing exotic sea voyages. Then, closing the book, she hugged it to her chest as she scanned the shelves for another. James Boswell's *Trip to Scotland*. That might trigger her memory and even contain accounts of where she was originally from. She would borrow just one more. *Gulliver's Travels*, Jonathan Swift. She opened the book and was immediately accosted by a man being set upon by tiny figures, a stranger in their world. The words pulled at her mind as though willing her to see the message they contained.

Feeling an instant affinity, she turned, smiling. 'I'll take these. Thank you.'

Freya returned her smile and led them back into the room where the others were now clearing tables. Owen looked disturbed, and as soon as Freya moved away across the room, he whispered urgently. 'Wolves are loyal to their kin, both blood and those they love.'

His mouth was inches from hers. If she leant forward, their lips would touch.

'Meg, I—'

'Help us clear the floor!'

Laylan was brandishing a fiddle. Standing near the fire, he began to play as the others cleared space for their impromptu ceilidh. Drinks flowed, and Meg danced until the stars faded, and the dawn birds began to sing.

CHAPTER 8

Sir John rose from his bed, yawned lethargically, and then shuffled across to the fireplace, where he stoked the fire with a long metal poker. He stared at the flames and then pulled the bell rope hanging from the wall next to the mantelpiece. Instantly the sound of a bell ringing came from the rooms below. Breakfast would soon be on its way.

Turning his back to the fire to let the heat soak into his spine, he glanced to the window and the view it offered. The mist had cleared, and he could see the island on the horizon. He scowled. The islanders were full of excuses. He deserved his dues. A ball of phlegm came from nowhere and caught in his throat. He coughed and cursed under his breath; the Highlanders on the island were bad for his health. *Damn them all. Damn them all to hell.* He turned his body round and reached out his palms to face the flames. *That blasted man. Where did he come from anyway?* Owen was the main root of his problem. Whenever he sought compensation for some discrepancy or other, it was Owen who came to confront him. *What right does he have? He's just …* There was a knock at the door.

'Enter.'

One of his footmen entered carrying a letter on a tray.

'A letter from Alexander MacDonald, sir.'

Sir John held out his hand, gesturing for the man to approach, and took the letter when it was within reach. His manservant bowed and left the room, leaving him to open and read what Alexander had written.

He did.

He exploded.

He screwed the letter into a ball and threw it onto the fire as a second knock sounded on the door. He shouted his response, in no humour for pleasantries.

The door swung open again, this time to allow access for a maid carrying a tray of bread and boiled eggs. He indicated the table with a nod and mentally undressed the maid as she turned and left. As he watched the door close, his mind returned to Owen. It was not just men that followed Owen. Owen was formed in a way that ensured no woman would ignore him. He hated him for that too. Shuffling his bloated body across to the table, he picked up an egg, pulled off its shell and put it into his mouth.

'No,' he said aloud, spitting out bits of egg as he spoke. 'I will not be intimidated by an outsider.' He threw the eggshell across the room into the fire where it began to crackle and spark. 'I will be rid of him!' he exclaimed in a raised voice. 'I will!'

There was a movement at the corner of his eye, and turning, he caught sight of a large crow taking off from the windowsill. He watched the bird fly into the distance, wondering if it had borne witness to his outburst. He had the strangest feeling not only that it had but also that it had understood every word.

CHAPTER 9

THE THICK ORANGE LIGHT SWIRLED across the desolate landscape of rock and burnt trees. Piercing the black slits of the castle windows, it caught on the white stone chess pieces, causing them to glint through the gloom.

'You can shine all you like, but you won't defeat me,' Scathchornail muttered in response to the unspoken challenge. Poising a finger over the black bishop, his eyes flickered through possible retaliations should he move the piece. Deciding it would leave the white force too many options, he pointed to a black pawn instead, causing it to slide one square forward. Minutiae, but sometimes small steps were necessary.

He switched his attention to a white knight but was distracted by wings beating near the window.

'Malphas. Any sign of the crystal?'

The large crow landed and transformed into his human form, white opaque eyes, skin devoid of colour, and dark hair formed from black feathers.

'No. How can you be sure they will send it.'

Scathchornail turned with a sneer. 'Strategy. The Atlantians will send the shard hoping it triggers her recall. It is pathetically predictable.'

Malphas cocked his head to one side and walked nonchalantly around the table, peering at the chessboard in a manner more befitting of his crow form. 'The white army has the advantage.'

'You know nothing of chess. Or strategy. You win by keeping your power hidden. Then you strike from all angles, leaving your opponent nowhere to run.'

'Yet there is an angle you haven't considered. The Dragon Fae is on the island in another era.'

'The woman you saw in Oxford is now on the island?'

'She is.'

An energy not dissimilar to a hurricane surged from Scathchornail's core and momentarily expanded to the edges of the room. Fate was drawing the women together. Problems. Weakness. When he was free from Shadow Side, there would be neither.

Irritated by the smirk on Malphas's face, he twisted a gloved finger, causing an electric static to whip round his mouth. Malphas did not flinch, but the smirk was replaced by a glare of loathing. *Better.*

He pushed the chair away from the onyx table, beckoning for Malphas to follow him from the room. Crossing the obsidian-floored hallway, they passed through one of its many archways to enter a long, dark chamber lined with faded tapestries, dust-filled scenes of bloody battles, stitched aeons ago in glory of a power that was weak and transient. Stopping by one displaying an armoured man on a rearing horse, eyes wide in terror and bloodied from battle, he ran his hand through the air, causing a stone panel in the wall to slide open.

Inside he removed his hat and gloves, placed them on an ornate black dresser, then crossing to the centre of the room took up position in the elaborate mandala etched into the stone floor. Closing his eyes, he began to mutter an incantation, moving his hands as though pulling energy up from the very depths of Earth. Then he drew a symbol and sent it, along with black electric from his hands, into the mandala and the ground beneath him. A dark mist began to seep from the floor, swirling in a vortex around him. Shadowy forms resembling wolves appeared, becoming more solid as they ran. Opaque eyes burned with hatred. The incantation was complete.

He regarded the snarling wolves now standing in the mandala. 'They can follow you through shadow. Hunt and scout dynamics. Find a link I can manipulate to separate the Dragon Fae from the animi.'

'I already have.'

Malphas related what he had overheard at Sir John's window and then disappeared into the shadow with the demon wolves at his heels.

It was time to tighten his grip.

CHAPTER 10

T HE WIND THAT HAD HOWLED through the trees all day had died down, leaving the air uncannily still. Something was going to happen. Something bad. Even the sea birds appeared to have sensed it and had fallen silent. Meg had finished *Gulliver's Travels*, which turned out to be a children's story that contained many undercurrents against the ways and prejudices of people. The story toyed with her mind, leaving her feeling even more of an outsider. She felt an affinity to the traveller who found himself washed ashore in such strange lands and with his difficulties in assimilating to their way of life.

To give her mind something different to focus on, she had been practicing writing and had written about her discovery of the symbol on the rock. She compared her drawing of it to the other symbols in her book. Neither she nor Owen had mentioned them since she had her fit, yet they were a clue to her past. Owen had called them Light Codes and had written that one of them meant air.

She recollected the image in her head when she had held the chess piece. It matched one on the page. Owen had said they were made of bone. If one symbol was air, then perhaps this symbol was bone. No. *Earth*. She wrote 'earth' next to the one she had identified and then stared at the others, willing an insight, but with no effect.

The symbol she had found on the rock was similar. Perhaps if she saw it in situ, she would get an insight into its meaning. There was still some daylight left. She would swim out to the symbol on the rock and take another look.

The tide was high, and with no wind the water looked flat and viscous.

She discarded her clothes and slipped into the water, losing her hair pin as she dove. Her hair began to flow around her like seaweed, and she moved her head this way and that, enjoying the sense of freedom it gave.

At a flash of movement Meg turned, but her hair moved slowly, obscuring her vision. She sensed another movement, nearer. Momentarily panicked, she shot to the surface and peered below. Something was hiding in the kelp, a long, slender creature that looked to be made from seaweed itself. *A kelpie.*

Diving back down, Meg lowered herself into the forest of kelp and slowly parted the wafting stems. The kelpie was beautiful and majestic. It remained motionless, gazing at her from eyes full of kindness and fun as a name drifted across her mind like sea mist.

Pendragon.

Slowly extending her hand, she touched Pendragon's cheek. She was galloping across the sand with the wind in her hair …

There was an explosion of pain in her heart and she kicked for the surface as her body began to judder.

She desperately tried to catch her breath, fighting against the water as the spasms got stronger. Seconds later her arms touched something solid. Pendragon was beneath her. She let her body rest against the support of his as he swam her to the shore.

Pendragon then lay in the shallows with her until her body stilled.

Her body now shaking with cold, she slid from his back to crawl for her clothes.

'Meg!' Owen and the wolves came running across the shore.

'For the love of God, woman, how many times do I have to do this?'

Scooping her into his arms, Owen carried her back to the cottage and laid her down by the fire. He wrapped a rug around her and stoked the flames. Then he sat down beside her as the four wolves entered and settled with them, as silent as shadows.

She told him she had met Pendragon, yet he did not seem surprised. 'You know more than you say, Owen.'

He remained silent.

'Don't deny it.'

His eyes flashed with emotion. 'I canna speak of it. It triggers the fits.'

There was a long pause. She studied his face as he stared into the flames, imagining him sitting in the same pose, but by a fire on the edge of a battlefield, reluctant to speak to the loyal men around him, lest the truth should dampen their courage. A wolf shifted its position, bringing her mind back into the room.

Owen spoke softly. Choosing his words carefully, he told her the light codes were healing and may mend a crystal called the Dragon's Heart that was needed to stop a dark force. He told her it's two shards were lost, that she had been looking for them, and that the kelpie Pendragon was one of her greatest friends. 'You have magic. You are meant to fix the crystal, and the demon wants to stop you. That's why the blasted thing hunts you.'

Too shocked to speak, Meg tried to take in what she had heard. It couldn't be true, and yet there was no denying the presence of the demon, or the connection she had felt to Pendragon.

'I don't remember any of it …' Her throat tightened, restricting her ability to speak.

Putting his arm around her, Owen drew her close. 'You are piecing it together. I can keep the demon away and give you the space to remember … If it's all the same to you, we will stay tonight.'

Nodding her consent, she leant against his shoulder, his warmth soothing her troubled thoughts. Exhausted, her eyelids grew heavy, and she was soon falling asleep in his arms.

CHAPTER 11

MEG WOKE THE NEXT MORNING to find herself lying on her bed, the cottage empty, and a note from Owen saying he had gone out with the wolves to track the demon. She stoked the fire, boiled water in the pot, and, when it began to bubble, poured it over a bowl of shredded seaweed. The pungent smell of salt and the sea rose with the steam. Closing her eyes, she took deep breaths, the smell carrying her to the ocean, to a ravine, a blue light …

There was a sudden knock on the door, and Meribeth's smiling face appeared around it.

'Lord. You made me jump!'

'Aunt Morag asked me to collect her remedy. I've brought you hazelnut bread, fresh baked.' Meribeth held out a parcel wrapped in a cloth.

'It's steeping. It will have to cool before I bottle it.' She untied the cloth Meribeth had given her to reveal a perfectly browned round loaf. 'Thank you. Surely you didn't row on your own?'

'Bran rowed me,' Meribeth said. 'He's fishing. Said he'd be back by in an hour.'

She picked up her shawl from the back of the chair. 'Then let's go for a stroll.'

Leaving the cottage, they took a narrow track leading into the forest. The fern had now fallen and lay on either of the track side like brown seaweed on the shore, but the larch trees were celebrating the season by their needles turning golden yellow.

'It's started to happen to me,' Meribeth said eventually. 'Sensing things.

Only little things. I know when someone will call by. Or if a thing is lost, I know where to find it.'

Meribeth stooped to gaze at a resilient yellow celandine still showing among the tree roots. Its colour illuminated her face. *Joy.* If she didn't regain her memory and the dark force destroyed everything, there wouldn't be such moments.

Meribeth looked up at her perceptively. 'You can tell me.'

'Some of my past has come back.' She related meeting Pendragon and how he had helped her.

Meribeth could not hide her enthusiasm. 'You saw a kelpie!'

'What do you know about them?'

'Fae water horses,' Meribeth replied enthusiastically. 'Some say kelpies are devious. That they eat flesh and seek to drown unwary folks, enticing them into the sea, but I don't believe that. Ma says with the Fae you get what you give. Treat them with respect, and they are good to you. What you have just said proves that. They live in the water but turn into beautiful white horses to come on land.'

Meg's heart skipped a beat. 'Like the one in your aunt's story.'

Meribeth suddenly looked serious. 'Aunt Morag has told me that story over and over.'

'Because it's your favourite.'

'It is now,' Meribeth said, 'but until a month ago Aunt Morag hadn't told it. Not once.'

'Then she only started after I turned up on the beach.'

Meribeth nodded, her eyes growing wide. 'There has to be a link … Pendragon.' She let out a squeal. 'Aunt Morag has been talking about you!'

Meg's legs suddenly gave way, and she leant against a tree for support. She wasn't from the sea, was she?

They continued along the forest track in silence, Meg breathing in the fragrance of the forest, the rich pine and the scent of the damp earth, willing the tension in her head to subside. Yet no sooner had she sunk into a sense of ease than there was a snap of a twig breaking on the track behind them.

Indicating for Meribeth to follow, Meg darted through a gap in the trees and broke into a run, ducking under low branches and pushing through fern to a small river. They paused. There was no noise, but instinct told Meg something still pursued them. She put her fingers to her lips, then pulling her skirts above her knees, she began to wade across the water, with Meribeth close behind.

The ploy to break their trail failed. They were barely halfway across the river when the demon wolf appeared on the bank behind them. It paced back and forth, its eyes burning with hatred, but did not get into the water. A shadow flickered across the surface, and Meg turned to see Meribeth clambering up the opposite bank.

'Wait!'

Meribeth let go of the water reeds she was using to pull herself up and fell backwards with a splash, as another demon appeared on the bank above her.

'What do we do?' Meribeth scrabbling to her feet.

'Stay in the water!'

They began to scrabble downstream to the shore, with the demons alongside on either bank, snapping and snarling in anger.

'Don't look at them; just focus on the river.'

Meribeth looked as white as a ghost. Meg thought of Owen out with the wolves. They had left to track the demons; they couldn't be that far away. In her mind she called out to Owen, envisioning the wolves pricking up their ears and smelling the wind as they sensed her need. *Movement.*

In what seemed like only minutes, a large male wolf came tearing along the riverbank. Hurling a demon to the ground it ripped its throat away, causing a dark mist to seep from it. Meribeth squealed as another demon appeared from the ferns, but at that moment four wolves came streaming through the trees. The demons immediately melted back into the shadows, and one on the opposite bank gave an angry snarl and then turned into a crow and took to the sky.

Meg scrabbled onto the bank and studied the pelt in the ferns. 'There's more than one demon.'

'They can change form,' Meribeth said, her voice trembling and eyes wide with shock.

'That explains how one got on my roof.' She put her arms around Meribeth, holding her until she stopped shaking. 'There were five wolves, yet Owen only has four.'

Meribeth nodded. 'The large alpha had green eyes, a bit like Owen's.'

'Like Owens?'

'Aye. Didn't you see?' Regaining her composure, Meribeth began wringing out the bottom of her dress and shaking it into shape. 'There's always been a mystery around Owen.'

'What do you mean?'

'Owen doesn't stay anywhere proper. A bit at Alexander's, a bit in the cottage you live in now, and the rest with his wolves. No one knows where he's really from. People speculate. You know how it is.'

'And what do they say?'

Meribeth shrugged. 'There's talk of him being ancient, more than human … like you!'

She ignored the reference to herself and looked intently at Meribeth. 'More than human?'

'He runs and lives with the wolves. That's hardly normal,' Meribeth observed.

They made their way back to the cottage, where Meribeth examined Owen's sgian dubh. 'This isn't a modern blade. Owen said it was a gift; I wonder who gave it to him?'

Meg screwed up her face. 'More to the point, when.'

CHAPTER 12

◆ ◆ ◆ ◆ ◆

Sɪʀ Jᴏʜɴ ᴄʀᴏssᴇᴅ ᴛᴏ ᴛʜᴇ fireplace, drained the last of the whiskey from its glass, then flicked through the pile of papers on his desk. Pulling out the indenture, he considered the implications of signing it. It would show villagers what to expect if rents were not paid, but there could be repercussions.

The chair in front of the desk let out a creak of objection as he let his weight fall onto its seat. Blast them all and blast Owen for stirring things up. Scowling, he picked up a quill and hovered his hand over the bottom of the page. He would sign and be done with it, and yet, the last thing he wanted, or needed, was villagers banding together. An uprising could mean losing everything. He was not an army man. It was not in him to fight. He put the quill back down on the table and poured himself another whiskey.

'You are pitiful.'

Sir John turned sharply to see a figure standing on the far side of the room next to the open window. He stared at the white opaque eyes, overcome with fear. 'Who are you and how the hell did you get in?' he stammered, glancing at the closed door.

'That's of no concern.' Malphas spoke in a manner befitting a cat toying with a mouse. 'What is … is your weakness. You are nothing. To be so intimidated by a few local peasants. You don't deserve the title of baronet.'

The words hit Sir John's deepest vulnerabilities, and his fear was instantly replaced by anger, which caused the skin on his face to flush a deeper shade of crimson.

'There is someone who wants to meet you.' Malphas smirked, seemingly

111

delighted by the reaction he had triggered. Sir John glanced towards the door again. 'He isn't coming through the door; he's already here.' Malphas pointed to an ornate golden gilded mirror hanging on the wall. 'You will see him there.'

Sir John did not appreciate being played for a fool. It was now apparent the intruder's intention was not to attack him, and he was not going to stand for being so openly scorned. 'I don't know who you are, but get out!' he said, raising his voice.

Malphas merely gestured at the mirror again. 'Most people would be curious,' he taunted. 'Are you really so afraid?'

Sir John cursed under his breath. How dare this … thing, turn up unannounced and challenge him in such a way? He would not have it. He strode over to the mirror and stared into it, only to see his own reflection staring back.

'What did you expect?' Malphas jeered. 'Look at yourself. So full of pomp and self-importance. You are laughable. You have no spine.'

Sir John spluttered, and he turned to face Malphas, his eyes becoming tiny beads as he screwed up his face in fury.

Malphas casually crossed the room, flicking his hand back towards the mirror. 'Save it for him.'

Sir John swung round to face the mirror again. It no longer showed his reflection but instead a dark and shadowy mist. He stared in shock as the mist parted, and a figure started to emerge.

'Your rage has invited him in,' Malphas whispered in Sir John's ear.

Sir John appeared not to notice. He stared fixedly at the figure, taking in the strange clothing. Slowly and deliberately the figure removed the gloves from his hands and held his palms towards Sir John's face. Instantly dark tendrils of energy shot out from the mirror penetrating Sir John's eyes. He jerked from shock, but he remained fixated, both unable and unwilling to move away.

The energy probed deep into Sir John's mind, rewiring neural pathways, manipulating thought patterns, and whispering action to be taken. The task finished, the energy contracted into the mirror, and Sir John's body slumped to the floor unconscious.

Looking from the mirror, Scathchornail addressed Malphas. 'Leave before he regains consciousness. He won't remember you were there. Keep it that way.'

Malphas grinned wickedly as the mirror disconnected from Shadow Side and returned to displaying a reflection of the room. Glancing down at Sir John in scorn, he changed into his crow form and left the same way he had entered.

Half an hour later Sir John came to. He lay on the floor bemused, aware of a violent pain in his head. Standing slowly, he staggered across to the desk and flopped into its chair, rubbing his head profusely. He must have blacked out. He glanced back to where he had lain on the floor and tried to recall how he had got there.

Then turning back to the desk, he regarded the whisky he had previously poured. He must have drunk more than he had intended, and all because of them. *They* had pushed him to it. It was all their fault. He had to be rid of them all.

Screwing up the indenture, he pulled a fresh piece of paper from the drawer of his desk. He would show the villages he was not to be trifled with and have revenge on Owen. He could silence them all. Owen was a dead man. With a smug smile of satisfaction on his face, he began to write.

CHAPTER 13

MEG HAD DECIDED TO RETURN across the loch with Bran and Meribeth, wanting to find Owen and question him about the fifth wolf. The mist was thick and swirling, hindering any chance of Meribeth spying Pendragon, who despite the odds had sat at the bow the entire time scanning the inches in front of the boat that were visible.

They left the jetty and made their way along the lane to the village, Owen's sgian dubh slung in a bag across Meg's shoulders. On land the mist was even more oppressive. Trees loomed through the mist, concealing and concealed.

Increasing their pace to a determined gait, they walked in silence, keeping their eyes locked on the path ahead. Meribeth, who had been slightly in front, suddenly turned, her eyes wide in fear. She pointed from the track into the trees.

Meg had heard it too. A stifled cry. *Someone's hurt.*

Leaving the track Meg cautiously picked her way through the trees. *Elsie!*

Elsie was unconscious with a deep gash in her thigh. A demon was standing over her and the area around them was splattered with blood, a lot of blood. Without thinking, Meg slid the sgian dubh from her bag, picked up a long stick in her other hand, and leapt.

Catching the demon off guard, she knocked it into the undergrowth as Bran and Meribeth rushed to help Elsie, who came round with a splutter. Her eyes were wide, and she tried to speak, but failing she put her hands to her throat, gasping for breath. The demon got back on its feet.

'Run!'

They did not need to be told twice. Each grabbing hold one of Elsie's arms, Bran and Meribeth pulled her to her feet and helped her stagger from the clearing.

The demon leapt, but Meg read its movements and deftly manoeuvred to the side, striking out with the sgian dubh. The blade struck home, but the blow was not fatal, and the demon turned to attack again as three more demons appeared from the trees to form a circle around her. A snarling ring of hatred.

'Meg, the blade!'

Owen ran towards them, leapt, caught the blade in mid-air, and dispatched a demon. Then he shouldered another to strike a third. He moved like the wind, and the demon wolves did not stand a chance. Moments later all that was left were pelts at his feet.

'It's the sgian dubh,' Owen said with a grin, cleaning the blade and passing it back to her.

Returning to the track they continued to the village. The sun finally burning off the mist. Shards of sunlight began to show through the trees, and as they passed the first dwelling, it was possible to see peat smoke rising from its chimney.

'I'm an animi, a demon hunter—' Owen announced.

'You're a what?'

The cottage door swung open, and Laylan came rushing out. 'Owen, I've been looking for you.' His face was flushed. 'They've served indentures on us all!' He paused as though reluctant to say more.

'What is it, man?'

'Sir John. He's put a price on yer head, lad!'

Owen looked explosive. 'On what grounds?'

They told us nothin', but they're searching the village. They fair near threw Elsie and her bairn out the house when she said she didna know where you were. And now the bairn's gone.'

Meg thought she was going to be sick. Elsie had been alone when they found her ... 'Elsie got back all right?'

'Aye, but she's hysterical. Owen, they were headin' for Morag's.'

Owen broke into a sprint and disappeared down the lane.

They caught up with him outside Morag's cottage where he was facing three of Sir John's men, all with drawn swords. One of them was the tax collector he had fought before. Owen drew his own sword.

'Holy mother of God.'

Two of the men attacked, simultaneously creating a barrage of blows. Owen deflected them all, somehow managing to disarm a man in the process. He picked up the fallen sword and brandishing a sword in each hand turned to face his other attacker.

The man recoiled, but the burly man stepped forward to join in, as Owen continued to fight with a sword in each hand. He disarmed another man, who then launched himself onto his back. Owen roared like a bear and shook him to the ground before turning to strike the burly man. Sword clashed sword, then the burly man knocked a sword from Owen's hand, catching him with his blade. Owen's eyes flashed dangerously. He fought like he was possessed, until his sword finally found a home in the man's chest.

'And there's Sir John's reason,' Laylan muttered as they stood over the dead man.

'He already had me condemned. May as well live up to it.'

Inside the cottage they found Morag leaning against a chair, drained of colour and staring into space.

'Morag!'

Snapped from her thoughts, Morag stared through them and started to shake. Supporting her arm, Owen helped her into her chair as Meg poured whisky into a glass. She passed the glass to Morag who took a sip, her hands shaking violently.

'Did they hurt you?'

Morag clutched the glass tightly and spoke in a faint voice. 'The village is being cleared.'

'Aye. We've heard.'

Morag's eyes filled with tears. 'The ship leaves in three days. We're to go to New Scotland, Nova Scotia.'

'Canada!'

Morag began to cough violently, suddenly looking frail and sick. Owen's thoughts were written all over his face and mirrored her own. *Morag will never survive the journey.*

CHAPTER 14

T HE WIND HAD PICKED UP, and although not yet raining, the sky was heavy with black clouds. Meg moored Owen's boat and hurried through the village to make it back to the cottage before they broke.

It had been eighteen hours since the news of the forthcoming clearance. The villagers had been preparing for their trip to the mainland and the awaiting ship that was to take them to Canada. Owen had ridden to Alexander's who had said he would appeal, yet time was not on their side. An appeal had to go to the Crown, and the distance was vast, they would be long gone before word got back. The situation was hopeless, and Morag's health had plummeted.

Arriving back at the cottage she found Haggis sitting on the doorstep. He gave her an intense look as she opened the door, gave a sorrowful meow, and then walked sedately away, melting into the bushes opposite the cottage. He was not coming back.

'Morag?'

Meg stood in the open doorway looking into the room in dismay. Everything was neat and tidy. Eerily neat and tidy. *Hollow.* She could hear whispers of old conversations, echoes of the past. A chill of dread crept into her heart. *Something terrible has happened. Haggis knew.* Forcing herself to be calm, she stepped inside. Every surface had been newly polished, and every item carefully placed. She could almost see Morag thoughtfully giving attention to her possessions, and she did not like the implications.

'Morag?'

There was still no reply. She tried to quieten her thoughts. *She's simply gone for an early walk to distract herself.* She crossed the room. Even Morag's

117

needlework had been deliberately arranged in the basket, the hanging threads all lined up in parallel, as though they had been brushed into place. Morag had finished the piece she had been working on for her. A lump stuck in Meg's throat as she surveyed the neatly stitched rolling waves crashing onto a grey-green pebbled beach and the head of a white horse reaching from the crest of the nearest wave.

Meribeth was right. The story Morag told was about her. Morag had stitched the picture for her in the hope it would help her memory. Shivering, Meg turned to the soot-lined opening of the empty fireplace, and her eyes fell onto the note on the mantelpiece. Forcing herself to pick up the yellowed piece of paper, she read what Morag had written. It was short.

'I feel like a piece of driftwood, battered by waves. Remember me for who I was to you. Love and blessings, Morag.'

She stumbled, vomit rising in her throat. Morag had gone to the water. Stuffing the letter into her pocket, she ran for the jetty.

Bran and Owen already there, Bran staring at his boat now moored next to Owen's.

'I've given her to fishermen from the mainland. I had half a mind to sink her,' Bran was saying as she raced towards them, 'but I couldn't bring myself to do it.'

'I'll make you another. I promise.'

She handed the letter to Owen, panting for breath. Owen read it and untied his boat.

'Get in. We know where the tide pulls.'

She felt faint but, rallying herself, stepped into the boat as Owen cast off. They searched the loch for an hour, eventually discovering Morag's body washed onto rocks, lying on a bed of golden-brown seaweed.

'It was like she was sleepin',' Bran observed as Owen gently laid Morag's body into the boat.

Meg placed her shawl over Morag and then sat staring out across the sea. *This has happened before … losing everything … and not just my memories.* A wind began to blow across the surface of the water.

'Damned vasanti,' Bran muttered. 'A storm is blowin' in. As if we need it.'

They buried Morag's body at the edge of the shore making a cairn of stone for her to rest in. The task finished, Meribeth picked a bouquet of late blooming moon daisies, tied them with ribbon, and laid them atop the stones. She looked haunted and older than her years, the joy gone from her eyes.

Sir John had laid claim to their livestock, including their horses, yet had permitted them to take a horse and cart to the harbour which would be handed over to his men once unloaded.

An hour after they had laid Morag to rest the wooden cart was packed. They had actioned Owen's design to smuggle him past Sir John's men and had stacked their belongings in a way that left a space he could crawl into when they neared the harbour. They would then create a commotion as they unpacked, distracting the guards and giving Owen the opportunity to slip aboard the ship.

Climbing onto the front of the cart, Laylan took up the reins as Lithe jumped up beside him. He gently flicked the reins along the horse's back, the horse strained in its harness and then there was a groan from the cartwheels as they gave up their static position. The cart began to roll forwards followed by a procession of haunted figures. Meg was suddenly aware of it being bitterly cold, she clutched her hand over Morag's finished embroidery, which was folded in her pocket, willing herself to keep looking ahead. The empty cottages mocked, and eyes of ghosts stared from every corner.

CHAPTER 15

THEY WALKED FOR SEVERAL HOURS, but their pace was slow, set by the horse and laden cart. Catching sight of Elsie walking in a daze at the rear of the group Meg had fallen back to walk with her. Elsie's face was grey and drawn. Meg stayed silent, sending Elsie thoughts of love and compassion, willing her to stay strong.

Eventually Elsie seemed to notice she was there and spoke. 'I haven't thanked ye for savin' me.'

'I wish we had found you sooner.'

'My bairn was an angel. Too good for this world. P'raps if it hadn't been the demon, it would've been the ship.' Her eyes filled with tears.

'I'm certain he is still with us, Elsie, and he's safe now.' Elsie nodded. 'You haven't eaten. Let's stop awhile at the next patch of blackberries and pick a handful.'

They came to a corner where they spied a heavily laden bramble bush and began to pick the dark purple fruit. Elsie put a berry into her mouth, ate it slowly, and then quickly ate another. Meg felt a sense of relief. It might only be a few berries, but some sustenance was better than none. She heard the cart rumble round the bend, steadily but slowly. They could gather berries and easily catch it if they walked briskly.

The berries were plump with juice, which oozed onto their fingers. *Like blood.* She stiffened.

It was over in an instant. The man rushed them from the trees, pushed Elsie to the ground, grabbed Meg by the waist, and carried her off. She kicked and lashed at the man with her fists, but her assailant was strong and held her fast.

Having come to where a horse was standing in the trees, he bound her hands together with leather cord and sat her on the horse in front of him. He rode hard, galloping across the moor to a burn at the base of a mountain.

Here the man dismounted and dropped her from the saddle. Then, as his horse drank, he took a chunk of bread from his saddlebag, sat on a rock, and began to eat. Meg tried to work her hands free, but they were tied too tightly. She glanced at the rocks nearby and seeing one she could wield, meandered to the water's edge as though to take a drink. Then, the rock in reach, she grabbed it and swung for the man's head.

It gave an uncanny crunch as she struck his skull. The man yelled in anger and made to stand, but she hit out again, this time knocking him out cold. Pulling the man's sword from its sheath she ran her bonds back and forth along its length to cut them. Then, once she was free, she rushed to the horse and scrabbled into its saddle.

CHAPTER 16

ARRIVING BACK AT THE VILLAGE she set the horse free and raced for the jetty as the clouds broke. Rain began to lash on her face, and she had to bend double against the force of the wind which howled through the empty houses, carrying with it an eerie baying. *Wolves hailing to hunt.*

She hurried to untie Owen's boat from its mooring. Yet the water was rough, and the boat had strained on its rope, tightening the knot that fastened it. *Come on*! She cursed the knot and the rain, which relentlessly stung her eyes, seemingly determined to make the difficult task impossible.

Abandoning her attempt to untie it, Meg leapt in the boat grabbing an oar as two demon wolves reached the jetty. One charged, baring teeth, its white eyes narrowing as she raised the oar to strike. Yet there was a sudden gust, the boat lurched, and losing her balance, Meg fell backwards into the loch. She let out a cry of surprise, her mouth instantly filling with water. The next moment she broke the surface, but her clothes were now heavy, and their weight started to drag her under. She grabbed for the jetty.

There was the sound of snarling and a sharp yelp. Meg caught sight of the large alpha wolf sending a demon spinning into the water as a second demon attacked, leaping onto the alpha's back. The wolf twisted his body to dislodge it, but then a wave broke over her, obscuring her vision. The loch was getting rougher, and she was tiring. She reached for the wooden post at the end of the jetty, but no sooner had her fingers touched it than there was a sharp pain at the back of her head as the wooden boat, tossed by the waves, struck against her.

Everything went black.

+ + ✦ ✦ + +

'Meg!'

Slipping in and out of consciousness, she was vaguely aware of being in the boat. She was wrapped in a rug and then began to feel heat from a fire.

'Meg.'

Owen was at her side. Her head was burning, and the pain muddled her mind.

'The demons?'

'Their pelts are in the loch.'

She sat up slowly. She was in the cottage with Owen and the wolves. She took the chunk of hazelnut bread and the bowl that Owen offered and began to eat, dipping the bread into the hot milk. Morag's embroidery was unfolded and dry by the fire.

'How is your head, your eyesight?' Owen studied her face intently.

'All good. It was Sir John's man. What did he want with me?'

'Sir John made me an outlaw …'

'Then he ordered his man to snatch one of us, to draw you out.'

Owen nodded. 'I think there may be more to it. The sudden increase in demons, Sir John's sudden act. Both reek of darkness and shadow. There is an orchestrator behind it, and Sir John is merely his puppet …' He broke off, listening intently to the sound of the wind. 'The demons coming! Stay inside and keep the fire lit.' He rushed to the door, gave a low whistle, and in the next instant both he and the wolves had gone.

The wind was howling round the cottage, threatening to put out the fire. Meg piled on more wood and then, feeling protective of the embroidery, laid it between the pages of her writing book, wrapped the book in a piece of oilskin cloth, and hid it under a loose flagstone, where it was safe.

She sat, absentmindedly picking at the bread, picturing Owen running with the wolves. The wolves had raced through the trees by the river like lightning. How could a man, even one so athletic as Owen, possibly keep up with their speed and agility? Unless – she froze, a bit of bread halfway to her mouth – the alpha wolf.

There was a sound from outside. Her eyes flickered to the shutters and door, but it wasn't a demon she had heard. It was horses' hooves. *Sir John's men.*

She staggered from the cottage. Her legs were leaden, and the wind snatched her breath as she fought against it to reach Owen's boat.

'I have you now.'

Meg turned to face the demon as others began to materialise at the far end of the beach.

'Now where have I seen this before?' The demon grinned cruelly.

Pre-empting his move, Meg twisted away and made a dash for the shallows, but the demon lunged, catching hold of her arm. She yanked herself free, tearing her flesh on the demon's blade-like claws, and then raced into the water, blood now pouring from her arm. The demon wolves were streaming along the beach, screeching in rage. She knew they were averse to water, but perhaps in their rage they would try follow.

She glanced over her shoulder. *Owen.*

The demons weren't shrieking because of her, but because of him. Owen was on the beach fighting, one against nine. Transfixed, she was oblivious to the enormous wave that came racing across the loch behind her until it lifted her from her feet and sent her crashing onto the shore. She lay on the ground spitting out water as an ice-cold hand clutched her neck.

'Got you.'

There was the sound of hooves. A white stallion lashed out. The demon released her throat but slashed at her stomach as he dropped her. She clutched at the area of pain as blood began seeping through her clothes and onto her hands.

'Meg!'

Owen raced towards her, his eyes widening in horror. His expression was easy to read, and she knew what he was seeing.

'It's too late for me.' She raised her hand to touch his cheek, wishing she had more time to be with him, to tell him how she felt.

He collapsed onto the shore beside her and lifting her shoulders slightly, put pressure on the gaping wound. She winced.

'Go, Owen. I know what you are. You can make it to the harbour.'

'I canna leave you, Meg.'

'You must. Run fast!' Talking exhausted her. Her strength was failing; she was bleeding out on the sand. 'Owen *please* ... Go!'

For one delicious moment Owen kissed her. Then he laid her back on the sand, his eyes filling with tears. As she watched he crouched alongside her and in the blink of an eye had disappeared, no longer a man but the wolf who had saved her so many times ... it gave her one last look from green eyes the colour of pine trees.

'Go,' she whispered.

The wolf let out a long howl that seemed to fill the shore ... and ran.

She clutched at the ground, closing her eyes, darkness drawing in. She thought she heard Owen shouting ... Then the world went black.

PART THREE

KAIA

CHAPTER 1

K AIA WOKE ON THE ISLAND as dawn broke. She slid the van door open, still lying in her sleeping bag, and gazed at the hypnotic display of early sunlight on the water, shimmering pink and orange. Deciding it was too magical to miss, she pulled herself from her warm cocoon and crossed the beach for a swim.

The cold instantly hit. Taking a few breaths to steady her breathing, she swam out to where it was deep enough to dive and made for the bottom of the loch. To her surprise, she could see as clearly as though wearing swimming goggles. She explored, in awe of her newfound vision. Then she returned to the surface and glanced across to the shore and her van. She did not relish being caught naked, but there was no one in sight, and she was a long way from any dwelling. Concluding she had some time before the beach attracted other visitors, she dove again.

Leidolf was a lean, muscled, well-built twenty-something man, with piercing green eyes set in a handsome and wise face, framed with unruly dark hair. Today he wore blue running trousers with his chest bare, showing a large tattoo of a wolf's head. He often took the coastal path back to his solitary dwelling by the loch after his early dawn run and had seen the woman getting into the sea. Deciding it would be prudent to wait until she left before arriving on the beach himself, he sat by some rocks to wait. She clearly assumed she had the spot to herself, and given the Baltic temperature of the water, he surmised it would not be long before she returned to the shore. Not only that, but he also had another cause to delay.

He locked his eyes onto the large, tattered crow circling overhead. It swooped low over the water, showing an unhealthy interest in the woman's activities. Moments passed, the bird flew away, and Leidolf turned his attention back to her. Not only did she seem unaffected by cold, but she could also hold her breath for an uncanny length of time. Yet she was not water fae, given the camper currently parked on the grass at the far end of the beach. He began to time how long she stayed under. Six minutes. Nine minutes. He stared at his watch in disbelief. Eventually she surfaced, only to dive again. Leidolf stood. He could not wait indefinitely and gauging now he would have more than enough time to pass by unseen, he continued down to the beach.

He walked quickly across the sand, unseen by her but not by her dogs, who tore across to dance excitedly round his feet. Leidolf fussed them, then passed the camper van towards the trees and the track that led to his house in the next bay.

++++++

Eventually the cold hit. Kaia waded from the water, wrapped herself in the towel she had left on the beach, then found a pretty pebble, which she kissed and placed in the breaking waves. Then she noticed the footprints. They were much bigger than hers, a size nine or ten. *A man.* Praying she hadn't been seen she absent-mindedly followed the trail. The sand turned to grass, damp with dew, and she could easily see where the prints passed the van heading for the forest. Yet just past the van the trail changed and instead of human footprints heading into the trees, the trail appeared to have been made by a very large dog. She tried to comprehend the mystery. Then, starting to shiver, she decided the puzzle would have to wait and hurried for the van to get dressed.

CHAPTER 2

*I*T *MUST BE FAULTY.* KAIA pulled on her dolphin hoodie and checked the dashboard. Its clock read the same as the one on her phone. She had been swimming for an hour. No wonder she was ravenous. Camp stove coffee and a cold croissant were not going to suffice. She tidied the van, converted the bed back into a seat, and headed inland to find alternative nourishment.

She drove for half an hour, passing several pretty croft houses professing to be hotels, but none offered food for non-residents, and all displayed 'no vacancy' signs. Seeing them made her realise that if she intended to be on the island for any length of time, she needed a permanent place to stay. Eventually spotting a pretty building built from stone, that professed to be a café, and with her stomach now growling like an angry lion, Kaia pulled into its car park. *Food first. Accommodation hunt later.*

The café was well lit, quaint, and rustic, housing a few wooden tables decorated with blue and white flowers set in glass jars. The exposed stone walls displayed local artists' work and were lined with wooden benches and stools. Behind the oak counter a chalkboard displayed the menu and special of the day, in this instance a vegetable haggis breakfast. The proprietor, an older lady with greying hair, dressed in loose-fitting pale grey trousers, a cream polo-necked jumper, and white apron, was busy adding fresh croissants and pastries to already well stacked cake stands set under glass domes.

'Morning, dear,' she said as Kaia entered. 'What can I get you?'

'A very large and very hot coffee, please, and something to eat, equally as hot!'

'You've been swimming! In this cold weather too!' the lady observed, her eyes sparkling. 'How about some porridge? Or one of these? They're still warm.' She lifted a glass dome, indicating the pile of fresh croissants underneath.

A delicious buttery smell wafted to Kaia's nose. It was an easy choice. 'Both!'

She paid and then, while the lady made ready her order, sat on a stool near the counter. There was a notice board on the wall, and she began to scan the advertisements. Some were for tourist trips around the island, one was for a lost dog, and another displayed caravans for rent. She began to note down the number.

'They're nice caravans.' The lady passed her a croissant on a plate. 'Chloe was in here yesterday saying how busy she is. You can check, but I think they're fully booked.'

'Everywhere I've seen has been full.'

The lady nodded understandingly. 'That's Skye. Always busy.' She glanced out of the window where a bus was currently manoeuvring into a parking space. 'Looks like you got here just in time. If you would like to find a seat, I'll bring the coffee and porridge over, else you might not get a table.'

The only other person currently in the café was a lady with greying hair, dressed in a skirt suit made from green tartan and a matching green felt hat with a feather fastened at the size by an ornate pin. Kaia walked over to another small table by the window and watched the passengers pile into the café. Most were on their mobile phones, taking pictures and logging onto the Wi-Fi. The tiny café was suddenly busy. The queue at the counter grew, and the customers began to harass the lady serving.

'What's the Wi-Fi code again?' one lady demanded in an officious tone, not waiting for a response. 'Did you get the code, Albert?'

The lady behind the counter passed her coffee. 'It's on the bottom of the board.'

Albert's wife critically scanned the chalkboard. 'I wouldn't call that a menu. There's not much choice.'

'It's just the breakfast menu at the moment,' the lady added, keeping up her cheery tone. She placed a bowl of porridge on the end of the counter, smiled at Kaia, and then turned to another tourist who was tapping on the counter, impatient to be served. 'I'll be with you in a jiffy.'

Albert's wife seemed determined to be provocative. 'Not enough choice and not enough staff! Honestly. These places!'

Kaia collected her porridge and was immediately accosted.

'Hey, don't push in, we were here first!'

The last thing Kaia wanted was confrontation. She smiled and reached for her porridge, but the lady who had spoken waved her phone aggressively to block her from the counter. As she did, it's screen glitched, showing a swirling black static, with immediate effect. Everyone in the queue jostled to get to the front and began helping themselves to items they could reach. The lady serving began to get flustered.

Kaia had seen enough. 'Would you like some help?'

The lady gave her an appreciative look, and without further ado, Kaia scooted behind the counter and picked up a pair of pastry tongs.

'If you would just like to wait your turn, it will be much quicker. Who's next? Now what can I get you?'

The nearest customer pointed at the croissants. Kaia placed two onto a plate and then put the plate onto their tray. 'If you would just like to move along and wait for the till to be free … What would you like?' she asked the next customer.

She proceeded to serve customers whilst the other lady stood at the till and took payments. Ten minutes later the madness had subsided.

'Thanks for your help, love. Did you particularly want a caravan?' The serving lady asked. 'Only I've a cottage. I've been looking for a long-term let, but I'm happy for you to use it. It's not very big; one bedroom.'

'That'd be perfect!'

'Then why not drop by and see if you like it, once you've eaten. It isn't far from here,' the lady continued. 'I'll give you the code for the key box. I'm Wilma, by the way!'

Thanking Wilma again, Kaia lifted the tray containing her breakfast and turned to her table only to see it now occupied by two tourists. She walked across to collect her croissant, receiving scowls from the two ladies currently in situ. There were no vacant tables, but the lady wearing the skirt suit waved.

'Thank you.' Kaia sank gratefully onto the chair the lady had indicated. 'It's gone a bit mad in here.'

'Och, it's always the same these days,' the lady replied. 'I didn't know you worked here. Where are you staying?'

'At Wilma's cottage.'

'Have we got a spare room then?' The lady looked confused. 'I don't remember us having a spare room, but then I don't remember lots of things.' She stirred a half-empty teacup and smiled apologetically.

'I'm Kaia.'

'Mrs Mackentyre, Marjorie Mackentyre, but most folks call me Mrs Mack. At least I remember that. You're local. I thought I recognised you. Where is it you stay?'

'At Wilma's place.' Kaia pulled off a large piece from her croissant and put it in her mouth. She momentarily closed her eyes, savouring the delicious buttery taste.

'Good, aren't they? No one makes croissants like Mea. She has magic in her fingers.' Mrs Mack suddenly looked more astute. 'You've been swimming in the loch again. I remember you as a swimmer. Just like the kelpies, always in the water.'

Kaia's ears instantly pricked up. 'You know about kelpies?'

'Aye. Of course. They're in the loch,' Mrs Mack said with affection. 'They've been here for as long as I can remember, and a good while before.'

There was a sudden outburst of noise as Albert stood up from his table, knocking into a lady walking past carrying a tray. The tray fell with a clatter, spilling its entire contents over the floor and over Albert, who then began to hurl insults. The disruption had an immediate effect on Mrs Mack, who returned to looking fuddled and confused.

'I think I'll go and sit outside,' Kaia said as both Albert and the lady began to shout. She picked up her coffee and bowl of porridge. 'It's quieter. Lovely to have met you.'

'Nice to see you again too, dear.'

Kaia sat at one of the wooden tables outside and had not been there long before Wilma appeared at a side door.

'Phew, I need some fresh air!' Wilma said, crossing to join her and sitting down with a sigh of relief. 'What a lot!'

'They're not exactly full of the joys of spring.'

Wilma returned her smile. 'Och, it takes more than that to break an old croc like me. People are glued to their phones. I swear it makes them bad. I don't use one,' she added. 'The signal around here is so poor, it's hardly worth having one.'

Kaia looked across to the café entrance where some of the tourists were now marching back to the bus, their auras prickly. 'I saw something else strange today,' she said, glancing back at Wilma. 'Enormous pawprints. Could have been made by a dinosaur dog!'

Wilma chuckled. 'That'll be Fraser.'

'Fraser?'

'Aye. Leidolf's dog. Leidolf emigrated from Canada about three years ago with two of his friends and brought Fraser with him. Looks rather like a wolf. You didn't see Leidolf this morning?' Kaia shook her head. 'Not surprising. Leidolf lets Fraser run free. Always wandering around by himself. Still, he tends to stay in the forests and never bothers anyone. Leidolf makes boats,' she finished, as if to answer a question Kaia had asked. 'You'll be bumping into him soon enough if you're staying local.'

She passed her a piece of paper. 'The directions to the cottage, the code for the key box, and the number for the café. If you like it, settle yourself in. I'll call by later, and we can sort out all the terms. Just give me a call if you're wanting anything.'

'Thanks.'

'It's no bother. Be nice having you stay. I had best go and clear the tables for round two. It is going to be one of those days.' She indicated the second bus pulling into the car park.

The bus was rammed. 'If you need help, I'd be happy to come and do some shifts.'

Wilma beamed. 'I won't say no to that. You just let me know when you want to start!'

Kaia looked at the tourists piling off the bus, picked up her tray, and walked back towards the side door of the café. 'I think I already have!'

CHAPTER 3

❖ ❖ ❖

KAIA HAD IMMEDIATELY FALLEN IN love with Wilma's cottage, a quaint, white croft, nestled into the hill at the side of a loch. The interior comprised of a hallway, a Quaker style kitchen, a small lounge with a wood-burning stove, and upstairs, a small bathroom and bedroom. Chalk white walls set the backdrop for coastal-coloured furnishings and soft grey throws. Original oak floorboards were exposed throughout, although partially covered in the lounge and bedroom by thick natural-coloured wool rugs. Deep-silled windows offered stunning views across the water and held either a rustic vase or a bowl containing a collection of pebbles and shells. A haven of peace and tranquillity.

Just back from her latest shift at the café, Kaia had collected the dogs and gone for a walk along the shore. The dogs were snuffling in seaweed nearby, and behind them stretched a vista of the open water, framed by forest and mountains on the far shore. Jim had said her parents loved Skye. Now she could understand why. *If only I could send them pictures.*

When she had started school, her parents had stopped travelling and had bought the car. They would still take Kaia on van adventures every holiday, but they had never brought her as far as Scotland. She shuddered, remembering the day Jim had met the school bus and told her about the car accident. He was a loving guardian, but she felt cheated that time with her parents had been cut so short.

A rancid smell distracted her from her thoughts. The dogs had found something disgusting among the seaweed and were rolling in it. Noticing

136

they had her attention, they tore towards her, looking mighty pleased with themselves. She grimaced and to escape the pungent smell of rotting fish, ran to the water's edge where she began jumping rippling waves. The dogs followed in delight and soon smelt decidedly cleaner.

Ianna.

She heard the voice in her mind like a whisper on the wind, and stared along the beach, but there was no one in sight.

Ianna.

The water. It was coming from the water. *Fae.* Curiosity getting the better of her, she took off some of her clothes and swam out.

She dove into a forest of sea kelp and pushed through the thick stems, seeking whatever had drawn her. At first there appeared to be nothing; then a movement caught her attention, the swirling kelp giving away just how large the oncoming creature was. *Shark! ... the Loch Ness Monster!* Shooting to the surface, she looked around frantically. *Get a grip. Wrong loch ... and there are no apex predators in Scotland!*

She took a few deep breaths to regulate her breathing and dove again. There was no sign of the creature, and assuming her imagination had got the better of her, she began to explore her new-found landscape and the array of coloured sea snails living there.

Ianna.

It was behind her. Turning slowly, she found herself looking into the face of a hippocampus shaped creature with a long fish tail, covered in seaweed, and with long fronds forming a mane that fell across its horse shaped neck and head. *A kelpie!* She slowly reached out to gently touch the creature's muzzle. Immediately there was a rush of energy through her fingers, her hand began to glow with soft blue light, and an image flashed through her mind. She was riding the creature before her, racing through the water so fast that the seabed beneath them was a blur ...

There was an explosion of pain in her heart. Kaia let out all her remaining air and kicked for the surface, but her feet entangled in seaweed, holding her fast. Her lungs began to burn, demanding she take a breath as she reached to free her ankle. Yet before she could grab the seaweed, the kelpie broke her free, and Kaia found herself whooshing to the surface, where she was left bobbing like a cork.

The kelpie broke the surface nearby, its frondlike hair matching the sea kelp in which it had hidden. It circled her slowly then disappeared. Kaia swam for the shore, so preoccupied with her encounter that she was unaware of a large dark bird circling above.

CHAPTER 4

❖ ✦ ❖ ✦ ❖

THE LUNCHTIME RUSH WAS FINALLY over. Finishing her shift, Kaia switched on the café dishwasher and hung her apron on a hook next to the kitchen door. Then she went to join Mrs Mack at her table.

'You've been busy, deary.'

'Just a bit!' She sank onto the chair. 'Would you tell me more about kelpies?'

'Och, it won't be kelpies causing all the trouble,' Mrs Mack replied, shaking her head.

'Trouble?'

'Now don't you go filling Kaia's head with your stories,' Wilma said affectionately, arriving at the table with a soya cappuccino and a slice of rhubarb cheesecake. 'For you. Well-earned.' She crossed to another table, answering the summons of a customer.

Mrs Mack was now looking confused. 'You only came to the island recently, but I had you down as a local.'

'I work here, so I guess I very nearly am.' She took a sip of her coffee, waiting for Mrs Mack to gather her thoughts.

Mrs Mack shrugged apologetically. 'Och, my memory. It gets all fuddled. Still, I know the truth of something when I see it. Like the attacks.'

'Attacks?'

'Aye,' Mrs Mack leant forward as though to disclose a secret. 'So-called accidents. Walkers calling in the air rescue, or turning up in town with unusual injuries, no memory of how they got them. Nasty injuries, too. Now if you ask me. I'd say it's demons.'

139

'Demons?'

'That's what demons do,' Mrs Mack said. 'Cause nasty injuries, then feed off the fear their prey projects. Unless of course they want to kill, but killing does not feed a demon. Oh no. It is the energy of fear they feed on.' She picked up a half scone from her plate and began to nibble its edge.

Demons. Maybe Mrs Mack was muddled, but she had been right about kelpies. 'Why do you suppose demons are suddenly showing up here?'

'No idea.' Mrs Mack lifted her empty teacup and sipped at it as though it was full. Then she replaced it back on the saucer, an astute look suddenly appearing on her face. 'I know one thing though, it's happened before. I used to teach history. That is what I love, history. Especially Scottish history. Similar attacks were recorded in the eighteenth century, here, on this very island, and demons were the cause. Demons looking like wolves. You mark my words, it's happening again. History always repeats itself.'

She started to get ready to leave. 'I had best be going; looks like rain.' She indicated through the window at the darkening clouds. 'I've no idea how long I've been here. Bless Wilma. She lets me sit here all day without so much as a grumble.'

Putting on her green Harris Tweed coat, Mrs Mack slowly did up its buttons. 'Kelpies,' she said, suddenly remembering the original question. 'There were lots of kelpie sightings in the eighteenth century too. Demons and kelpies. What a mix, and what an interesting time to live in!' She looked around as though she had forgotten something but couldn't remember what.

'Have you ever seen a kelpie?' Kaia asked, passing Mrs Mack her hat, which had fallen from the back of her chair.

'Aye. They're in the loch. You must see them, you swim ...' Her voice trailed off, and she looked more intently, as though seeing her differently. 'Why are *you* asking me about kelpies? You of all people!'

She must have looked confused because Mrs Mack suddenly smiled. 'Now people say I get befuddled! Looks like I'm not the only one.' She let out a chortle, straightened her hat, and turned away from the table.

Demon wolves, and they have been here before. She thought of the illustrations in Jim's book. 'Mrs Mack, one last question, because you're right, I can't remember. Do kelpies look like people or horses?'

Mrs Mack turned sharply. 'Horses, of course, and turn into white horses on land.' She lifted her hand in farewell and walked across to the door, blowing Wilma a kiss goodbye.

Wilma was taking the opportunity to tidy the counter, unaware that she was being observed. Kaia was suddenly aware of how troubled she looked. Finishing her cheesecake, she carried her coffee across to join her. 'Is everything Ok?'

'I heard enough to know what you two were talking about,' Wilma said, wiping down the counter glass. 'Usually, I'd tell you to take what Marjorie says with a pinch of salt, but in this instance …'

She paled, and Kaia guessed the reason. 'You've seen something.'

Wilma put down the cloth and lowered her voice. 'Yesterday.' She glanced around the café, making sure that the customers were engrossed in their own conversations. 'As you know, I came in early to clean out the fridges and take the delivery. After I'd finished, I went out the back with the rubbish, and there it was.'

'What?'

'A large crow, or so I thought,' Wilma replied. 'I thought it was going through the bins, and I tried to shoo it away, but it changed – right there, right before my eyes – into a man, with a wicked-looking face and white eyes.' She shuddered. 'Grinned, he did. I thought he was going to attack me, but then a bus drew up in the car park.'

'What happened then?'

'His attention turned to the bus. He turned back into a crow and flew over the café while the customers milled about outside, like he was looking for someone. I went in to serve, and later there was no sign of him. I wasn't sorry. It all seems ridiculous when I hear myself say it. If I were you, I'd think I was crazy.'

'I don't think you're crazy. I wonder why it came to the café?'

Wilma's reply was instant. 'Like I said, looking for someone. And whoever that someone is, I pity them.'

CHAPTER 5

K AIA HAD TOLD BELLA ABOUT seeing the kelpie and was beginning to wish she hadn't. The pause in their conversation was starting to make her feel uncomfortable.

'You still there?'

'Maybe it was a big fish.'

A big fish rescued me. 'That's as far-fetched as it being a kelpie.'

'Fish are real.'

Time to change the subject. 'How's things with you?'

'I'm not sure.' Another pause. 'JD didn't come home last night. No message. Nothing.'

'That's not like him. Did he explain why?'

'No. I was beginning to get worried. I even rang the local hospital to see if he'd been in an accident. Now I wish I hadn't. I got a message this morning, saying he was at work and that he'd be home the usual time.'

'Rattish, but that's good.'

'It wasn't sent from his phone. I didn't recognise the number.'

'Perhaps he's lost his phone.'

Yeah maybe.'

Bella didn't sound convinced and a few minutes later their conversation ended. JD's strange and sudden change in behaviour, was almost as impossible to accept as her encountering a mythical creature.

Leaving the cottage, Kaia took a track along the loch shore, heading for where she had seen the kelpie, in the hope she might meet it again. She felt rather than saw the black shadow stepping onto the shore behind her, but the sudden adrenaline spike was signpost enough. Breaking into a

142

sprint, she raced through the trees toward the main road in the hope that passing vehicles would deter whatever was behind her. She kept running. No sign of the road.

Realising that she had miscalculated, she leapt onto a fallen tree and looked around to get her bearings, but the pine plantation looked the same in every direction. Panic started to set in; there was nowhere to hide.

She crouched. *Breathe ... think.* She was suddenly aware of the protective bark of the tree and ran her palms across it wishing it could cocoon her too. *Wood.* A strange symbol flashed through her mind. Almost immediately there was a rush of energy through her hands, then everything hazed as a column of energy the colour of wood, rose from the tree to surround her. The energy thickened to look like sap and then took on the look of bark. The tree *was* hiding her, and just in time.

A large wolf came into sight. It ran back and forth nose to the ground, sniffing for her scent, then, pausing next to her hiding place, it raised its head. Kaia stared in horror at the two blind eyes and held her breath, willing herself not to blink.

Moments later the wolf dropped its head, walked to the far end of the fallen tree, and changed into a human form. *A demon!*

She stifled a scream, and the demon sensed it. Instantly he was back, a few inches from her face, sniffing as though still a wolf. Then, at the sound of footsteps among the trees, in the blink of an eye he turned into a crow and took to the sky.

Kaia moved her hands, and the energy of the tree contracted. She slid to the ground shaking and shivering from cold sweat.

Yet she had no time to focus on the demon. The footsteps were getting nearer accompanied by the sound of two men speaking. They sounded angry and not in the mood to be accosted, Kaia squeezed next to the tree trunk alongside a fallen branch, praying they wouldn't notice her.

'It's not that hard to work, Regalis. It's a sodding GPS. You set the destination and press go. The only difference being the addition of a year.'

Kaia recognised the voice. She peered over the top of the tree trunk but could not quite see the man who had spoken. She could, however, see the one called Regalis. A tall lanky fellow with black eyes. She squinted. *Solid black.*

Terror-stricken she remained motionless, ready to run should they catch sight of her.

Regalis checked a gadget strapped to his wrist. 'I don't need your sarcasm, Agaricus. I set it right.'

'Then how d'you explain us being in the wrong era? We may as well have taken a bloody bus. Try again, and this time add, one, seven, five, two.'

Regalis muttered something and tapped on the gadget which milliseconds later projected a red symbol into the air. The air around the symbol appeared to warp, forming a triangle five feet high.

Regalis disappeared into the triangle as the man stepped out from behind the trees. She couldn't see his face, but his body and posture, his hair ... *Rick?*

Rick followed Regalis into the triangle. Without giving it a second thought, Kaia ran from her hiding place and leapt through behind them.

CHAPTER 6

KAIA STEPPED FROM THE TRIANGLE into a thicket of fern in what appeared to be the same forest. Cautiously making her way through tangled branches, she came upon the track that led to the shore. It was different. There were trees that hadn't been there before, and what was even more puzzling was the sudden presence of the peninsula, that now stretched out into the water. She was so engrossed in trying to figure out how a lump of land could suddenly appear, that she didn't notice a figure stepping from the shallows.

'Ianna.'

That same name. Turning sharply, she regarded him as he approached. Tall, slender but well-muscled, golden hair twisted into a knot at the top of his head, fish-scales, wearing some sort of green body armour and a leathery looking bag slung across his chest. *Water fae. A merman*!

'Ianna.'

He was distracted by the sound of footsteps and indicated for her to hide.

She looked around frantically. Options were few, but ducking back into the treeline, she squeezed in between some overgrown rocks as the merman turned and walked away.

Seconds later Regalis and Rick stepped onto the beach and without any warning Regalis shot a gun. He marched across the beach as the merman crumpled to the floor, then opening the leather bag, took out a large crystal shard which caught the light and began to flicker like purple fire. Immediately the horror of the scene seemed to lessen. The crystal called her, a magnetism drawing her in.

Kaia gripped onto the rocks. Yet Rick sensed her movement and pulling a pen-like device from his pocket, pointed it in her direction. She tensed but he did not investigate. Regalis had tapped the gadget on his wrist and the same symbol appeared opening another triangular portal into which they both disappeared.

Creeping from her hiding place, Kaia raced to the fallen merman. Blood was pouring from a wound in his side, but he was still alive. She pulled out her phone to get help, but he spoke a strange word and pointing to the water, tried to stagger to his feet.

Her mind was overwhelmed, too full to speak. Placing his arm across her shoulders and her own arm around his waist, she helped him stand. They stumbled to the shallows, then waded out until the water was well up their thighs. The merman paused, gave her an intense look and she let go. He slid forwards, stretched his hands and feet to reveal webbing, then in a flash, he had gone.

Portal!

Ignoring the one still open on the beach, Kaia raced for the portal she had used. Its edges were looking less defined and as she sprinted towards it the triangle started to shrink. She leapt through milliseconds before it shut and carried on running until she reached Wilma's cottage. Letting herself in, she bolted the door and collapsed on the hall floor, her body shaking in shock.

There was the patter of feet on wood, and her two dogs appeared from the kitchen. Sensing her distress, they sidled close as though to warm her. *Heat.* She needed heat. Staggering up the stairs, she ran a deep, hot bath, and sank gratefully in.

———————— +++++++ ————————

An hour later she was starting to feel less dazed. She still felt like ice, so after dressing in multiple layers, she returned to the kitchen to make a hot drink. Mrs Mack was right, there was a demon on the island, and it could change form … but what had happened to Rick? *Was it really Rick?* Rick's eyes had flickered when he attacked her in Oxford … Now he, like the man he had called Regalis, had solid black eyes. She messaged Bella. Moments later her phone rang.

'Girl you're having a breakdown. Come back to Oxford; you've gotta get some help.'

'It *was* Rick Bell. He was there with another guy—'

'Rick shot someone on the beach?'

'No, the other guy did.'

'Have you called the police?'

'To say what? There was a peninsular that wasn't there before. I don't think it was in this era …'

There was an awkward silence.

'Kaia, listen to yourself. Your mind is messing with you. Where's the body?'

'Gone.'

She hadn't disclosed what he had looked like, or the fact he had swum away with webbed hands and feet, nor for that matter that she had been hunted by a demon or that a tree had hidden her. She groaned inwardly.

'Look. As much as I love the guy, I wouldn't like to think something bad has happened to him either. I'll call by after work on the pretext I'm picking up something for you, and make sure he's alive and kicking.'

'Thanks. … Have you spoken to JD? Has he lost his phone?'

Bella let out a long sigh, and when she spoke again the zest had gone from her voice. 'No. I called his number after we spoke, and he answered. I don't know. There's a thick shell around him I can't get through, and he's gone all grouchy. I'm starting to think the worst.'

'An affair! Not a chance. He adores you.'

'You say that, but—'

Kaia heard Layna barking a question off screen and grimaced. Everything was on Layna's terms, even employees' so-called free time.

'Kaia, I'll call you back later.'

CHAPTER 7

REGALIS QUICKENED HIS PACE, CLOSING the distance between the man in front of him. This section of the base was unusually deserted; it was too good an opportunity to miss.

The man stopped by a panel on the wall, clicked it open, and began to examine switches that regulated electrical flow to the transmission tower on the floor above. Regalis took a step nearer.

'Is there a problem?'

The man recoiled, stumbled against the metal panel which then swung to hit against the metal pipes that ran along the wall. The jarring sound was the tipping point. There was a crack as the man's neck gave way, then black tendrils reached from Regalis's body as he began to feed. For an instant he looked distorted, then his body assimilated the increase in mass, and he looked as he had before, except for his hair, which was now the same ginger shade as his host. He stretched, closed the panel, and then returned to the floor above to seek out Gracilior.

Gracilior was speaking to Agaricus.

'They're all hidden?'

Agaricus crossed to a computer and tapped a code into the keyboard. 'It beats me why the original design did not factor in their concealment.'

'Humans are not as smart as they think they are.' Gracilior began to study a map showing the topography of the country, marked with clusters of red dots, as it appeared on a nearby screen. 'They never consider implications, only fulfilment of a brief.'

Agaricus let out a snort. 'The human I occupy was self-obsessed, riddled with jealousy and self-pity.'

'Which is why he was such an amiable host. Remnants of thought processes within neural pathways … they don't always fade.' He smirked and continued to study the dots. 'There's some missing.'

Agaricus pointed to the blank area over the Isle of Skye. 'I have ensured the final monoliths meet updated specifications. I will oversee installation.'

Gracilior grunted in satisfaction. 'Soon every human in the third dimension will succumb to the power of the crystal, and the doorway will open. There is a new age dawning, Agaricus.' He suddenly noticed the change in Regalis's hair. 'Again! There is flesh in the substation, Regalis. If you had some excuse before, you've none now!'

Regalis scowled. 'It's one human.'

'It only ever is!'

To deflect the rebuff, Regalis indicated a nearby computer as it began spewing data onto its screen. 'The first monoliths have begun fracking then.'

Before Gracilior could respond, they were approached by a man wearing a military uniform.

'You are wanted at the communication chamber, sir,' he said, addressing Gracilior. 'The colonel wants an update.'

'Tell him Regalis is on his way,' Gracilior replied. He turned to him. 'You seem to have an aptitude for playing against the odds. You can tell him we have the crystal.'

Regalis made to move away.

'Wait. There's something else to report. There was someone else at the collection site, or rather someone else. A woman.'

'I didn't see a woman.'

'Agaricus logged her energy signature.' Gracilior handed him a pen-like device. 'I'm sure the colonel will want to know who was sniffing around his operations.'

⋅⋅◆◆◆⋅⋅

There was a surge of energy, and the human checking the data on the device behind Regalis cried out in pain as black static energy hit his body. He fell dead, his eyes still wide in shock.

On the communication device the colonel's hologram rippled dangerously. 'How did the woman from the twenty-first century get there?'

Regalis shuffled uncomfortably. 'I went there by mistake. I—'

There was a second crackle of energy as the Colonel sent another surge of black energy through the communication device. This time it hit him full in the chest to slam him against the wall. Another bolt came. Regalis slid to the ground, oblivious to the gaping hole in his chest and the fact that his innards were now splattered on the wall behind him.

CHAPTER 8

LEIDOLF RAN FAST, LEAPING OVER fallen trees and pushing through the undergrowth to follow the scent trail. He had run through this same section of the forest, following the exact same scent, many moons ago, only then he had been accompanied by his wolf pack. Wolves were long gone from Scotland. They belonged to a past age, an age when life was raw and free. He pushed the thought from his mind. He was not new to change. He had learnt a very long time ago that you could not hold back the tide of time.

He came to a place where his quarry had stopped. Demons were figures from the shadows. They did not need to rest. Scanning the area, he caught sight of a patch of red on crushed fern fronds. Blood. Human blood. He pieced events together. The man stumbling across the demon, his shock and the demon attacking, exhilarated by fear.

Pushing through the bank of fern, Leidolf picked up the man's scent. He had run. He was still alive. He scouted for the scent of the demon, but there was no trace of it having followed. It was long gone.

Leidolf found the man sitting by a burn using a moors scarf to bathe a deep wound to his leg. He was dressed in walking boots, a checked shirt, and black hiking trousers with the fabric of one leg completely shredded. Leidolf took in the pale face and the trembling hands.

He stepped from the ferns. 'Are you okay, mate?'

The man visibly started and glanced at his leg. 'I'm not sure what happened. I must have fallen.'

'Pretty rough wound. It needs stitches. Best get you to the hospital.'

'I would appreciate it. I don't know where the hospital is.'

'On the other side of the island. Here, let me help.' Taking the man's scarf, Leidolf deftly created a makeshift bandage.

'Looks like you've done that before.'

He gave the man a knowing look. 'I've had to deal with some major battle wounds in my time.'

The man looked puzzled, sensing a seriousness underlying the flippant retort, then gingerly stood, assessing the strength of his leg.

'You can't remember how you did it?'

'I remember walking through the fern and then …' The man tried to recollect the chain of events that led to his injury but simply shrugged. 'The next thing I know, I'm lying on the ground with this gash.'

'I'd say you were lucky. Perhaps if you could remember, it would turn out you got off lightly.'

'Maybe a branch fell on it, or maybe I fell and knocked myself unconscious.' the man suggested, attempting to rationalise what had happened.

'More than likely,' Leidolf replied. 'This way. My truck's not far from here.'

He drove the man to outpatients, waited for him to have the wound stitched, and then dropped him back to where he was staying on the island. Arriving back at his own house, Leidolf pulled his pickup onto the drive to discover another vehicle already parked there. 'Alex!' he said raising his hand to the middle-aged man with wavy rowan hair, casually dressed in a loose grey T-shirt and faded jeans, who got out of the battered-looking blue car. 'How's things?'

'Good.' Alex sauntered across to the front door with him. 'Just calling by to make sure you're still alive, as we haven't heard from you in a while.'

'You know me. A loner.'

They entered the light, airy kitchen, made so by the wooden beamed, vaulted ceiling and A-frame window with its view of the forest. Crossing to a large Smeg fridge, Leidolf took out two bottles of cider and handed one to Alex, before pulling off his T shirt. Grabbing a clean one from a washing basket on the worktop, he pulled it over his head, covering the wolf's head tattooed across his chest. 'Bottle opener is in the work shed.'

'Loner or not, we still have to keep an eye, make sure you not going off the rails,' Alex said jovially as they walked along the track to the shed. 'May is concerned,' he continued, his tone becoming serious. 'A lot of tourists have ended up at the surgery lately, with nasty injuries.'

'Demon attacks?'

'May reckons so,' Alex answered. 'None of the patients have any recollection of how their injuries happened.'

'Stereotypical attack. Feed on fear and wipe their victim's memory. I came across a guy myself. Just back from dropping him off. Bad gash to the leg, needed twenty-two stitches.'

Arriving at a large wooden barn, Leidolf pressed a code into its padlock. Then he pulled open the door, crossed to the well-used wooden workbench, and picked up a bottle opener. After uncapping his cider bottle, he passed the opener to Alex. 'Cheers.'

Alex took a long draft and then strolled across the sawdust covered floor to the back of the shed. 'My God, you've finished it!' He surveyed a large, highly polished wooden rowing boat with an unusually scrolled bow and stern. 'I've never seen anything like it.'

'It's how I've always seen her.' Leidolf followed Alex to the boat. 'Pretty much how she was back then.'

'A labour of love,' Alex remarked in admiration. 'Who would have thought that heap of rotten wood could be restored into this!'

'Aye.' Leidolf regarded the boat in silence. Then he looked back at Alex. 'I finish this boat, and that demon shows up on the island. Nothing is ever by chance, Alex. History is repeating itself. It's the same bloody demon as before.'

Alex raised his eyebrows. 'That can only mean one thing.'

'She's alive and somewhere near, perhaps even on the island. If the demon is looking for her, she's in one heap of trouble!'

'That she may not know she's in.' Alex spoke in a low voice, concern showing on his weathered face. 'She won't know you, mate. Chances are, she won't even know who she is herself.'

That was true enough, but he had waited a long time. A very long time. 'Nothing new there then. Like I said, history repeats itself.'

CHAPTER 9

✦ ✦ ✦

Kaia had not set foot outside for twenty-four hours. Instead, she had huddled by the fire, with the door locked and bolted, terrified lest Rick or the demon should show up.

To try and unravel the mess in her head, she had written out everything, from Jake's headaches to her recent experiences, onto several sheets of paper and had spread them out on the coffee table. Pieces of a puzzle that she felt certain somehow linked together, to create a not very pretty picture.

She shivered violently and stood to put more wood on the fire. She was assessing the dryness of three pairs of thick slouchy socks hanging on the radiator when her phone pinged a FaceTime request from Bella. She grabbed two odd socks and put them on with one hand as she studied Bella's worn face.

The situation with JD had not improved. 'You're a goddess, remember. You can deal with anything.'

'I'm a goddess who is losing her allure … It's rapidly becoming a nightmare. That's not the reason I'm calling, though. Two things … Strange things have been turning up on Dartmoor; it's been on the news.'

Her interest was piqued. 'What sort of things?'

'Monoliths … appearing out of nowhere. There are pictures of them all over the Internet. The first was discovered by a sheep farmer, and since then walkers have come across several others.'

Clicking the phone screen to Google, Kaia typed into the search engine. Immediately images of tall, grey-flecked, monoliths appeared on the screen. One had been taken with a walker standing nearby. It towered over him. There was something ominous about the audacity of it.

She clicked back to Bella's face. 'They just turned up?'

'Overnight,' Bella confirmed. 'The tallest is eight feet high. People are speculating; some say they're a prank, but it's an expensive prank.'

'What are they made of?'

'Some sort of metal. What d'you think? Dartmoor is the perfect place for shady goings-on. High up on the moor, wildest place left in England, not to mention it's partially firing range, so the military can control when people go. What a great cover: put the red flags up to keep people away. Who is going to venture across a piece of land if they think they are going to get shot?'

She had to agree. 'I wonder if the red flags have been up more than normal.'

'Checked,' Bella replied. 'Not, as it happens. They'll be building on Dartmoor soon, though, extending the prison, after all the recent arrests.'

There was a noise off-screen that sounded like the office lift being activated. Bella glanced to one side and began to speak quickly. 'Damn. That might be Layna. The other thing is, I went round to see Rick. It was weird. The door was unlocked. There was a funny smell, like rotting veg all around the house. I couldn't make it out, and no sign of Rick. Something else, Kaia – there was sick all over the bathroom floor.'

The lift arrived and opened its doors.

'I've got to go.'

Kaia sat studying the pictures, then wrote *mysterious monoliths* on a piece of paper and laid it out with the others. Perhaps the monoliths weren't connected, but they could be transmitting some sort of signal. Wilma and Sue had recognised it, and she had seen evidence of it herself. Mobile phones were bringing the worst out of people, causing headaches, and worse … *Sick on the floor!* She made sure her phone was off and put it under a cushion. Bella was right. The remoteness of Dartmoor, with its military connection, was the perfect place for secret goings-on.

CHAPTER 10

THE RAIN HAD SET IN and was hitting hard against the windowpane. Reaching for the woollen throw at the end of the bed, Kaia wrapped it around her shoulders, its snugness instantly making her feel more secure. Throwing a look of defiance at the raindrops running down the glass, she turned her attention back to her mobile.

She had been scanning the Internet for accounts of demons. There were several illustrations, mostly stereotypical figures with horns, or beings that looked like vampires. Nothing looked like the figure she had seen, and no accounts suggested demons could change form. She considered the injuries Mrs Mack had mentioned and wondered if the demon was behind them. Wilma had thought it was going to attack her ... but it was looking for someone else.

Me.

She FaceTimed Jim.

'Best get a wee dram,' she said as he answered. 'You might need it.' She spent the next twenty minutes relating her adventures.

'Whoa! You went through a portal. I do need that whisky! I wonder where you went?'

'I think the same forest. Just in a different time.'

'I'm surprised you didn't investigate more,' Jim said.

'I was kind of distracted by seeing the water man shot.'

Jim looked sheepish. 'Shouldn't encourage you to go looking for trouble,' he mumbled. 'Although it seems to follow you around.'

She had to agree. 'Do you think it was a demon that followed me through the forest?'

'I reckon so.' Jim rubbed his fingers on his chin contemplatively. 'Ancient texts describe the universe as a continuous dance of light and dark. Everything has its place. Yet dark forces continuously seek to expand and gain supremacy over the light. All stories of good against evil reflect it.'

'And demons are part of the dark. I am almost certain the demon showing up is linked to the thing with the mobiles and Rick ... Do you think there's one power orchestrating everything?'

Jim didn't hesitate. 'Has to be. Someone high up, too, if they've got the capacity to dabble fingers in both technological and supernatural pies.'

This was rapidly becoming more complicated. 'It was bad enough thinking there were people being manipulative on a third dimensional level. Now there's other-worldly forces at play too ...' She pulled the throw tighter around her body.

'I don't like it one bit.' Jim muttered something inaudible under his breath. 'Rick and the other fellow could have been possessed. You say Rick saw you?'

'He pointed a strange device at my hiding place.'

'The demon was tracking you prior to that, though.' Jim's brow furrowed in concentration. 'It has locked onto you for some reason. I agree, you're only going to get answers by going through more portals. I researched portals years ago, when I was embroiled in discovering truth in the myths around Atlantis. Some records I unearthed spoke of doorways, and others, dimensional gateways. The doorways appear to be just that, doors leading from the third dimension to other realms. I couldn't find much information on the gateways, but sources described both as being huge physical structures, not like the portal you saw, created with a symbol. Can you remember what the symbol looked like, by the way?'

Doorways. The word resonated. Taking a photo of her drawing of the symbol she forwarded it to Jim and then watched as he tentatively copied it in the air with his finger. When nothing happened, his face fell, as though someone had offered him a gift and then demanded it back.

She grinned. 'You really thought that would work?'

'I don't see why not.' Jim shrugged. 'Our bodies are made of electromagnetic energy. It's what you channel when you do your healing. It's not too much of a stretch to surmise we could potentially create and activate energy symbols ourselves. There are records of it in Egyptology, very interesting actually.'

He spent the next ten minutes enthusiastically describing what he had unearthed in Egypt. Kaia was used to her godfather going off on a tangent, and it was reassuringly familiar to see his animated face and hear the enthusiasm in his voice as he described catacombs under pyramids and ancient scrolls containing esoteric symbols.

'Someday I will go back and explore it all more,' Jim concluded. 'I'm certain there are links to the lost city of Atlantis.'

'Atlantis. Do you think there's a link with the merman?'

'Maybe.'

The call ended. Raindrops were still lashing against the window like gravel. She half listened to the sound, digesting their conversation. She might not know why the demon was interested in her, but she was not going to sit around and wait to find out. She needed to discover what the conspirators were doing, and the first thing was to figure out where the base was.

Huddling down in the bed covers, she reached to turn out the lamp and then suddenly realized the dogs were very quiet. *Too quiet. They're still outside.* Letting out a groan, she grabbed the rug and, wrapping it around herself, hurried downstairs.

Able to see by the light from the upstairs landing, Kaia unbolted the front door. Two very bedraggled dogs scampered into the kitchen to sit looking at her reproachfully. Muttering an apology, Kaia pulled a towel from the oven rail and began vigorously rubbing the nearest dog. It wagged his tail, enjoying the attention, but then suddenly began to growl, staring towards the hallway. Startled, Kaia leapt through the hall, bolted the door, then crawled back into the kitchen on her hands and knees as the dog turned its attention to the window, with its hackles raised.

Kaia crouched on the floor and peered up. All she could see was a black rectangle with rain streaming down it. *A black hole to hell. Perfect for a demon. I can't see you, but can you see me?* Hugging the rug around her body, she squashed herself against the kitchen units, grateful she hadn't used the light. Yet she had no sooner had the thought when a strange symbol flashed in her mind, she felt an energy rush through her hand, and the kitchen light began to glow a soft yellow. She stared at both the bulb and her hand as the dog stopped barking, gave a woeful whine, and trotted over to give her a reassuring lick.

Her mind leapt back to her conversation with Jim. Tentatively reaching out a finger, she drew the portal symbol in the same way that he had. Another rush of energy shot from her fingers, this time shattering two glasses on the draining board, and the dogs disappeared under the table, yet she barely noticed.

She stared at the floating symbol as it rotated, flashed, and then morphed into an orb that expanded, like a balloon being inflated, to four feet in diameter. *Theirs was triangular. Perhaps this isn't a portal at all …* Her question was obligingly answered by one of her dogs, who trotted over to investigate the unusual rabbit hole by sticking her head into it. *Now that's very disconcerting.* Kaia grabbed the seemingly headless dog by the collar and yanked her back, thankful she was in one piece. Yet her relief was short-lived. The dog let out an angry growl as shadowy forms started to appear within the orb.

Wolves!

Leaping to her feet, Kaia grabbed the frying pan from the top of the stove and turned back to the portal as the muzzles and white eyes of demon wolves appeared in the kitchen. She lashed out with the frying pan.

Get … your face … out of … my space!

The demons gave angry snarls and pulled back. To Kaia's relief, the portal then contracted and disappeared. She sank to the floor.

Upset by her demeanour, both dogs came and sat beside her, wagging their tails reassuringly. Kaia began to stroke their heads, her hands trembling. Her aura looked different, lighter, as though something had been activated. *The kelpie. Touching the kelpie activated something in me. Something the demon senses too.* She stared at the space where the portal had been. *I can get to the base. I can get answers.*

159

CHAPTER 11

* ◆ ◆ ◆ *

KAIA HAD BEEN PRACTISING THE portal symbol when Jim FaceTimed. She had shown him what it did, and they were both equally surprised when an orb not only appeared in the cottage kitchen, but also in Jim's study.

'I can't believe it!' Jim's shock turned to exuberance, as she stuck her face through the orb. 'Come on through; it's a bit discombobulating seeing you without a body!'

She stepped into his study, tripping over a pile of books stacked on the floor. 'None of the orbs have led anywhere since that first one.'

Jim stuck his own head through the orb, stepped through, momentarily disappeared and then reappeared seconds later. 'Tea. I need tea.'

He made two mugs of herbal tea, handed one to her, and then stood contemplating the hovering orb, seemingly shocked into silence.

'Talk about the elephant in the room.' Kaia took hold of the teabag's string and made it waft through the water. 'Why do you think the portal led somewhere this time?'

'Anchors,' Jim said, still staring at the portal, deep in thought.

Anchors. Large metal devices … hold ships in place. 'Something was outside the cottage. The demon was on my mind when I first used the symbol. Maybe that anchored the portal to where they were.'

'I'm not liking that you saw a whole pack.' Jim turned away from the orb and rubbed his fingers over his unshaven chin. 'I'm guessing you were in a highly emotional state at the time. Shock, fear … Take this study. You know what it looks like inside out. I think, to direct the portals, you need a highly charged emotion or a detailed knowledge of where you want to

160

go. Without such an anchor, I reckon getting them to go somewhere will be difficult, if not impossible.'

'As I've already found out. Do you think they could open through time?'

'Linear time is an illusion.' Jim sipped his tea, suddenly looking more aware of her and not the orb. 'You of all people know that. Quantum physics states everything exists within the same space, simultaneously. I reckon they could, only like I said, if you don't have an anchor—' He broke off, his eyes twinkling. 'Just think what fun a historian could have.'

'You call yourself a historian. You've just smashed the whole notion of history to pieces!' A wave of regret washed over her at the lost opportunity as a columnist.

'Things only change if people are curious. Don't regret quitting,' Jim said, guessing the reason for her sudden subdued look. 'Once you have the measure of something or someone, if it's not right for you, it's time to act, before you get stuck.'

'I just don't know what to do next.' She took a sip of tea and watched the portal fade to nothing. 'Although I seem to have enough to keep me busy right now.'

Jim chuckled. 'Destiny led you to Scotland. You've found work. You'll figure it all out.' He shuffled through some books on his desk and pulling one out, opened it to a photograph of an ancient handwritten document. 'Records from the estate of a Sir Alexander MacDonald, who lived on Skye in the eighteenth-century. Your Mrs Mack was right. There were demon attacks back then.'

Kaia scanned the page, but didn't understand a word.

'It's in ancient Gaelic,' Jim said, guessing the reason for her silence. 'I don't read it either, but there's a translation on the next page. Considering what I've just said, it could be the same demon, weaving through the third dimension. I doubt demons are restricted by linear time.'

'If it's looking for someone or something in both eras simultaneously, who or what could that be?'

Jim looked at her incredulously. 'Kaia, you are currently standing in my study having come through a portal you opened, without the aid of a device, like those other beings. I think you can figure that out for yourself.'

An uncomfortable hot prickle raced down her spine. 'Me. In both eras.'

'Has to be. You exist in both parallel realities, a past life if you want to call it that. It explains the pull you had to Scotland. There's something huge that links you there. Something that someone else knows about too.'

'And that same someone could be behind whatever is going on with the phones.'

Jim let out a breath to release the tension he was feeling. 'I don't like it one bit. So much for looking out for you. Your parents would have a fit.'

Kaia put down her mug and drew the symbol. Another orb immediately appeared. 'I don't know. They had a sense of adventure. I reckon they would be all for it.'

Blowing Jim a kiss, she stepped through.

CHAPTER 12

✦ ✦ ✦ ✦ ✦

K AIA TENTATIVELY PUT HER HAND through the portal, only to see it appear out from the other side. She let out a sigh of frustration, drew the symbol again, and watched the portal contract to nothing.

She had been trying to open a portal to where Rick and Regalis were based for an hour, but Jim's premise about her needing a strong image or emotional charge to direct a portal was proving correct. She had no definite proof of there being a base on the moor, and she certainly had no idea what it looked like. As a result, she had spent an hour opening portals that led nowhere, yet the exercise had not been entirely fruitless. She had discovered if she used the symbol a second time when a portal was open, it served to close it.

She flopped onto the sofa, glancing at the dogs as they poked their noses round the lounge door. 'It's safe to come in. There's no chance of demonic wolves coming through these.'

One dog disappeared, only to follow her sister into the room moments later, carrying a lead. She sat down to regard Kaia dolefully.

'You're right, fuzzy face. Fresh air is long overdue.'

Moments later she and the dogs left the cottage, heading for the shore. Kaia jogged along the beach, then followed a track alongside a river that twisted and turned through banks of heather, before rising over a small hill to reveal a secluded pool. Rowan trees laden with red berries framed the banks, yellow wagtails bobbed among the rocks looking for insects, and the water was so clear she could see the colour and shape of every pebble within it.

The chance was too good to miss, so discarding her clothes, she slipped in. Angst and frustration were soon washed away to be replaced by a sense of calm. Flipping over onto her back, she lay like a starfish, watching clouds drift past overhead. *Magic. The realm of the fae.* The strange words she sang when she sent healing began drifting through her awareness, and she softly began to sing.

The symbol she had seen in the kitchen when the light glowed, and the one she had seen before the tree hid her, flashed across the screen of her mind. She had almost forgotten about them. *Wood. Light.* They must be significant.

Her tranquil moment was broken by the dogs catching the scent of a rabbit. Yelping in excitement, they tore across the heather in pursuit. Kaia swam for the bank, dressed, scattered some fallen rowanberries at the edge of the pool in thanks, and was lacing her running shoes when one of the dogs came racing back, looking incredibly pleased with herself.

'Leave the rabbits be! Where's your sister?'

As if to answer her question, a brown streak tore past her in the direction of the estuary. *Great. She'll have swum to the mainland before I catch her.*

By the time Kaia arrived on the shore, the dog was indeed way off in the distance, now chasing seagulls. When the birds took to the air, it changed direction again, disappearing into undergrowth at the far end of the beach and then reappearing on a track leading round the coast, still running like the wind. Letting out a groan, Kaia set off in pursuit.

The narrow track track swept along cliff tops before plunging down to a second beach. The tide was out, and the dog was now running back and forth in the distant shallows, chasing yet more birds. Kaia picked her way down the rugged track, scanning for suitable places to step. As her attention was on her feet and not the beach, she was shocked when she finally reached the shore.

It was covered in plastic. Plastic bottles, bits of rope, unidentifiable broken plastic objects, and even a plastic cement sac. Kaia looked around in dismay and, her dog momentarily forgotten, aimlessly walked along the beach, her heart sinking with every step.

A prickling sensation suddenly crept down the back of her neck. Glancing behind, Kaia saw a large black crow flying low over the cliff. *The demon!* It had to have seen her, but spying a cave in the cliff ahead, she sprinted for it.

She crawled through the cave's narrow entrance, screwing up her nose at the pungent smell of seaweed. The interior proved to be large. From its rear came the sound of a waterfall that clearly created the stream which ran along the cave floor to collect in a large rock pool near the cave mouth. Kaia waded into the rock pool and then, scrabbling along the stream, made her way deeper into the cave, looking for a hiding place. She found one. Climbing from the stream she pulled herself onto a narrow ledge and squeezed among some jagged rocks, just as a shadow appeared at the cave entrance.

'There's no escape. You may as well come out.'

She did not intend to make it easy. Clasping her hand around a loose rock, she tensed, ready to lash out when discovered. There was a moment's silence; then claws came scrabbling on the other side of the stream. The water had obscured her scent.

'Malphas. You're wanted.'

Rick. She watched the demon return to the cave entrance, turn into its human form, and go outside. Leaving her hiding place, Kaia crept to a position near the cave entrance to hear what was being said.

'—the eighteenth-century woman, Meg.'

'I have business here.'

'You have business where the colonel says you have business. He wants the loose end tying up.'

The demon muttered a curse, and then everything went quiet. Peering onto the beach, Kaia saw the demon, now in crow form, disappearing into the clouds and Rick stepping into a triangular portal. This was her chance. She broke into a sprint, but the portal closed just as she reached it. Letting out a cry of annoyance, she stared where it had been. *I can follow Rick, use him as an anchor.* Holding an image of Rick in her mind, she drew the symbol to open a portal and cautiously stepped through.

CHAPTER 13

✦ ✦ ✦ ✦ ✦

KAIA FOUND HERSELF IN AN enormous hangar. To either side were military style jeeps, and up ahead Rick was entering a large corridor. She closed the portal – and retched – the air was rank, thick and damp, with a putrid smell of mould. Willing herself not to be sick, she scurried after Rick, ducking into the shadows when he was accosted by another man, who also had the same soulless black eyes.

'Agaricus, did you send Malphas?'

Agaricus?

Rick nodded. 'Have the new Skinwalkers arrived?'

'Ten minutes ago. There were twenty.'

'Is that all!'

'I say it's a design fault. Humans are so ridiculously incompetent.'

'Yet they are our hosts.'

'For now. Get the new Skinwalkers orientated.'

Rick strode away, leaving Kaia to follow the other man into another huge hangar, lined with pieces of equipment, computer stations, and housing an enormous metal construction resembling a lighthouse, which looked to have been made from the same, grey-flecked metal as the monoliths. The man stopped at a metal box connected to the tower's base, opened a control panel, and began to check settings. There was the sound of crackling electricity, a crystal set within a spiked grey dome at the top of the tower darkened and then began to fill the dome with dark, swirling energy. *The crystal they took from the merman!*

The energy surge subsided, and the swirling energy contracted back into the crystal. Kaia crept nearer. Skirting round the base of the tower to get a better view, she leant back against it when the man glanced in her direction. A surge of energy raced up her spine, and to her horror a strong electric charge pulled her against the metal, like metal filings to a magnet. There was a loud crack from above as the crystal filled the dome with the dark energy. Then dark energy shot from the dome's spikes into another device connected to the ceiling.

The man looked up in surprise and saw her. 'Hey!'

Yanking her body from the tower Kaia ran for the vehicle hanger, with the man in pursuit. She twisted and turned through several vehicles then managed to give him the slip by rolling underneath a large military-style truck. She waited until his legs and feet were out of sight, then rolled to open a portal.

Back on the beach she closed the portal and stood in a daze. Rick was no longer Rick but one of those *things*. She wasn't sure exactly what Skinwalkers were, but if they were created by some sort of parasite that used humans as a host, then how long was it before that host died? *Solid black eyes. Does that mean Rick is dead?* Her body went to jelly, and she collapsed to the ground.

Catching a movement in the corner of her eye, she turned sharply, but this time it proved to be nothing sinister, simply her dog tearing across the beach, followed by an enormous dark grey dog resembling a wolf.

'About time!'

Her dog sat beside her looking sheepish.

'You're a prize pest,' she said, rubbing the dog's ears, *but a sight for sore eyes.*

The wolfdog whined as though hearing and understanding her thoughts. He was a beautiful dog with deep green eyes the colour of sunlight through a pine forest and a bright yellow aura that looked like rays of the sun. She held out her hand.

'Hello, boy. It would have been nice to have met you before. I don't think I'd have felt so scared with you around.'

The dog licked the back of her hand and wagged his tail.

Feeling more in control of her legs, Kaia began to walk for the cliff path with her dog, and the wolfdog, following close behind.

CHAPTER 14

K AIA'S PHONE PINGED DECLARING JIM had replied. She pulled into the café car park and read his latest message.

'Lecture about to start. Catch you when I've finished. If you do try to warn Meg, be wary. If she is your past life, I'm not sure what would happen if you were to meet.'

She responded with a frown emoji and entered the café.

'We're all set for the lunchtime rush.' Wilma placed the last pastry under its glass dome and turned to face her with a smile. 'Would you like one of these before you start?'

'Just coffee, thanks.' She sat down on one of the chairs near the counter in somewhat of a daze.

'You look like you've got a lot on your mind.'

She took the cappuccino Wilma was holding and stirred its chocolate powder into its froth, wondering how much to say. Trying to explain yesterday's escapade at the base would not be easy, nor would her conclusions about the fate of her old boyfriend. Better to stick to what Wilma had witnessed herself.

'You said you pitied whoever the demon was looking for. I think it's looking for me.'

Wilma pursued her lips and let out a burst of air. 'If that's the case, you could use some help, but who is going to listen and not think we're crazy?' She took a cloth and began to vigorously polish the front of the glass counter as though it helped her think. 'Marjorie would believe you, but I don't know what help she could be. It's a pity she isn't here, but she was particularly fuddled this morning. I encouraged her to stay at home.

168

Have you seen the paper, by the way?' She stopped polishing and picked up a folded newspaper from a nearby table just as the door of the café opened to let in a group of tourists. 'I'll get these; check out page two.'

Wilma greeted the tourists and set about taking their orders, leaving Kaia to open the paper. She scanned the article. Two forestry commissioners had mysteriously disappeared. Their vehicles had been found abandoned in the forest, and no one had seen the men for three days. She read through the article a couple of times, instinct telling her the disappearance was linked. Perhaps the men had turned into Skinwalkers and were now at the base. The photograph showed the reporter standing near to the abandoned vehicles. Her blood ran cold. It was obscured by the trees, but there, nevertheless, a cuboid shadow. *A monolith.*

The café got busy. It was not until the end of her shift that Kaia's thoughts returned to the article. Deciding to investigate, she crossed to her van, changed into her running shoes, and moments later set off along the lane with the dogs at her heels.

Passing through a small wooden gate, she continued along a wide gravel track that led into the forest. For a while it was a pleasant run; birds were singing, a woodpecker was drilling into a tree trunk, and everything felt tranquil and benign. However, at a split in the track, she took the trail leading to the vehicles and immediately began to feel uneasy. Instinct screamed objections about her being alone in the forest and of her not telling Wilma where she was going.

Pushing through her discomfort, Kaia eventually arrived at the abandoned vehicles. She walked round them slowly. Everything looked normal, so she turned her attention to the forest, looking for the monolith that had cast the shadow.

Nothing.

Puzzled, Kaia returned to the vehicles. Then, noticing a track of trampled ferns, she followed the makeshift path to where the trail stopped. The crushed ferns formed the shape of a perfect rectangle. Something cuboid must have stood here, and not so long ago. She took a step forward, stumbling against something hard as her toe hit against metal.

She had no time to investigate.

Shadows flickered among the trees, becoming demon wolves. Kaia turned and fled, racing past the forest vehicles and calling for her dogs to follow as the demons began to bay. They were hunting her and were gaining. Pulling on all her reserves she raced for the split and reaching it, she took the shorter trail towards the shore.

There was a spine-chilling growl as another shape came racing towards her. Her heart leapt into her throat, but this time it wasn't a demon but the wolfdog. He tore past her towards the oncoming demons, his teeth bared. There was the sound of a fight and a yelp, but she did not stop. Leaping from the trees onto the shoreline, she sprinted full pelt for the water and waded out fast. Then, throwing her body across the surface, she began to swim. Immediately the threat subsided, and sensing the demons had gone, she turned to face the shore. It was deserted.

++++++++

Back at the café car park, Kaia collapsed on the van floor and sat staring into space.

'I saw you were wet through!' Wilma came to a halt next to the van. 'I take it you hadn't planned to swim, given you have all your clothes on.'

Kaia roused. 'I went to check out the abandoned vehicles … only I got spooked and swam back.'

Wilma regarded her shrewdly. 'The demon?'

She nodded.

'What is the island coming to?' Wilma said in a cross voice. 'Come back inside. You need something hot and sweet. We need to find someone who will watch your back, Kaia. This is all getting a bit one-sided.'

CHAPTER 15

RATHER THAN RETURNING TO THE cottage after her latest shift, Kaia had taken a drive to explore more of the island's coastline. Parking near a loch shore, she walked for a couple of miles along its beach. It was like being in a painting – stripes of white, grey, and reddish pink pebbles, interspersed with stripes of golden brown and green seaweed dropped by the falling tide. The perfect environment for wildlife and no doubt home to a multitude of seabirds and otters. She glanced to where her dogs were scampering back and forth. 'You have no chance of seeing an otter,' she told one dog as she raced towards her, leaping joyously in the air before scampering into the ferns edging the beach. *And neither have I.*

The wind had dropped, and the surface of the loch had become a mirror, reflecting the surrounding mountains. She stood transfixed as a sea eagle glided past, its enormous unusually shaped wings, extended out like barn doors on either side. Catching a thermal, the majestic bird soared higher.

Kaia closed her eyes and stretched her arms to either side of her body, imagining that she was the eagle and could see herself standing far below. The scene in her mind changed. She was soaring over a different part the loch. Far below now she could see a man cutting away bracken and brambles near the shore, revealing what looked like the hull of a boat.

The eagle cried out, and Kaia opened her eyes, but her mind was hyperactive. He had looked like the man from her previous vison, the one wearing a plaid kilt, only this time he was in modern-day clothes. Her mind suddenly made a connection. Great plaids were a type of kilt worn by men in the eighteenth century. It couldn't be by chance she had envisioned him in that era too. He was linked to her past life.

She was distracted from her thoughts by her dogs playing tag, much to the annoyance of a gull which was displaying its objection by flying low across the water, calling menacingly. One dog instantly took on the challenge and ran into the sea in a vain attempt to catch the bird before swimming back, looking defeated and deeply sorry for herself. Kaia picked up a stick of dried seaweed and threw it. Instantly forgetting its soggy escapade, the dog retrieved it, then raced away with the seaweed dangling from its mouth.

Kaia caught up with the dogs at a ruin where they were now running back and forth among dead ferns. Her heart began to pound as she explored what was left of the cottage. It had a dry stonewalled construction, its walls virtually intact, despite being covered in moss and the miraculous growth of ferns and grasses which had taken root in the cracks. Stone lintels marked where the door and a small window had been, and it was possible to see where wooden beams would have sat to support a roof.

The inside of the cottage was not so well preserved. The floor was entirely covered in cotton grass and thistles, but there was an area that would have been the fireplace. She crossed to where her dog was now scratching at the ground near it. 'Not much chance of a mouse there, I'm afraid.'

Yet the dog was persistent, pausing only to give her a Paddington stare of disapproval. Kaia chuckled and crouched to investigate. The dog had scraped away the dirt and plant roots to reveal one side of a small flagstone. She traced the stone with her fingers.

The hiding place.

Collecting a driftwood stick from the shore, Kaia scraped away the rest of the dirt from around the stone and then prised it up. Her eyes instantly fell on the concealed package. The cloth had the consistency of cardboard, and as she tried to unfold it, huge sections fell away, to reveal a leatherbound book and an embroidered picture of a white horse leaping from the sea.

She opened the front cover and saw a name written on the inside. *Meg.* There was no energy portal, but it was as though she had gone through one to the past as she slowly turned the pages, taking in the Gaelic writing.

She couldn't understand the meaning, but voices whispered in her head, echoes of those times. One page contained five symbols, two of which she recognised. *Light. Wood.*

She closed the book and sat lost in swirling thoughts, until her dogs came up and touched her arm with their noses, bringing her attention back to the moment. The light was fading and not relishing being out in the dark with demons on the prowl, she headed back to the van, taking the book with her.

CHAPTER 16

'ALL OF THEM? ALL THE monoliths have vanished?' Kaia clicked her phone to speaker phone, drained the remnants of her hot chocolate and stood to put the mug in the sink.

'So it seems,' Bella confirmed. 'Everything has gone offline. Pictures. Interviews. It's as though the whole thing never happened.'

'I bet they're still there.' Kaia pulled a disgruntled face as she rinsed the cup clean and turned it upside down on the draining board. 'They've done something to make them invisible, like the one in the forest. They were attracting too much attention.'

'Unless they have done what they were put there for, and really have been taken away,' Bella suggested.

There's only one way to check. 'I could go back and see if the one in the forest is still there.'

'No way!' Bella said in alarm. 'I may be getting my head round that what you've been describing is actually real, but that doesn't mean I'm in favour of you going out looking for it! Besides, even if the monolith is still there, it doesn't prove anything … What makes you think you were in the eighteenth century when you met the figure with the crystal?'

'One, seven, five, two. Those were the numbers I heard. Jim confirmed there were demon attacks in the eighteenth century. I think they opened the portal to seventeen fifty-two. I think the man was trying to warn Meg … Bella, he wasn't human either. He was some sort of merman.'

'Oh.'

She tensed, expecting ridicule, or some sarcastic remark regarding her mental health. Yet to her surprise, she got neither.

'I can't believe you found the book. Pity you can't read Gaelic … Geez. If you're right, and the crystal contains an evil parasitic energy, why would a merman want to give it to Meg, or Ianna, and why would it be wanted in our time?' Bella let out a groan. 'I'm sounding as crazy as you, girl!'

'Meg had the embroidered picture of a kelpie. Maybe she had seen the kelpie too. If I can get back to the eighteenth century, I can have a snoop around, maybe I'll get some answers.'

Their call ended. Pulling a grey throw from the couch, Kaia tied it around herself as a makeshift eighteenth-century dress and then opened the diary to where the embroidery was lodged in its pages. Placing her hand on the embroidered picture, she focused her mind on the shore where she had met the merman and opened a portal.

The wind immediately took her breath. It was blowing a gale, bending the tops of the trees as though they were grass. The portal hadn't opened on the beach but on the rise of a small hill. Below was open moorland and, beyond that, a cluster of dwellings set back from a different loch shore. Shadowy forms were circling the moor. *Demon wolves.* As she watched, two broke away from the pack and doubled back, approaching the dwellings under the cover of gorse and shrubs, as the others raced away across the moor. They might not be hunting Meg, but they had locked onto someone. She had to warn them or try to help. Securing the rug more tightly, Kaia ran to join a dirt track which she could see offered a direct route to the buildings.

She arrived at the first cottage. It was built in a similar way to the ruin she had discovered, only the stone had been lime-washed and bulged outwards near the ground, giving the impression of melting ice cream. It had a thatched roof that had clearly been done by a craftsman, with laced stones to keep the straw from blowing loose, and a small planked wooden door that was currently banging in the wind.

Kaia cautiously stepped inside. The cottage was uninviting, cold and damp. It had furniture, but the shelves next to the fireplace were empty. She walked into an adjacent room that turned out to be a kitchen. This was also empty aside from two wooden chairs and a few jars and a mixing bowl which had been left on a wooden table. She frowned. Something was not right.

Leaving the cottage, she hurried down the lane to two further cottages. The door of the nearest was shut, but peering through the windows, she could see it was also empty. The shelves had been cleared and there were no personal items that indicated that it was being used. It was odd. *It's a ghost town.* The thought made her shudder. If the dwellings were empty, then what were the wolves hunting?

There was the sound of hooves and startled, she ducked round the side of the building as a beautiful white stallion galloped past. It ran away from the cottages, jumped a gate, then tore across a field towards the moor.

She peered back onto the lane as the door of the second cottage opened. A woman stepped out into the rain. Kaia stared: the woman's body shape, the colour of her hair, her posture …

My God. It's me!

She froze, too stunned to call out. It was like looking in a mirror and seeing herself dressed for a historical play. Meg didn't notice her; doubling against the wind, she raced away down the lane. Seconds later the wind carried the sound of howling wolves, they had sensed their quarry.

Kaia caught up with Meg and the wolves by the shore. A strange-looking boat was moored to a wooden jetty by a thick rope which Meg was desperately trying to untie. Two demons, seeing they had her cornered, were slinking towards the end of the jetty with teeth bared and hackles raised.

Seizing a boat hook leaning against a wall, Kaia ran for the nearest demon. The demon turned its attention on her, snarling viciously and its white eyes burning with anger. She stabbed out to force it back as a cry and a splash came from the jetty. Meg had fallen into the water.

Kaia's chest suddenly tightened causing her to gasp for air. Gripping the boat hook tighter, she battled against the sudden heaviness of her body as the demon poised to attack. Then a sudden streak of grey raced past, charging for the other demon which was now perilously close to Meg. With a blood-curdling snarl, the newcomer, an enormous dark grey wolf, ripped the demon's throat clean away. In an instant the second demon turned from Kaia to race along the jetty. It leapt onto the wolf's back, but the wolf twisted its body to dislodge it. The demon went sliding along the jetty, and before it had time to stand, the wolf dispatched it. As dark mist seeped from both fallen demons, the wolf stared into the water as though looking for Meg.

Kaia's lungs were burning, screaming for her to take air, but she could not inhale. She began to panic. Everything started to spin. It was as much as she could do to draw the symbol. When a portal opened, she staggered through, collapsed on the doorstep of Wilma's cottage, and blanked out.

CHAPTER 17

MAY TIPPED THE REMAINING SPARKLING wine over the bow of the rowing boat then waded alongside to clamber in. 'God bless all who row in her.'

Leidolf smiled at the companions who had followed him through so much. Alex, suave and rugged in his T-shirt and jeans, and May, energetic, her greying hair plaited above a carefree face with sparkling eyes. She wore a loose shirt, and trousers rolled up in defiance of the water. They complemented each other, two sides of the same person. He could think of no better people to call friends or share this moment.

'It's so roomy. To take all three of us. It's going to take a lot of effort to row.' May ran her hands along one of the wooden benches admiring the polished wood. 'It's a pity you haven't given her a name.'

Leidolf waited for Alex to climb aboard and then got in himself. 'I will. I just haven't found the right one.' He slotted the wooden oars into their locks. 'Perhaps this maiden voyage will help.'

He began to row. He had done what he set out to do, and the boat was now restored in memory of her. Finding a steady rhythm, he rowed out across the loch with his friends surveying the water and surrounding shoreline in appreciative silence.

'I can't believe she used to row this across the loch,' Alex observed eventually. 'On her own too.'

Leidolf flinched. For an instant he was back on the jetty, with her standing before him, looking defiant. 'If there's one thing I've learnt about women,' he said, 'especially strong women, it's never to underestimate them. Or be seen to be challenging them, by implying they can't do what they've set their mind to accomplish.'

Alex let out a chortle. 'Ain't that the truth.'

'It's like she's with us,' May astutely observed. 'Her time is merging with ours. In other ways too, aside from you finishing this boat. The demon attacks are getting more frequent, Leidolf.'

'I hadn't noticed there'd been an increase.'

'No disrespect, mate, but how would you? You live off grid,' Alex stated. 'The media is full of reports of violence too. It's like an unseen force is deliberately stirring up the populace.' He paused. 'D'you think what we're thinking?'

Leidolf stopped rowing and looked at them in turn. 'Scathchornail. Christ. If he is up to his old tricks. She really is in trouble.'

'Right up to her neck,' Alex agreed.

May said, 'Perhaps he's broken out of Shadow Side.'

Leidolf considered her words and then shook his head. 'If he had, we'd know about it. He could be preparing the field for harvesting Skinwalkers, but how is he doing that from Shadow Side?'

May screwed up her face. 'My guess would be the grid. Most people are deeply entrenched in it. Perhaps he's found a way to hack the communication network.'

'If he is doing that then he definitely has a plan to break out from Shadow Side,' Alex added. 'If he succeeds, there's going to be one hell of a storm, Leidolf.'

Leidolf began pulling on the oars with vigour, and the rowing boat began to shoot through the water. 'I need to meet her.'

'I don't think you need to worry about that,' May replied, raising her eyebrows at the bow wave Leidolf was now creating. 'If history does repeat itself, then she'll find you.'

CHAPTER 18

⬩⬩⬩

KAIA STEPPED FROM THE RHODODENDRON thicket in a secluded area of the Oxford park. Bella was already there.

'Girl, that is the most freakish thing ever.' Bella stared in disbelief as the portal closed. 'It's one thing hearing you describe them, but another seeing one for real!'

'I've kinda got used to them now. It's funny how one minute something can freak you out, and the next your brain accepts it as normal.'

She had opened a portal to meet up with Bella after receiving Bella's SOS. It was now Bella's lunch break, and she was currently carrying a cardboard takeout tray holding two very large coffee cups and a bag of what looked to be pastries.

Stepping from the bushes they crossed the grass to a path and followed through an avenue of beech trees until they found an empty bench. She had to admit Bella was right. It was surreal to be sitting together in the park, when seconds ago she had been on Skye. Taking the almond croissant that Bella offered, she took a bite. It was good, but not a patch on the ones the girl on the island made.

Bella finished her own croissant. 'I still can't believe it. How long were you out for?'

'About an hour, I think.'

Bella looked shocked. 'Thank the Lord you were all right. What d'you suppose caused it?'

'I think I felt what Meg was experiencing. Jim had warned me. I should have been more careful.'

She took the lid off her cappuccino. Then she emptied the paper bag of croissant crumbs and threw them to the pigeon sitting expectantly on the arm of the bench.

Bella took a sip from her latte. 'If it'd been me. I'd have passed out when I saw that Rick had turned into one of those Skinwalker things … and you think they're behind the monoliths on Dartmoor. Christ.' She shuddered. 'Do you think Meg drowned?'

'I didn't see her getting out of the water.'

'You and she must be the same person. It's radical. People talk about past lives, but that's what they are, in the past. To think you have seen your past life self *and* felt what she was going through.' She took the lid from her latte cup and gently swirled it. 'I don't know why, but I find it odd that there's demon wolves and the good wolf that acts like a protector.'

Kaia absent-mindedly watched the pigeon finish its breakfast. *It's true. The wolf on the jetty with the green eyes. It was strong, a protector … and familiar.*

'What are you going to do next?'

'I need to find out more about Meg.' Kaia picked up her now cool coffee. 'Jim can't read Gaelic, but I'm sure one of his colleagues at the university will be able to. If not, there's always Google translate. I overheard Rick sending the demon to the eighteenth century to hunt her, there must be a link between Meg and the modern-day thing with the phones, though heaven only knows what … And the wolf I saw on the jetty. I'd swear I've seen it before.'

'Perhaps you remember it from when you were Meg, or maybe it's an immortal wolf!' Bella chuckled, tapping her nails on the side of her coffee cup. 'Maybe wolves have past lives too!'

'Maybe they do, but I've seen a wolfdog on the island, and it looked the same. …'

A man jogged past. They waited for him to be out of earshot.

'I never thought I would be sitting in the park chewing over a conspiracy that could be linked to a different century,' Bella stated.

She had to agree. 'If the crystal sends out that dark parasitic energy through the mobile network, which ultimately turns people into Skinwalkers, my question is, what are they doing it for?'

Bella shrugged. 'Why does anyone want control of the masses? Power. It must be some sort of takeover bid. A silent invasion … with a supernatural twist.'

'So that begs the question, who is behind it?' Kaia fell silent, sipping coffee as the pigeon, giving up on second helpings, flew to scavenge underneath the next bench. 'What about you. What are you going to do?'

Bella's face immediately fell. 'Leave. Now I know for certain the rat is having an affair.'

'Are you absolutely sure he is?'

Bella crossed to the waste bin and deposited her cup. 'To my shame I looked at his phone when he was at the gym.' She sat back down and began to fiddle with a hooped earring. 'His behaviour has been so different. Working late, being snappy. Part of me wishes I hadn't read his messages.'

'What did you find?'

'Nothing too incriminating on the face of it. Flirty texts to a female colleague, but since then … he has had to attend more meetings.'

'Meetings don't necessarily mean he's having an affair.' She was doing her best not to think the worst.

'Not when they're in a different town and require an overnight in a hotel. Come on, Kaia, neither of us was born yesterday.'

Kaia screwed up her face as Bella went on to tell her the details and relate her feelings. She knew well enough what it was like to be treated with disrespect and JD's behaviour stank. She was not about to tell Bella that she was being paranoid.

'I'm packing up,' Bella concluded, 'before it drags me right down. Work is already suffering, and you know how supportive Layna will be. If I keep making mistakes, she'll fire me and then I will be in a pit.'

'I bet his sudden change in behaviour is linked to the crystal. From what I've seen, there's different stages. Initially there seem to be headaches and feeling ill, then you see changes in behaviour that get increasingly severe. Then eyes flicker from their normal colour to black and finally stay black all the time. My guess is that's when the parasite takes control.' She paused, thinking of Rick. 'I don't know whether there is any coming back from it once that happens.'

Bella looked grave. 'I didn't like the guy, but I don't like to think of some evil parasite taking him over any more than you.' She forced a laugh. 'If JD *is* turning into a Skinwalker, then I'm best off without him! I could never trust him now, even if he came clean.' She looked at her watch and stood up reluctantly. 'I had best get back to work.'

They headed back through the manicured park to the ornate iron gate at its entrance. 'Keep me updated,' Kaia said. 'If you need to get away, I can come and get you. Anytime, just let me know.'

'It means a lot, you coming to see me.' Bella took a deep breath, rallying herself for her return to the office. 'What a fantastic way to travel. I can see the advert. *Portal Power. Instant. Free. No carbon emissions.*'

Kaia hugged her friend goodbye and then returned to the thicket of rhododendron bushes. Weaving among them, she thought of the trees next to Wilma's café and opened a portal. Seconds later she crossed the car park and opened the café door. Wilma had been clearing tables and was in the process of carrying a precariously balanced stack of plates and cups into the kitchen. Catching sight of Kaia, she jumped and nearly dropped them.

'Lord, you nearly gave me a heart attack. I thought you'd gone home.'

'There was something I wanted to ask Mrs Mack.'

Wilma smiled. 'I'll join you in a jiffy. Just let me get rid of these!'

Kaia crossed to the corner where Mrs Mack was sitting at her usual table sipping tea. 'Hello, mind if I join you?'

Mrs Mack's face lit up, and she indicated one of the vacant chairs. 'There have been more demon attacks.' She said, instantly continuing a previous conversation. 'A group of climbers were found in the hills, yesterday, with nasty injuries. One died in hospital, lost too much blood from a wound to his leg. None of them can remember what attacked them apparently. They're blaming a stray dog. Really, whoever heard of a dog attacking a group of men!'

'I was wanting to ask you about the attacks.' Kaia took off her coat, hung it over the back of her chair, and sat down. 'I was wondering if you could tell me more about the demon attacks in the eighteenth century and which villages were specifically involved. Are there any local historical records I could look at?'

'There's no records, because of the clearances.'

'Clearances?'

Mrs Mack picked up her teaspoon and pointed to the map of the island pinned to the notice board near the counter. 'Most of the villages on there are from after the clearances. Prior to that, there were lots of tiny settlements, but most were abandoned because the inhabitants were ordered to leave. Criminal.'

The empty houses. 'Why?'

'Politics. Power. Big wigs wanting land for their own reasons. The locals were in the way, so they were sent packing.'

Kaia stared at the notice board. *Meg ran to a rowing boat. She must have lived away from the village. If the villagers were sent away, did she go too?* She walked over to retrieve the map and laid it out on the table.

'Here.' She pointed to a loch slightly south from the café. 'Were there any settlements here?'

Mrs Mack leant forward in her chair and ran her finger over an area near the shoreline. 'There was a small village here once upon a time. You can still walk in the ruins and see the fireplaces. It's interesting, but sad.' She sat back on the chair and looked at her knowingly. 'You think the demon attacks were linked to the clearances.'

'They could have been, if both events happened at the same time.' Kaia pointed at a different area on the map. 'Tell me, was there a cottage across the loch, here?'

Mrs Mack screwed up her face and then shook her head. 'Not that I know of.'

Wilma put down the tray she had been carrying and pointed to a spot on the map. 'There's an old ruin right by the loch shore, just here. You remember, Marjorie.' She gave Mrs Mack's hand a squeeze. 'There's quite a lot of it left too,' she added. 'It's a tiny place, but then that's all you would want. With all the rain blowing in with the south-westerlies, one room would be enough to keep warm. What a location!'

'Is it right next to the water?'

Wilma nodded. 'It is now. The land has eroded a lot. Now the water fairly laps on the doorstep.'

Where I found the diary. It was Meg's cottage. She could picture it in her mind not as a ruin, but as it would have looked in the past. *The smoking chimney. The screen that separated the bed. The red rug on the flagstones by the fireplace. Writing the names of the villagers in the book, Morag, Owen …* She let out a gasp, suddenly aware she had been holding her breath.

Wilma was looking concerned. 'You have gone pale, Kaia. I am getting to know you now, and that usually means you're about to get yourself into a whole heap of trouble.'

CHAPTER 19

JIM MOMENTARILY DISAPPEARED FROM THE screen, and Kaia heard a shuffling from the other end of his desk. 'Here it is.'

He reappeared, holding an open book. 'It's very similar.' He held the book so that she could view the symbol. 'It's said to represent earth dragons.'

She was sitting at the kitchen table in Wilma's cottage talking to Jim on Zoom after sending him some photographs of the symbols from Meg's diary. Jim had drawn a blank on them all except for one, which had reminded him of an old Druid symbol. She compared the symbol he was currently displaying to the one drawn in Meg's diary.

'It looks the same. What do you suppose the Druids meant by earth dragons? Ley lines? Do you think they used the symbol to mark sacred places?'

'Possibly.'

She sensed he had different ideas. 'You don't sound convinced.'

'Language and words used to have a more literal meaning than nowadays. I think the symbol could have referred to actual dragons.'

She let out a chuckle but cut it short, seeing the seriousness on his face.

'Ancient traditions across the globe speak of dragons,' Jim continued. 'There's always truth in myth. Dragons are no exception.'

Can't argue with that. I've seen demons, a merman and a kelpie. 'I know now that beings from other realms exist, so why not dragons.'

'Exactly. On the premise that other realms interconnect with ours, it follows that beings from those realms can potentially intermingle with

185

us. Dragons included,' Jim stated. 'They are seen, and before you know it, you have stories about those sightings. They are retold and over time become myths.'

'If Meg knew about Druid symbols, I wonder why she didn't draw more.'

Jim looked thoughtful. 'Either she didn't know of any others, or she didn't think they were worth recording. Have you tried using it?'

'I've tried them all, but nothing happens. Either they're not created in the same way, or I'm missing something.'

'Shame.' He was silent for a moment and rubbed his chin in his usual fashion. 'Perhaps that's why the merman wanted to give the crystal to Meg. Maybe the crystal is needed to work the symbols.'

'Maybe, but he called me Ianna. If he had meant the crystal for Meg, then surely, he would have used her name. … If other realms interconnect with ours, the symbols could be from someplace else!'

'Eighteenth-century Meg came across them somewhere.' Jim went on rubbing his chin, reflecting on the conundrum from different angles. 'What if Meg was an incarnation of Ianna?'

'It would explain the merman's confusion. She, either Meg or Ianna, could have had interactions with beings from another realm and got the symbols through them.'

'Or another possibility. People have recalled lives in other dimensions, remember. Perhaps Ianna was from another realm. The symbols could be nothing more than part of that realm's written language.'

Kaia stared at the symbols. 'I'm sure they are more than that.' She sat back in her chair, doing her best not to lose herself down the rabbit hole. 'If Meg had a past life in another realm, then it follows, as an incarnation of her, I do too.'

Jim nodded, his face showing that he was also joining the dots.

Kaia involuntarily whistled through her teeth and rubbed her hands across her face as though to wake herself from a dream. 'I need to know more about Meg and Ianna, but the only anchor I have is that point in time when Meg died, and I feel what she feels—'

'Absolutely not!' Jim interrupted. 'You mustn't go back.'

Perhaps there are clues in the book. She glanced at the strange language. 'If only I could read Gaelic.'

'Leave it with me,' Jim replied. 'I'll ask one of my colleagues to look at the photos you sent.'

'Thanks. I'll take the diary with me to the café too. Mrs Mack may be able to help.'

CHAPTER 20

SOMETIME LATER, KAIA ARRIVED AT the burn with the dogs. The swim spot was just as Wilma had promised: a sunken paradise on the moor, home to frogs, water-boatmen, and the occasional otter. She swam back and forth along the length of the pool several times. Then, positioning herself where the water came bubbling down over rocks, she let her neck and back be pummelled.

She closed her eyes, her mind drifting through random thoughts, and remembered the pool she had discovered just prior to her dogs running off after rabbits … *the symbols!* She opened her eyes. The symbols she had seen in her mind, light and wood, they were the same as two in the book. She whooshed underwater and emerged. Then she dressed, placed dried heather flowers on the water in thanks, and hurried back to her van.

She sat on the van floor looking at the symbols. There were three others aside from the ones she had now recognised and the Druid one, and two of these had words next to them. She would bet anything the translation would be an element. Yet Meg had only labelled two. If she had known their meaning, surely, she would have known what the others represented?

Entering the café, she discovered Wilma looking pale and worn. Wilma clearly hadn't slept well, and her aura was dull muddy yellow. *Sluggish. Worried.* Yet despite how she was feeling, Wilma was doing her best to be bright and breezy. She began making Kaia a coffee and on noticing her wet hair, asked her about her visit to the pool.

'It was sublime!' Kaia glanced at the empty table by the window. 'No Mrs Mack? I was going to ask her to look at this old book I've found.'

Wilma's smile faded. 'Marjorie was suddenly taken terribly ill. She has been sent to the hospital on the mainland. Water on her lungs.' She passed her the cappuccino. 'I'm going to close after lunch and go across to see her. I'll tell her you were asking after her.' She wiped her hands down her apron. 'Want me to take a look?'

Kaia handed her the diary and the piece of embroidery, explaining where she had found them. 'Mrs Mack said there were demon attacks back then too. I was hoping this would provide some answers.'

Wilma examined the picture. 'I'll be. A kelpie. Marjorie would love this!' She turned a few pages of the book. 'My, this is an odd dialect ... hard to read. It seems disjointed, as though the person wasn't very confident with writing. I know what these words mean, though.' She pointed to two words in the middle of a page and raised her eyebrows. 'This word means demon and this one here ... wolves. I'll tell Marjorie; it'll spur her to get well. She'll want to see.'

So, the book did contain information that could throw light on things. Kaia wrapped it and placed it back in her cloth bag. 'I can stay on this afternoon if you like and close the usual time.'

Wilma looked as though she was going to cry. 'You are such a pet. That would be grand.'

A flurry of tourists entered the café, ending their conversation. Later, after the lunchtime rush, Wilma set off to see Mrs Mack. 'If any issues arise, just ring,' she said, giving Kaia a hug. 'And if a bus of tourists gives you grief, kick them all out, and close up!'

Kaia assured her she would be fine. She was more resilient than she used to be. 'After demons, a few grumpy tourists don't seem that intimidating!'

As it happened, there were no buses and no grumpy tourists, and the afternoon went like clockwork. Hours later Kaia crossed the café, carrying an order to a middle-aged woman with sparkling brown eyes and long greying hair tied in plaits. *Pocahontas.*

'I'm originally from America – well Canada actually,' the lady responded, as though reading her thoughts. 'You seem a bit preoccupied.'

'I was, a bit.' She was somehow not surprised by the lady's perceptiveness. 'I was thinking about Mrs Mack.'

'Alex and I saw the ambulance last night. I came by to check on Wilma.'

'She has gone to see her. She was putting on a brave face this morning, but she was very worried. They're such a sweet couple.'

'It can't be good if Marjorie has been sent to Raigmore.' The lady lifted the things from the tray as Kaia set it down on the table. 'They were childhood sweethearts. Wilma told me once that Marjorie did marry, but her husband passed away when she was in her forties. A few years afterwards she finally moved in with Wilma. They are both real characters, hearts of gold.' She paused and looked at her astutely. 'What's your name?'

'Kaia.'

'That's pretty. I'm May. Are you here with someone?'

'On my own.' *Men*. She grimaced.

'Mr Right is out there,' May said with a knowing smile. 'In my experience it's important to be yourself; then the right person shows up because they can see you!'

'Be real and open to a new life. What an article that would be!'

'Is that what you do?' May responded. 'Write?'

'Not at the moment.' An image of a praying mantis flashed into her mind. Which proceeded to plant its head onto Layna's body. 'I'm in between things. It turns out I have deep links with the island. I want to explore where they lead.'

If May had sensed the negative image she didn't show it. Instead, she beamed a smile. 'The island does that. Sneaks up on you when you least expect it, and draws you in. We came here from Canada. This is such a tiny island after living there, but like I said, Skye gets under your skin, and before you know it, you're hooked.'

Kaia moved on to the next table to clear away the empty cups, but suddenly struck by a thought, she turned back to May. 'Canada … then you must be the couple who came across with Leidolf.'

'Yes. Do you know him?' May's eyes were dancing as though she was bursting to say something.

'No. Wilma mentioned him after I saw large pawprints in the sand. She said they were probably made by his dog, Fraser. I—' She broke off.

The wolfdog on the beach had the same green eyes as the wolf on the jetty in the eighteenth century. She nearly dropped the tray.

'You don't tend to see them together,' May said. 'Fraser hangs around our place quite a lot. … Would you like to come and have lunch with Alex and me sometime?'

Another person offering the hand of friendship. *Jim was right, the island is a magical place.* 'That would be great!'

CHAPTER 21

THE WIND HAD FINALLY DROPPED and the sun was now doing its best to break through the thick cloud. Leidolf removed his blue woollen hoodie and hung it over the side of the boat. Then, kneeling on the pebbles, he marked out four letters onto the bow in chalk.

He stood back to check the positioning and then began stirring the pot of white paint with a stick. He wondered why he hadn't given the boat a name back then. It could have been a way to help her remember. A list of names he could have used flashed through his mind.

A gaggle of geese flew in a V above him distracting him from his thoughts. He watched the bird at the front of the group relinquish its position, falling back to the rear as another took the lead. The birds worked together, helping one another survive the journey just as they had done all those years ago.

The geese disappeared over the escarpment. Adjusting his beanie Leidolf turned his attention back to the work in hand. Reflection was no bad thing, but it could ensnare if permitted to have free rein over thought.

He dipped a brush into the paint and carefully scrolled the letter K, then he stood back to review it. The style of the lettering he had chosen suited the boat and her, epitomising a free and flowing spirit. He touched up one of the brushstrokes then squatted and painted the next letter. Twenty minutes later, the complete name was on the bow in beautiful scrolling script.

He was replacing the lid on the tin when he heard a vehicle driving along the lane. It slowed and turned onto the track that led to the shore and his house. Moments later Alex and May came walking along the shore to find him.

'A bad storm is due in,' Alex said as they drew near. 'We came to make sure you knew.'

He had been unaware of the warning. 'Another one. The Met Office will run out of names. I'm not intending to stay out in the forest tonight though, the trail's gone cold. Been any more attacks?' He looked at May questioningly, but she shook her head. 'I don't know what game it's playing. It's so inconsistent.'

'Perhaps it's travelling to different time eras,' May suggested. 'It's not limited to linear time after all.'

'Christ, I am dumb.' Leidolf grabbed his hoody and put it back on. 'That's exactly what it is doing. Still, I can't time jump. ...'

'When you do catch up with it, it won't be able to go back and be a problem back then.' Alex said. 'But you've got to be careful, mate. They're blaming the attacks on a stray dog, and there's only one large dog roaming the island solo that I know of.'

Leidolf held Alex's gaze but didn't comment.

'Just watch yourself, hey.'

'Oh!' May had been walking round the boat and had suddenly noticed the name Leidolf had painted. 'That's unusual. The meaning rings a bell. Purity?'

'Purity from the sea.'

'Very apt.'

'They say the storm will have blown over by tomorrow night,' Alex said. 'You may not have caught the one you're after, but I take it other demons have met their demise.'

'You know Fraser. One or two have met a sticky end.'

Alex chuckled, but May was still staring at the painted name.

'Do you still feel she's on the island?' she asked. 'If she is, then she must be aware of the demons by now.'

He turned to the boat. 'Aye, she's here.' He indicated the name he had painted. 'What's more, I'll bet you anything that's her name.'

Kaia.

CHAPTER 22

IT WAS LATE EVENING. THE wind was howling round the cottage like an immense unseen creature determined to get in. Yet the resilient little croft was impenetrable, and the kitchen remained defiantly snug and cosy. Placing the blue mug of hot chocolate on the kitchen table, Kaia folded her calves and feet, currently housed in thick pale grey woollen socks, onto the seat of the chair. She had drawn out the five symbols onto a piece of paper, had written wood and light next to the two she recognised and then wrote the Gaelic words next to the two that Meg had named. Wilma might know what the words meant; she would take the paper with her tomorrow and ask her.

Picking up her phone, she scanned her new emails and after opening one from Jim, clicked on his contact number. Seconds later he appeared on her phone screen.

'You've discovered something about portals?'

'Gateways.' Jim's enthusiasm lit up his face. 'Interdimensional gateways in fact. Verifying the other account. According to this document there were five, one for each element. It describes them as huge physical structures that accessed vast amounts of light energy. It doesn't say what they were for or where they were located, but I'm determined to find out.'

'That'll keep you busy!'

Jim was in his element. *Like a dog with a bone.* He loved an ancient mystery to get his teeth into. His image froze. Taking a sip of the hot chocolate Kaia involuntarily glanced at the window. The rain was falling in rods, sounding like grit against the glass. Her screen remained frozen. She spoke, unsure if Jim could hear.

'The Wi-Fi is unstable. This storm is sending it AWOL.'

Nothing changed. She waited for a few minutes. Switched off her phone, picked up the mug of hot chocolate, and went through into the lounge. The dogs were currently laid out in front of the wood burner toasting themselves, oblivious to the turbulence outside. Kaia opened the little stove's door and put on another log. The fire crackled and spat, but the dogs' only response was to thump their tails against the floor. *A new type of hotdog.*

Her phone pinged, and sitting down on the floor next to the dogs she opened Jim's email. She had frozen on his screen too, and guessing the storm was putting a premature end to their conversation, he had forwarded the translation of two pages from the book. She clicked on the first attachment.

She wasn't sure what she was expecting to read, but it wasn't this. Large sections of text seemingly copied from *Gulliver's Travels*. She read over it again, trying to understand Meg's reason. Then she clicked on the second attachment, a translation of the last page in the diary. It was short: an account of someone called Morag having drowned and of how they had buried her.

It wasn't much. Perhaps the translations of the other pages would shed light when they were finished. She stared at the Gaelic, willing herself to understand it, but nothing made any sense except names.

She googled village clearances and then flicked through several accounts describing how villagers were forced from their homes to make way for grazing land for landowners. It explained the deserted dwellings she had seen. Yet if the villagers had already left, why had Meg still been there, and if Meg hadn't left in the clearance, did that mean that Owen had stayed too?

The clearance was too convenient. To have happened when demons were hunting Meg ...

Kaia sat staring at the fire, her mind piecing the puzzle together. Her thoughts turned to Mrs Mack. *Mrs Mack has deep links with Skye; her family has been on the island for generations.* A piece clicked into place. Mrs Mack had water on the lungs and Morag had drowned. *Morag is one of Mrs Mack's past lives. She's drowning!*

Leaping to her feet Kaia, opened a portal to the hospital and stepped through.

+ + ✦ ✦ ✦ +

She found Mrs Mack awake. Her breathing was laboured, her chest rattled with fluid each time she inhaled, and her aura looked thin and wispy. *Not good*.

Recognising Kaia, Mrs Mack's face lit up.

'Hello,' Kaia whispered. 'I've come to see if I can help.'

Drawing the curtains around the bed, she set to work strengthening and balancing Mrs Mack's aura. Forty-five minutes later, Mrs Mack's breathing eased, and she fell asleep.

+ + ✦ ✦ ✦ +

Back inside the cottage Kaia returned to the fire, praying Mrs Mack would pull through. She watched the blue and orange flames flickering across the now glowing embers. She was supposed to stand against the orchestrator of all this. She needed answers ... *Morag ... Meg ... Ianna ... Owen* ... She began to see slender figures dancing within the flames, her thoughts began to blur, and her eyelids grew heavy ...

She was lying on a wooden jetty. The sky was blue, she was aware of the texture of the wood beneath her and the smell of its sap having been baked in the sun. It was an evocative smell, reassuring and homely. Dangling her legs over the side of the jetty, she kicked out her calves, splashing cool water onto the jetty and onto herself.

'Hello.'

Her heart leapt as she looked up into the greenest eyes she had ever seen, set in a face full of fun and light. ... He wore a plaid kilt and had a wolf's head tattooed to be looking straight out at her from his chest. He pointed across to the shore. Sitting up, she saw the same man on the beach only now in modern, outdoorsy clothes: a blue woollen hoodie with a hole worn at the elbow, and a deep red beanie hat slouched at the back of his head with a certain *je ne sais quoi*. He was using a hand plane to shape a plank of wood to fit along the bow of an upturned boat.

196

'Owen?'

He couldn't hear her.

'Owen!'

Her calling out woke her. The flames in the fire had now completely died out. Pulling a throw around herself, Kaia headed upstairs for bed.

CHAPTER 23

THE STORM HAD BLOWN ITSELF out during the night, and dawn brought with it a clear, pale blue sky. Picking up her cardigan, Kaia put it on over her dress and closed the kitchen door, shutting the dogs inside. They whined. She relented. The dogs shot into the hall where one pulled on a lead slung over a coat hook. The lead fell to the floor and the dog stood next to it looking hopeful.

'More like. You sleep in the van and behave.'

Yet on opening the door Kaia changed her mind. It was too good to miss – the scent of the sea and pine trees – everything looking vibrant and renewed. She grabbed her running gear from the hall radiator, picked up both dog leads, and shoved the items into a cloth bag.

'We *might* go for a run afterwards.'

It was not far to Alex and May's house. Kaia took in the coastline and the distant mountains as she drove. It was easy to imagine a scene in the past when the clearances had been enforced, with laden horse-drawn carts taking the villagers away.

She turned onto a smaller lane. This one passed through a forest before running alongside another loch with a single house on the far shore. She could not take her eyes off the building.

A car horn sounded. She swerved to miss the oncoming car, cringed, and waved apologetically to its driver. Then she stopped the van and took another look at the house. It was a modern wooden construction yet blended with the trees in a non-obtrusive way as though it had always been there.

'That'll be Leidolf's place.'

They had eaten the vegetable soup and Buddha bowls May had prepared and were now sitting in the kitchen by the log burner. May and Alex's house had turned out to be a croft, set at the mouth of a glen by a small burn. It was larger than Wilma's croft by far and yet seemed smaller, given it was rammed with an array of pot plants and cosy furnishings. The kitchen worktops were filled with cookware items and objects that May had gathered on her walks, pretty pebbles, pieces of driftwood and numerous shells. May had insisted that she bring the dogs in from the van, and they were currently flat out on a red patterned rug by the fire, enjoying May making a fuss of them.

Alex paused as though filtering what to say. 'He's a talented carpenter, Leidolf, specialises in boats, but can turn his hand to pretty much anything. He built his own house, the one you saw.'

My dream. 'What sort of boats?'

'Any type,' Alex replied. 'Although he likes smaller, personable projects the most. He's just finished rebuilding an old wreck he found. Couldn't help himself, he told me when I asked him what motivated him to drag an old heap of rotten wood into his work shed.' Alex glanced at May. 'Named it too, hasn't he, May.'

'Yes. Quite an unusual name.'

'All boats deserve to have a name, especially if they're made with love.'

May gave her a knowing look, but she couldn't fathom why.

'I'd best be going. I promised these guys a run if they behaved themselves, and I want to drop by and see if Wilma has news of Mrs Mack. Thanks again for lunch. It's been lovely to meet you, Alex.'

'I've a feeling you'll be around these parts for a long time!'

'Hope so!' She gave them both a hug. 'Come on, you two, time to go.'

The dogs looked at her reluctantly, half wagging their tails, as if to say they would rather stay by the fire.

'Run.'

It was like flicking a switch. Ears pricked, excited barks, and the dogs became a bundle of energy, much to the amusement of Alex.

'Where are you planning on running?'

'Storr Rock. I saw a picture in my godfather's study. It was the first thing that drew me to Scotland, but I still haven't been.'

CHAPTER 24

SHE BEGAN HER DRIVE NORTH and, calling in at the café, found Wilma in the process of closing early.

'How is Mrs Mack?'

'Marjorie has pulled through!' Wilma's relief lit up her face. 'She made a remarkable recovery last night and is being discharged today. I'm just off to collect her, as it happens. What a turnaround!' She looked at Kaia knowingly. 'I spoke to Marjorie earlier, and she swears she saw you last night. Now I know she gets confused about things, but I have a feeling there may be something in it.'

'I did send healing,' she said truthfully. 'Perhaps Mrs Mack was picking up on that.' Her phone pinged, and she saw Bella's number. 'I'd best get this,' she added, grateful for the distraction. 'See you both soon.'

Back in her van, she listened to her answer phone and then clicked on Bella's number. Bella answered immediately.

'Hi, Bel. I can't quite believe it.'

'He left. Just like that. Walked out without so much as a by-your-leave. I should have left first. I said I would, and now he has left me. I feel so stupid!'

'He's the one who's stupid. Have you told Layna?'

'I rang her this morning. I couldn't face going to work.'

'And what did she say … write an article about it?'

Bella managed a chuckle. 'Not exactly. She was super cool as it happens.' Her voice began to sound decidedly lighter. 'She has emailed me a voucher for a luxury health spa and told me to have the day off tomorrow. I'm to get myself pampered and remember how gorgeous I am.'

Layna is bound to have her own agenda. No doubt not wanting to lose the best P.A. she has had, has something to do with it. 'I agree with her sentiments. You're not to slump, you're worth a million of him. Goddess Kali, remember!'

She went on to say what she had discovered from Meg's diary and how she had made the connection between Morag and Mrs Mack.

'Wow, another past life connection. No wonder Mrs Mack thought she knew you when you met her. In another lifetime she did!'

'Morag must have played a big part in Meg's life. I'm going to ask Mrs Mack about it when she comes back. Perhaps if she reads Meg's diary, it will trigger her to recall something.'

She hung up, pulled out from the car park, and continued north. The tide was low, and as she drove past the long stretches of beach, which in places edged the road, she was drawn to the seaweed lying in swathes across the shoreline. She glanced at her watch and noting that she had plenty of time before it got dark, she parked and then took a stroll along a length of the beach. The seaweed had looked so different when she swam through it. Then it had been a swirling forest, whereas now it looked sad and lifeless.

She began to harvest seaweed from the rocks and popped some sea lettuce into her mouth. She screwed up her face. An intense salty taste, yet strangely, she could feel a vibrancy as though her body relished it. One of her dogs ran towards her, looking hopeful. 'You're welcome to try.' The dog sniffed the seaweed suspiciously, then looked at her as though she were mad. 'Not your thing. What about this?' She picked up a piece of driftwood and threw it, at which the dog let out a yelp and raced across the beach in pursuit.

Kaia's attention was drawn to the water and a rowing boat in the distance. Her heart skipped a beat. *Leidolf.* She stared, fixated, until he disappeared around a headland. Then she walked back to the van carrying the seaweed she had harvested.

──────────── ✦✦✦✦✦ ────────────

Leidolf had been enjoying the solitude the loch offered. Pulling on the oars, he headed past the headland and further out into the loch. The boat brought memories flooding back, a roller coaster of experiences and emotions. He had gotten used to not clinging and embracing the transience of time, except when it came to her.

He suddenly became aware of a snuffling sound, like a dog on a scent. Thinking one had swum out and gotten exhausted, he stopped rowing and looked around at the water. The sound stopped too. There was nothing near the boat, but on the distant shore, he caught sight of a woman walking along the beach. His heart leapt. It was her. He knew it. Yet she was too far away to hear him, and by the time he reached the shore, she would be long gone.

He returned to rowing and the sound came back. If not a dog, it must be a nosy seal, drawn to the sound of oars. He kept going, and the noise got louder, until finally the creature came into his field of vision. It was not a seal.

'Pendragon!'

In the next instant, Pendragon had disappeared, leaving Leidolf to row slowly back to the wooden jetty near his house. Nothing for three years, now in less than two weeks, demons and Pendragon. Pendragon had sensed her on the shore too. She was like a comet on a trajectory: after aeons of being deep in space, she was finally back in sight.

CHAPTER 25

✦ ✦ ✦ ✦

LEAVING THE VAN IN THE lay-by, Kaia ran with the dogs along a twisting stone track towards the mountain and the jutting Storr Rock. A popular tourist spot, the track would usually be a stream of mobile phones and cameras, but with it nearing the end of the day, visitors had left, and she had the place to herself. As she rose higher, the sea below began to glint gold in the dropping sun, and she felt an urgency, an inner prompt as though something sensed her approach and was hurrying her along.

The track passed through an old wooden gate and became a winding, rocky path that rose steeply through dense forest. It was uncannily silent and feeling uneasy, Kaia ran fast, only slowing her pace when the track broke from the trees.

She was now near the rock, which stuck out at its precarious angle from the mountainside. It looked familiar. *I've been here before. Perhaps as Meg.* Hoping the rock would trigger a recall, she left the dogs to their investigation of banks of heather and picked her way across to touch it.

Kaia.

The voice came from deep within her mind, an echo of rumbling thunder. The rock had spoken.

I am not the rock.

It had read her thoughts. *Then what are you?*

The symbol will show you.

The symbol. Not the portal symbol. She racked her brains. *The druid symbol ... earth dragons. You can't get more earth than a big lump of rock on the side of a mountain.* She closed her eyes, recalled the symbol, and slowly drew the shape on the rock with her finger.

Dragon.

In her mind's eye she saw an enormous creature moving through the earth. It was nothing more than a shadow at first, but then suddenly she saw an enormous golden eye. Opening her eyes in shock, she saw the rock had changed. It was now etched with lines that gave it the appearance of being an enormous, closed doorway and, as if that weren't enough, she could see the golden eye looking through it right at her.

Perhaps I'm simply imagining it.

She had no sooner had the thought when the eye shifted, and something blew out smoke which drifted through the rock to surround her.

You will get answers in the library. Come through.

There was a blast of hot air, which caused the surface of the rock to ripple. Then the lines on the rock moved, and the doors swung open.

Seeing a dragon was one thing. Trusting one was another. *It could be on the same side as the Skinwalkers. This could be a trap … although Meg could have gone through. There's only one way to find out.* She stepped forward.

At first nothing looked different. She turned.

I'm going to die.

Seeing dragons on films and drawn in picture books was one thing. Standing within reach of fearsome teeth set in a ferocious-looking green-scaled jaw was quite another. She swallowed, her heart pounding in her chest, as the dragon lowered its head to her level.

You look small.

Bite-sized. She caught the glint of merriment in its eyes and relaxed. It might look terrifying, but the dragon was no threat to her.

Where am I?

Alfheim. Home of the Akashic Library.

The dragon drew her attention to the castle situated at the top of a grass slope. Built from the mountain, its turrets and spires gleamed as the sun reflected on the stone. Colours and textures shone, golden browns, silvers, and greys, it was stunning. She looked at the dragon questioningly.

Go. The Old Man of Storr is expecting you.

Kaia scrambled up the slope and entered the castle courtyard. Noble figures had been carved into its rock walls. Some looked human, others did not, and yet all were giant sentinels that marked the place as sacred. Making her way across the courtyard, she passed through an arched doorway and then entered a high vaulted hall. Marble columns intricately decorated with carved leaves were positioned in rows along either wall as though holding up the ceiling, from which hung a large chandelier housing crystals that glowed with light. The room demanded respect and silence, yet it also felt warm and welcoming. At the far end of the hall was an overly sized arched wooden door, split down the middle into two halves. Coming to it, Kaia gently pushed one of the halves ajar and peered inside.

The library.

An enormous room was lined with bookcases that were crammed with large leather or clothbound books. In the far corner stood a large oak table, and sitting next to it was a wizened-looking man who reminded her of a wizard from a fantasy novel, with his round glasses, flowing robes, and white beard, which he wore groomed to a point halfway down his chest.

The Old Man of Storr.

The Old Man of Storr caught her gaze and beckoned her into the room.

'I can never find what I am looking for when I need it,' he said, indicating a large leatherbound book that lay open on the oak table. 'I've read these books times over, and I still can't remember the relevant pages and chapters when I need them.'

'Maybe you could write them down?' She drew level with the table.

'Have you seen how many Akashic records there are?' He chuckled, gesturing to the books on their shelves. 'If I wrote references, they would be as great a volume as the books, and I should spend just as much time looking through those!'

What he said was likely to be true. The shelves rose high into the vaulted ceiling, making it almost impossible to see those at the top, and they were shifting. Shelves appeared and disappeared all by themselves, causing a ripple effect which reminded her of waves on a beach.

The Old Man of Storr was watching her intently. 'Records. Past and present … and all simultaneous. A lot to keep track of, don't you agree?'

She nodded, mesmerised by the books and crossing to a row that had just appeared, she pulled one free. It had a blue cover, which changed in a moment from being light blue, like a summer sky, to being the darkest blue like the ocean. Holding the book between her palms, she let it fall open.

She recognised the writing. *Meg's diary.*

The words disappeared, and she was surrounded by blinding light. She caught the smell of the sea and then found herself gasping for air. Her chest tightened. Her lungs burnt and dropping the book, she crumpled to the floor.

The Old Man of Storr helped her into a chair. 'It's your record,' he explained as her breathing returned to normal. 'You will feel the recollections it contains. It can be rather overwhelming if you're not expecting it. ... Better?'

She regarded the book on the floor. 'I think I just felt Meg's death.' *Again.*

'Perhaps,' the Old Man of Storr said softly. 'Yet things are not always as they first appear. Akashic records only ever show what serves you in the now. Whatever you saw will aid in the fulfilment of your destiny.' He picked up the book and held it towards her. 'Want to take another look?'

She tentatively reopened the book. Prepared this time, she steadied herself as she was momentarily blinded by the light. As it faded, she was aware of a large rock behind her and leant against it until her vision cleared. She was by Storr Rock, only now it was lit with lanterns. Men dressed in woollen-looking tunics were standing in a stone circle, formed from huge slabs over eight feet high. In the centre of the circle was an altar, constructed from four narrower slabs laid on their sides topped by a further slab around a foot thick. *Druids.*

One Druid, wearing a crown of leaves, stepped before the stone altar. He began intoning an incantation as the others began to chant. The deep resonance of their voices was amplified by the stones, and a vibration of sound rippled through her body. The energy began to build. Her body felt like it was opening, expanding, and she was suddenly aware of enhanced sound – the movement of insects in the grass, the beating of birds' wings high in the sky – then the large slab that formed the top of the altar moved, as though it were as light as a feather. It slid to one side, and as the others continued to chant, the Druid wearing the crown stepped forward and took two crystal shards from their hiding place.

She jolted as something in her mind tore open, but before she could grasp any understanding, the vision faded, and her awareness shifted back to the library. She closed the book and handed it back to the Old Man of Storr.

The Old Man of Storr returned the book to the shelf, where it was instantly replaced by another. Picking up the book, he studied the cover and then turned it to show her the title.

Dragon Fae. The gold lettering scrolled across a luxurious cover that looked to be made from overlaid red scales. 'Dragon Fae?'

'Highly perceptive individuals destined for great things.' He looked at her intently over the rim of his glasses. 'When such a child is born, if a dragon chooses, it will cast great magic and bless them. From that point the child is linked to dragon-kind and can access their magic. The dragons become their kin. ...'

The Old Man of Storr fell silent, looking troubled. Kaia was about to probe when the book flared with light. Crossing to the oak table, the Old Man of Storr set the book down and let it fall open.

'Many moons ago there was a prophecy. It spoke of the last Dragon Fae, who would reunite the Dragon's Heart Crystal and stand against a great evil from Shadow Side. Scathchornail.'

'Scathchornail?'

The Old Man of Storr indicated the open book. 'Gaelic. It translates to the Shadow Colonel.'

Kaia studied the illustration on the open page. It depicted another ornate doorway, this time carved into the side of a mountain. 'I am sure I've seen that before.'

'Just prior to the turn of the eighteenth century Scathchornail used his magic to twist the mind of the beast that held the doorway to Shadow Side shut. He broke into the third dimension and used the power of the dark seed crystal to send the Skinwalker parasite into the bodies of men. His intention was to overthrow humanity and then use his army to invade the interconnecting realms. All looked lost and would have been, were it not for one brave warrior. Forcing Scathchornail back into Shadow Side, the warrior killed the beast. The door slammed shut, trapping him and Scathchornail in Shadow Side. For centuries it has stayed shut, but Scathchornail did not give up. He has found a way to open the doorway, and it is now crumbling.' The Old Man of Storr turned the page and pointed to another illustration. 'The Dragon's Heart Crystal as it would look if it were whole.'

Scathchornail. A silent invasion. Bella was right.

'Does the Skinwalker parasite kill the host?

'Once it fully takes hold, there is none of the human left.'

She swallowed and looked down at the open page. 'What does this crystal do?'

'There is much myth surrounding it, but all I know for certain is that when whole, it can seal the doorway to Shadow Side.' A shadow passed across the Old Man of Storr's face. 'The Atlantians had one shard, but they sent it back to the third dimension.'

'Atlantia?'

'Atlantia is another realm, accessed by an underwater doorway.'

Hence the merman. 'Meg was the last Dragon Fae wasn't she and that's why the demons are hunting me, because I can somehow unite these shards and seal the doorway?'

The Old Man of Storr opened his mouth to respond but seemed to change his mind. 'A Pict Druid hid the second,' he said instead. 'He may have left a clue to its hiding place … or maybe not.'

The answer to my question is yes then. She opened her mouth, but the Old Man of Storr spoke first. 'You must allow the path to unfold. Take the steps you can, without overly concerning yourself with those you can't. You are the Dragon Fae. You must trust your intuition and let love lead.'

Let love lead. She had heard that before but couldn't think where.

The Old Man of Storr closed the book and replaced it on the shelf, where it instantly disappeared. 'Demons are not a nice bunch. No conscience. No soul.' He turned back to face her. 'If you do happen to cross paths with them again, remember, they don't like water.'

'The demons stopped chasing me when I went into the sea.'

'Water is cleansing, purifying. Anything dark cannot abide it.'

───── ·+♦♦♦+· ─────

Soon afterwards Kaia left the castle and returned through the doorway. *Farewell, little Dragon Fae.*

The words rang a bell. She turned abruptly. Yet the dragon had vanished, and the rock was now back to being solid granite, glinting in the setting sun. She waved at it anyway. Then, whistling for her dogs to give up their rabbiting and follow her, she jogged down the mountain track, going over everything in her mind.

CHAPTER 26

✦ ✦ ✦ ✦ ✦

Back at her van, Kaia discovered that someone or something had tried to break in. She stared in shocked dismay at the deep gouges now running down the door. It couldn't have been a demon. She knew enough about demons to know they were vicious in the open, but they would not, or could not, break into a third-dimensional object. A demon would have seen the van empty and hidden. It wouldn't advertise its presence and ruin the element of surprise. Whoever had done this must have been either totally deranged, or very angry. ... *Rick.*

Rick knew she was here. *But it isn't Rick. Rick is dead.*

She drove back to the cottage on high alert. Yet there was no sign of any trouble, and she didn't appear to have been followed. Hurrying into the cottage, she locked the door and leant against it, her head spinning. If Rick had located the van in the lay-by, would he be able to locate it at the cottage? She decided it was unlikely. The lay-by had been on the main road, whereas the cottage was well off the beaten track.

She needed to unwind. She needed to think. She washed the sea kelp she had gathered and put it into a hot bath. Then she soaked up to her neck in sea weedy water, letting out a sigh of relief as her tension began to melt. Feeling more at ease, she pieced together what she knew. *Find the shard the Druid hid. Get the one from the base. Unite the shards. Seal the doorway to Shadow Side ... before it fully opens. Note to self: You don't want to be meeting Scathchornail ...* She groaned, took a breath, and sank her head underwater. *The answers are in me somewhere. Perhaps being underwater will help.*

It didn't.

Stepping out of the bath, she threw on clothes and went downstairs. The dogs were now flat out by the fire and thumped their tails against the floor in their usual fashion. Taking up her laptop and the guidebook Jim had given her, Kaia pulled a chair near to join them. Then opening the file containing photos of beings in the water off the Scottish coast and flicking open the book to the illustration depicting the kelpie woman. She sat comparing the images.

The photo and the illustration were similar. Both showed merfolk not with fish tails but scaled legs like the merman she had met. She looked at the dates. The book had been published twenty years prior, the photograph, two.

Proof that they've been seen around Scotland for at least two decades and … She stared into space as a realisation hit. *They're Atlantians. The doorway to Atlantia is off the Scottish coast!*

Meg must have met the Atlantians. That could be where the symbols were from, but if they knew Meg, why had the merman had used the name Ianna? … The only way she was going to get answers was to find them, but how? *The kelpie.*

She switched the screen to Zoom and tried to connect to Jim. There was no response, so she typed an email filling him in on her recent adventures and sent it. The next morning, she would grab supplies from the local store and then explore the nearby lochs to see if she could find the kelpie.

CHAPTER 27

THE NEXT MORNING WAS BRIGHT and sunny. Kaia pulled into the car park outside a small store, a single-storey brick building with large windows topped by green and white striped awnings. Sitting by netted bags of logs stacked by the door was the wolfdog she had met before. She held out her hand. The wolfdog sniffed it and wagged his tail along the ground. Crouching, Kaia stroked his head, stunned again by his deep green eyes. She would swear this was the wolf who had rescued Meg. Yet even if this *was* a real wolf, how could he have been in the eighteenth century, unless he had a way of opening portals too?

At that moment the wolf growled. Kaia quickly withdrew her hand, but it wasn't her that had upset him. The wolf crossed to her van, hackles raised, to sniff at the deep gouges in the door. Then he looked back over his shoulder as though asking how they happened.

'Someone I used to know has a grudge. Lucky for me I wasn't around, but they took it out on my van.'

Inside the shop, Kaia browsed its narrow aisles, which were crammed with essentials: locally baked goods, fresh fruit, locally grown vegetables, a variety of ready-made sauces, random kitchenware, car accessories, hair accessories, socks, and thermal tights. She had visited the store a few times now and loved the Aladdin's-cave vibe, which ensured you left with far more than you intended to purchase. She selected the items on her mental list, then added a homemade tray bake of chocolate orange tiffin and a pair of thick teal blue thermal socks to her basket for good measure. Next, she considered what could attract the kelpie. Guessing kelpies grazed on seaweed, she thought at first carrots or apples could be a treat. Then she remembered that land horses had a partiality for mints. Deciding kelpies might like mints too, she picked up a packet from the sweets rack, added a bar of dark chocolate containing crisped rice, and took her selection to the counter.

The storekeeper, a middle-aged man with curly hair, dressed in a faded green polo shirt and putty-coloured loose cords, was his usual chatty self. 'Been a bit stormy lately, lassie. Still dipping?'

'Yep. You know me by now. D'you think kelpies like mints?' She emptied the contents of her basket onto the counter next to the till.

'You want to watch out for those kelpies. They'll whisk you away.' He picked up the three paper bags she had filled with fruit, peered into them, and placed them onto the scales one at a time. 'Nasty things that seek to drown unwary folks.'

'I've read that, but then lots of things get bad press … like dragons. Have you ever seen one?'

'A dragon or a kelpie?'

'Kelpie.'

The man scanned the packet of mints. 'There's a lot around here, but I've not seen one meself.'

'Is there a loch where they're seen the most?'

He picked up a tourist leaflet from a rack on the counter, opened it out to a cartoon map of the island, and pointed to a small loch not far from the store. 'There's lots of tales about this being a kelpie loch. It's where most kelpie hunters go. Mind you, it's not like it used to be. It used to extend right up into this part of the glen, but it's mostly bulrushes now, more like a marsh. I'd go and see Marjorie Mack. She'd be the one to ask. This cheese is free, out of date today. Would you like some?'

'Yes, thanks. I've got a shift later. Hopefully Mrs Mack'll be at the cafe.' She tapped her card to pay.

'Are these yours too?' The storekeeper picked up another bag from the counter containing avocados. She shook her head. 'Then May must've left them by mistake.'

'I'll drop them round after my shift if you like.'

Putting the avocados in her shopping bag she left the store.

Seconds after Kaia had driven away, Leidolf ran across the car park.

'If you're lookin' for that dog of yours, he's not here,' the storekeeper said as Leidolf raced in. 'Although he was outside not so long ago.'

'Thanks.' Leidolf glanced around the inside of the shop, looking disappointed at finding it empty. Crossing to the shelves, he picked up a packet of coffee and a bag of chocolate waffles. 'They're for Fraser. He likes them,' he explained, tapping his card as the bemused storekeeper put the items into a paper bag, along with two blocks of free cheese.

CHAPTER 28

❦ ✦ ✦ ✦ ✦ ✦ ❧

FOR AN HOUR KAIA SWAM back and forth in the loch where she had met the kelpie, but if it was still there, it did not want to be found. The cold finally getting to her, she dressed and drove to the loch the storekeeper had pointed out.

He had been right. The designated kelpie loch was now mostly marsh, filled with bulrushes and water lilies. A pair of swans were gliding across the only section of loch free from vegetation, and small brown wading birds were scurrying among the pebbles on the shore, but there were no signs of kelpies. Time was getting on. It was nearly lunchtime, and she was due to start her shift at the café.

She made her way back to her van, feeling a bit despondent. It was all well and good the Old Man of Storr telling her to focus on what she could do rather than what she couldn't, but that really didn't help very much. She wasn't exactly brimming with ideas or avenues to explore.

She let the dogs into the van and was about to get in herself when there was a loud growl, followed by men's voices, coming from nearby trees. She scurried up the bank and then keeping to the trunks of the scrubby oak trees, she crept nearer to investigate. It wasn't a demon. Instead, she discovered two men, wearing black caps, black trousers, and bomber jackets, standing over Fraser, one aiming a gun.

She immediately stormed towards them. 'What the hell are you doing?'

The men turned to see who was accosting them.

'What have you done to my dog?'

Fraser was lying on his side with what looked like a tranquiliser dart in his shoulder. She crouched next to him. He recognised her scent and whined dolefully. She glared at the men.

'We're only doin' our job. A stray is responsible for the attacks on tourists.'

'That's an assumption! Maybe you should speak to locals first? Ask around. Find out what they know, before you go ahead and shoot someone's dog!'

The man muttered an apology. 'But he shouldn't be runnin' around on his own.'

'Why not? I live here! There's no law that says a dog can't run around common ground near his own home! What have you shot him with?'

'A mild sedative. We were—'

The other man cut him off. 'Just a mild sedative. He'll be right as rain in a couple of hours.'

'No thanks to you! The least you can do is help me carry him to my van.' She scowled at the men. 'Be careful and I want your contact. If there's a big vet's bill involved, your organisation is paying.'

One of the men scooped Fraser up, followed her back to the van, and laid him on the floor. Kaia grabbed a throw from the seat and covered him.

'He's a mighty fine dog,' the man said, stepping back from the van.

'Yeah, but he very nearly wasn't!'

She took the man's card and drove away. A vet lived not too far from the café. She would call in and let Wilma know what had happened. Then she would take Fraser to the vet to see if he would check him over.

CHAPTER 29

I T WAS ONLY A FIVE-MINUTE drive to the café, but by the time she pulled up in the car park, Fraser had miraculously recovered from his ordeal, and when she slid open the van door, he leapt out to jump around her like an excited puppy.

'You are very welcome. It's good to see you back on your feet.' She placed a hand on either side of his head. 'You're very handsome. You keep out of the way of those nasty men, d'you hear? We don't want anything bad to happen to you.'

Soon afterwards she entered the café, delighted to see Mrs Mack had resumed her usual spot. Wilma was busy with customers, so helping herself to a pre-shift croissant and coffee, she joined Mrs Mack at her table.

'Been for a swim?' Mrs Mack gave her a beaming smile.

Kaia explained she had been kelpie hunting and why. 'Apparently Atlantians come through an underwater doorway to get here. Have you ever heard of it?'

Mrs Mack looked blank. 'It doesn't ring a bell.'

'These symbols might be their language. Do you know what these Gaelic words that describe them mean?' She took a folded piece of paper from her pocket and showed Mrs Mack the symbols.'

Mrs Mack looked at the paper with as much enthusiasm as Jim over a newly discovered historical document.

'Ooo. Now this word means air, and this, earth.'

'So, they *do* represent elements. Then this last one is either fire or water. What about Dragon Fae? Have you ever heard of them, or heard of a link between Dragon Fae and kelpies?'

'Ianna.'

Mrs Mack had spoken without thinking. She stared at Kaia, mirroring her surprise.

Mrs Mack is recalling Morag's memories. Morag knew Ianna was linked to Meg. 'What do you remember about Ianna?'

'A tale.' Mrs Mack spoke slowly. 'I forget where I heard it. Ianna left her water world to be with her lover. Come to think of it, if I remember right, the tale originated in the eighteenth century. I can't remember the significance of Ianna being a Dragon Fae though.'

'Ianna. Are you sure that was her name?'

Mrs Mack nodded. 'As I remember, she came from the sea and turned human so she could be with her lover, a good-looking Scottish laddie.' She chuckled. 'Nothing like a good love story. I forget where I heard it,' she repeated apologetically.

Kaia's synapses were firing rapidly. Perhaps the story Mrs Mack was speaking of was a true narrative of events. If so, Meg couldn't have been a reincarnation of Ianna because she was a young woman in the eighteenth century too. It didn't fit together.

'Are you all right, dear?' Mrs Mack asked in concern. 'You've gone a bit peaky.'

The door of the café opened, and customers began to pile in. Kaia assured her she was fine. 'I'd best get working. It is getting busy. Are you wanting anything?'

'A nice pot of lemon tea would go down a treat.'

'I'll bring it over.'

Ten minutes later, when the queue had gone from the counter, Kaia made a pot of lemon tea and carried it back to the table.

'Do you know anything about Druids?' she asked, placing the cup and the teapot on the table. 'I'm interested in their symbols. Courtesy of Wilma,' she added, putting down a plate containing a hot buttered scone.

Mrs Mack's eyes lit up. 'One of my favourite things.' She surveyed the scone. 'Along with the Druids and the Dark Ages. All myth and magic. The territory of King Arthur. Totally stolen by the English, of course. Scandalous.'

'*The* King Arthur? As in Camelot and the Round Table?'

Mrs Mack picked a piece from the scone and put it into her mouth, savouring the taste. 'The very same. There's no doubt Arthur spent time in England of course, but a lot of his story took place this side of the border too, in southern Scotland. There's lots of connections to Merlin and Druids there.'

'What about on Skye?' she asked, bringing Mrs Mack back to her question.

Mrs Mack looked thoughtful. 'Hard to say, because nothing's written down. All sources are oral, so get distorted over time, just like King Arthur's tale. Some of the old names echo of Druids though. Storr Rock for one.'

'I've been there … an interesting spot.'

'There used to be a stone circle,' Mrs Mack continued. 'But that's gone now, eroded, fallen into the sea.' She stirred her empty teacup absent-mindedly. 'Then there's the Fairy Pools, and the Fairy Glen, both at the north of the island. Druids considered those places sacred.'

After finishing her shift, Kaia returned to her van and pulled the map book from under the seat. The locations Mrs Mack had mentioned turned out to be on opposite sides of the island. She stared at the names and picking the Fairy Pools, purely on the premise it offered another dip, she pulled out of the car park.

CHAPTER 30

◆ ◆ ◆ ◆ ◆

The Fairy Pools turned out to be a set of pools created by a burn which gushed down the mountainside, before meandering away down the lower part of the glen. Leaving the dogs in the van, Kaia set out to explore.

The pools were deep, filled with ice-teal water and connected by small waterfalls, ranging from ten to fifteen feet high. One of these fell through a natural rock tunnel, plummeting like thunder into the pool below. Kaia climbed past them all, surveying their different shapes and sizes, as she clambered among rocks and crevices looking for a potential hiding place for a crystal shard.

Finding nothing, she stood at the topmost pool looking down into the glen. It spread before her like a green and brown carpet. It was easy to imagine Druids walking amidst the heather bushes. She could even hear them screaming. She jolted and turned to stare at the mountain behind her.

Screaming.

She could hear screaming, and what was more, it sounded like her own voice. A chill ran through her body, and in a trancelike state, she continued her ascent. It was clear to see that at some point in time, huge rocks had fallen from the summit to create a veneer effect and in one place they had left a dark, narrow cleft. As Kaia stared at it, a deep sense of unease crept down her spine. Somewhat reluctantly, she clambered across to the gap and squeezed through.

The sound of the wind and of birds instantly ceased, to be replaced by a deathly stillness. The cleft let in very little light, and she could sense, rather than see, that the fallen rocks had created a huge cavern. *It's like a tomb.*

She pulled her phone from her pocket, switched on the torch, and stepped deeper inside. The floor of the cave was littered with what she assumed were sheep ribs. Yet the cleft was very narrow. A lamb might get through, but not a fully grown sheep. Come to think of it, they were the wrong shape for a sheep. *Human!* She shone her torch around the floor. There were an awful lot of rib cages ... *the battle.* Her heart began to pound. If these were the remains of fallen warriors, then this mountain and glen could have been the battleground when the doorway to Shadow Side was last opened.

Oh God!

She stared in horror as her torch illuminated the carved frieze of figures. Strange forms with elongated limbs, which seemed to have bone and muscle but no skin, were depicted as scrambling over one another in a frenzy. She craned her neck to see the top and saw that the frieze was in the shape of an enormous arch. This was what she had seen in the Akashic library. *The door to Shadow Side!*

In places the carvings looked fresh, but elsewhere they were worn and weathered. She ran her fingers over one area, instantly causing large pieces of stone to fall away and smash at her feet. The noise echoed through the stillness like a bomb exploding, and a bolt of hot electricity shot through her.

Ianna.

The voice cut through her mind like an ice-cold knife. Recoiling in horror, Kaia squeezed back through the opening and scrambled down the mountain. Moments later a screech came from the cleft above her, and glancing back she saw black shadows seeping from the opening. *Demon wolves!*

Remembering what the Old Man of Storr had said, she skidded down scree to the first pool and threw herself in.

The force of the water thrust Kaia around rocks to the top of a fall and then plunged her into the pool below, where she was churned like clothes in a washing machine. Yet adrenaline gave her extra strength, and kicking free from the pull of the water, she swam for the next waterfall. This one was higher, and hitting the water below was like hitting against stone. Winded, she half swam, half sank to the next waterfall, and then the next.

Water splashed in her face, and every time she tried to breathe, her mouth filled with water. Her battle was not simply to stay above the surface but to catch a breath. Her body was now screaming in objection to the abuse and the pain. She consciously detached, focussing only on the momentum of the water and the next waterfall, as the demon wolves streamed down the mountainside in pursuit.

Had she been on foot, they would have caught her, but the water flow was strong and whipped her down the mountain. Ahead now she could see the entrance to the tunnel. The water roared as it spun like water down a giant plug hole. Terror flooded through her as she fell through rock to crash into the foaming pit below. The water churned, sucking her under, but somehow, she managed to kick free. Breaking the surface, she let her body crash down the last fall then made for the bank, battered and bruised. Yet there was no time to assess any injuries; the wolves were nearly upon her. Summoning every ounce of remaining energy, she dragged herself onto dry land and sprinted for her van.

She was shaking with cold and exhaustion, but her van, unaware of any urgency, refused to start. She muttered a curse and then, realising in her haste she had not pressed the clutch, she rectified her mistake. Slamming her foot down she turned the key again and this time the engine sprang to life. She put the shift into first, pressed hard on the accelerator and screeched away, just as the demons reached her.

CHAPTER 31

KAIA PULLED UP OUTSIDE MAY and Alex's house to see May standing at the kitchen window. On seeing her step from the van, May's face beamed, and she waved enthusiastically, beckoning her inside.

'What a delightful surprise!' May said appearing at the front door moments later. She gave her a hug and then stood back, in dismay. 'My word. Have you been swimming with all your clothes on?' The smile faded to a look of concern. 'What the lord have you done to yourself? You look like you've been chewed by a dinosaur!'

She had driven straight from the Fairy Pools, not stopping for an instant. She was not only still wet through, but her arms – and probably her face – were covered in deep grazes and she could feel that it wouldn't be long before they also displayed colourful bruising. 'I've been waterfall diving. It wasn't exactly an experience I intended to have.' She handed May the bag of avocados. 'I'm just grateful I didn't break anything.'

'Demons?'

Kaia nodded. 'You know about them?'

'Yes. There's someone here I think you should meet.'

Kaia glanced down critically at her apparel. 'Maybe some other time.'

'Now is the perfect time,' May assured her. 'And if you think I'd let you drive away after what you have clearly just been through, then you've got another think coming. Come on in.' She gestured for her to step inside. 'Have a hot shower and assess the damage. I can lend you fresh clothes.'

Kaia followed May into the hallway. There was a pair of walking boots that hadn't been there the last time she was here. *Men's, size nine or ten.*

There was the sound of voices coming from the kitchen, Alex and another man. She didn't recognise who the voice belonged to, but its deep resonance was calming and somehow reassuring.

'You were bloody lucky, mate.' Alex's voice was saying. 'We knew they were blaming a dog.'

She heard something being poured, and from the smell wafting into the hallway guessed it was coffee.

'Too bad though. Should've run faster.'

She didn't catch the man's reply; she was now halfway up the stairs. May passed her a fresh towel from a cupboard and ushered her into the bathroom.

'Here's arnica cream, it will help with any bruising, and if you discover anything needs dressing, then give me a shout. I've always plenty of first aid supplies; it comes from being a nurse! I'll leave you some dry clothes by the door so you can grab them when you're done.'

'Thanks, May.'

'It's the least I can do. I'll make more coffee, and how about some warm scones?'

Kaia nodded her thanks and then spent a good ten minutes standing under the shower. She turned up the heat every time her body got used to the temperature, but her body craved more. *Fire … I need fire.* The last symbol in Meg's book flashed across her mind, and she absentmindedly drew it on the tiles of the shower wall. The symbol flared red and looked as though it would burst into flames.

What?

Cupping her hands, she threw water over the symbol and then wiped her hand over the tiles to wash away the reside it had left. *Soot.*

She rubbed the oily ash from her fingers. What had changed? The symbols hadn't worked when she had tried drawing them before. *The Akashic library. The Druids chanting.*

The Old Man of Storr had told her that Akashic records only ever revealed what a person needed to know. Her record had had shown her the Druids opening the altar with sound, and the sound vibration had also opened something within her. She hadn't thought it would be quite that literal.

Stepping from the shower, she dried, put on the leggings, white T-shirt, and patchwork zip-up hoody that May had left for her, and returned downstairs.

CHAPTER 32

T HEY STOPPED SPEAKING AS KAIA stepped into the kitchen. Alex beamed, and May's eyes were dancing. The other man was facing away from the door, but she recognised him instantly. The same blue hoody and broad muscled body. It was the man from her visions. An invisible energy tremored, and it was clear he felt it too. He stiffened, turned sharply, and she sank into eyes the colour of a pine forest.

Owen.

He took a step towards her, as though to lift her from her feet, then checked himself.

'I don't believe you two have met,' May said. 'Kaia, this is Leidolf. Leidolf, Kaia. Are you feeling any better?'

'Heaps thanks. I'm just so cold!'

'Come over here by the fire!'

She was aware of Leidolf's eyes burning into her as she crossed to the wood-burning stove. May pulled a chair as near to it as she could get, wrapped a rug around her, handed her a coffee, and then went to fetch her dogs in from the van. They scampered into the kitchen and immediately began making a fuss of Leidolf.

'Hello, trouble. Still running then.'

He hadn't met her dogs before. He must have seen them from a distance, maybe that day he was rowing.

He seemed to guess what she was thinking. 'They can run fast for such whippersnappers and seem to believe they can catch anything.' He flashed an adorable grin. 'I need to thank you for what you did to help my dog, Fraser.'

She hadn't told anyone. How did he know, unless Fraser had experienced a delayed adverse effect to the tranquiliser? 'Is he Ok?'

'Very well, thanks to you.'

'I think you should tell us what just happened to *you*,' May said. 'You said demons were involved, and when it comes to demons, Leidolf is somewhat an expert.'

She related her trip to the Fairy Pools, only leaving out the reason behind it. They took it in their stride, not even seeming surprised when she mentioned the doorway carved into the rock.

'It's where demons come from,' Leidolf said simply. 'Shadow Side.'

'You know about Shadow Side?'

Leidolf was about to speak, but May fidgeted, clearly uncomfortable, and interrupted. 'Leidolf is one for stories and *myth*. There's always truth woven within myths.'

'My godfather says the same. He's obsessed with sniffing out the truth they contain.'

'*Myth* says the doorway leads to a realm called Shadow Side and that an evil shadow colonel, called Scathchornail, found a way to open it.' Leidolf said. 'He invaded but was driven back into Shadow Side during a great battle, and the doorway was closed. Yet myth also states that one day the shadow colonel will find another way to open it.'

He was clearly trying to protect her. They all knew more than they were saying, as did she. It was time to come clean. She told them what she had learnt about the battle, how an eighteenth-century woman, Meg, was supposed to seal the doorway using two crystal shards, and finally that as a reincarnation of Meg, the task had fallen onto her. 'I was looking for a shard and discovered the doorway. ... It's crumbling.'

Leidolf's eyes were fixed on her, so unusually green. 'Hardly surprising there was no sign of it. I don't think a Druid would leave it on Scathchornail's doorstep like some special delivery.'

She smiled. It was nice to be able to speak openly about things with people who seemingly had experience with what she was talking about. As supportive as Jim and Bella were, they had no real context as to what she was going through – not that she wished the demons anywhere near them.

She hugged the mug, grateful for its warmth soaking into her hands. The movement was not unmissed by May.

'You're still cold! Alex, stoke the fire. I'll make some hot scones. Let's get this lady warm.'

An hour or so later she left the cottage, Leidolf and May walking her from the door to her van.

'Watch out for the demons, Kaia. Try not to make it easy for them,' May said, passing her an old ice-cream tub that she had filled with some of the remaining scones. 'Take Leidolf up on his offer tomorrow and pick up Fraser.'

Leidolf opened the van door for her. 'Do. They may think twice about bothering you if he's around.' He examined the marks on the door. 'Not to mention whoever did this.'

Kaia pulled onto the main road and then let her face explode into a grin. She was still grinning when she parked on the gravel in front of the cottage. Turning off the engine, she made to pick up the tub of scones but then froze, seeing the events of the afternoon in a different light.

She had been so lost in the euphoria of meeting Leidolf, she had not stopped to think how it was that he, Alex, and May knew so much about Shadow Side. Or why Leidolf sent Fraser out roaming the island hunting demons.

She carried the scones into the cottage kitchen, her head in a whirl. Twenty minutes later she was still staring into space, trying to grasp the implications. Eventually she reached for her phone and called the magazine.

'Good afternoon. *Real Woman* magazine. Layna Fynch's office,' Bella said in her formal tone.

'Hi, Bell, can you talk?'

Bella's voice instantly changed. 'Not right now. Gimme five, and I'll be on my break.'

Kaia put her phone down and opened the tub of homemade scones. A warm, buttery smell immediately filled the kitchen. She eaten at May's, but suddenly craving more sugar, she cut two in half, spread a thick layer of jam across the top of each, and made a pot of coffee. She had just finished as Bella rang her back.

'Sorry about that.'

'No problem. Are you feeling any better?'

'Heaps,' Bella admitted, sounding her usual bubbly self. 'I've concluded that although JD's behaviour may have been triggered by the phone thing, he must have had it in him to cheat in the first place. I'm only glad he did it sooner rather than later to be honest. I've seen him for what he is and can move on.'

That's Kali talking right there. 'You deserve more—I've met him, Bell … the guy I kept seeing in visions.'

'In this lifetime? You're kidding!' Bella's voice mirrored her own delight. 'Is he a dish? My God. How did you meet?'

Kaia explained about her dropping off May's forgotten avocados. 'I had just had another encounter with the demons. I told them all about it. Had to, I was still wet through.'

'Wet through?'

She filled Bella in on her escapades. 'I didn't find a shard, but I've discovered where the doorway is. Maybe I'll find something in the glen tomorrow. I feel like I'm running out of time. The doorway is starting to break apart.'

Bella muttered something about holy mothers.

'I'm going to take Leidolf's wolfdog with me as backup.'

'Leidolf?'

'That's his name.'

There was a short pause before Bella replied. 'Descendant of wolves.'

'Pardon?'

'Descendant of wolves. It's what Leidolf means,' Bella stated. 'I just googled it. He's going to have a close connection with wolves if his name is anything to go by. Explains him having one.'

'There's something bothering me. They knew all about Shadow Side … everything. May said that Leidolf was one for myths, but …'

'What are you trying to say?'

'That Leidolf must remember his past life, and I think he has told Alex and May. That's why they know about demons and things … Leidolf sends Fraser out hunting demons.'

'He does what?'

Kaia repeated what she had said.

There was a muffled sound as Bella momentarily put down her phone and did something on her desk. 'Layna's on her way again,' she said, picking her phone back up. 'She is really on form today. Coffee break or not, I'd best not be caught crossing her proverbial line. I just think the whole wolf thing is odd. Something doesn't weigh up.'

Bella rang off, leaving Kaia nibbling at the scones. Bella was right about things not weighing up. Leidolf couldn't have gotten the information about Shadow Side from a written source, else Jim would have found it. If he did remember it from his past life, then he must recall an awful lot … *and recognise Meg in me.*

CHAPTER 33

EVENING WAS DRAWING IN, AND the cottage was starting to feel cold. Kaia scrunched up some scrap paper, laid kindling in the fireplace, and reached for the box of matches. *I wonder.* Sitting back on her heels she drew the symbol she had drawn in May's shower. There was a flare of light, and the symbol appeared, but it just hung in the air expectantly. Kaia breathed out hard trying to blow the symbol onto the wood, but instead of moving, it burst into flames and vanished.

Hands. I use my hands when I send healing energy. She tried again. This time when the symbol appeared, she pushed at the air and visualised it moving onto the laid fire. Instantly the symbol flared, shot into the kindling, and set the sticks alight. Kaia laid on larger logs, and soon the fire was roaring.

Five symbols. Fire, Air, Earth, Wood, and Light. *So where is water?* She was about to create another symbol when the dogs suddenly rushed to the door barking. Seconds later there was a frantic knocking.

'Kaia! Kaia, are you there?'

Wilma was standing on the doorstep, wide-eyed and pale. Her coat was badly torn, her hands covered in blood, and blood was seeping onto her torn jumper from a wound to her chest.

'My God! What has happened!'

'We were on our way to see you! They've got Marjorie! Demons!' Wilma staggered into the cottage and collapsed onto a chair.

Kaia passed Wilma her phone and grabbed another long-sleeved top from the radiator. 'Ring May! I'll go and find Mrs Mack. Where did you last see her?'

Wilma told her which lane they had walked, and where they had turned off to pick up a track that led to the cottage via the loch shore.

'I'll go. Ring May!'

Shoving on her running shoes Kaia raced for the loch. There was no sign of Mrs Mack or the demons by the water, so she ran on through the trees, retracing the route that Wilma had described. She heard a scream.

Leaping into the trees, she came upon them. Mrs Mack was on the ground, her hat and a bag were in brambles nearby, along with fragments of cloth that had been slashed from her coat. Two demons were standing over her, their claws extended like knives at the end of their paws, toying, like cats playing with a cornered mouse. As Mrs Mack tried to crawl away, one slashed at her leg, and then both seemed to suck in her expression of fear and pain. They were feeding off Mrs Mack's aura, and it was starting to look transparent.

Kaia charged. Drawing the fire symbol, she blew it at one demon. The ground near it burst into flames, but the fire didn't harm it. Instead, the demon stood amid the flames, narrowing its eyes to slits, and curling its lips back in a snarl.

She grabbed a stick from the ground as the demon leapt, but at that moment Fraser launched himself from the ferns and knocked the demon onto its side. In an instant he was next to her, hackles raised, teeth bared, and eyes flashing in anger.

The demons retreated, melting into the shadows, and Kaia rushed to Mrs Mack's side. Her leg was a mess, and she was losing a lot of blood. Taking off a top Kaia tied it around the wound, trying to stop the bleeding. 'We've got to get you to the cottage.' She grabbed Mrs Mack's hat, slung her bag across her shoulder and helped Mrs Mack to her feet.

Mrs Mack stumbled a few steps and then stood still. 'I don't think I can lassie. Wilma—'

Mrs Mack was as white as a sheet, and her voice barely more than a whisper.

She's going to faint. Keep talking. 'Wilma is safe. She is already there. She is ringing May. May will be with her by now. Come on, it's not too far. Take it steady. Fraser here can keep the demons away. Fraser?'

Fraser had gone.

'Fraser is chasing the demons. They'll be far away by now.'

'Need some help?' Leidolf was running towards them. In an instant he had scooped Mrs Mack from her feet and was carrying her back to the cottage in his arms.

CHAPTER 34

B Y THE TIME THEY GOT back to the cottage Mrs Mack was barely conscious. Alex and May had arrived and were in the kitchen. There was an open nurse's bag on the chair, and May was assessing Wilma's wound.

'It's not too deep, but it needs stitching.'

Alex scooped up his car keys. 'May and I will take you both to the hospital. It's only seven miles. It'll be quicker than waiting for an ambulance!'

Kaia passed Wilma Mrs Mack's bag, but she refused to take it. 'You keep hold of it. There's a book inside. Majorie said you were asking about Druids and remembered an old book that we had in the loft. She wanted you to have it, as a thank you for sending her healing in hospital.'

'Thank you. Please ring, keep us updated.'

Wilma looked blank.

'It's Ok. I've got my phone,' Alex said, opening the door.

There was a flurry of activity getting Mrs Mack comfortable in the car, and then they were gone. The adrenaline spike over, Kaia's energies began to slump. She returned to the kitchen and flopped into a chair.

'How are you holding up?' Leidolf was at her side.

She stared through him in a daze. 'All good.'

'Sure.'

She was aware of him pouring soya milk into a saucepan, and soon he presented her with a mug of steaming hot chocolate. After a few sips, the sweet drink worked its magic.

'Thanks.' She focused on the green eyes that were surveying her face. It wasn't the look you would expect from someone you barely knew. Rather it was the sort of look you would expect from a concerned close friend, from someone who held you in high regard, from someone who …

Leidolf looked away. 'I'll go and find Fraser. I'd feel happier if you kept him here tonight. Would that be all right? He won't be a problem.'

'That would be great. I would feel a lot happier if he was around.'

'It's no bother. When I find him, I'll send him here, but I won't call back myself. I'll carry on to the hospital and see if May or Alex wants a lift home.'

'How—'

'Fraser is sharp. He'll know what I'm saying when I tell him.'

In the next instant Leidolf had gone too. After locking the door, Kaia carried her hot chocolate and the book from Mrs Mack into the lounge. She sat on the floor with the dogs, feeling suddenly very alone. Leidolf was one of those rare people who gave you a feeling of strength and of anything being possible.

She frowned. Leidolf had said that May had called him after hearing from Wilma. He had no mobile on him, so he must have taken her call at his house. He hadn't come to the cottage in a vehicle, and he hadn't got a lift to the cottage with Alex and May. He had come on foot, yet his house was miles from the cottage, there couldn't have been time. It didn't make any sense.

There was a bark from outside. *Fraser.* She let him in, bolted the door and then returned to the lounge where Fraser joined her, and her dogs, by the fire.

'Leidolf is a mystery,' she said addressing Fraser. 'I wish you could talk. You could answer some of my questions.'

Fraser lay down and listened as though he would happily reply to any query she had.

'You really are a beautiful dog … and brave too, taking on those demons like that. It isn't the first time either, is it? I saw you on the jetty with Meg. I know it was you.'

Fraser whined. Then, flopping on his side as if he was exhausted, he lay soaking in the heat of the fire.

Kaia reached for Mrs Mack's book. *The Druid Path.* It had a faded red cloth cover with delicate dark brown writing on its spine, and its contents page declared it to contain beliefs and practices of Celtic Druids. She let the pages fall open and spent the next few hours absorbed in a world of elementals, circle casting, the Ogham alphabet, and the language of the trees.

CHAPTER 35

⟡ ✦ ✦ ✦ ⟡

THE REST OF THE NIGHT had proved uneventful, save for a call around midnight from Alex saying that both Wilma and Mrs Mack were fine, but Mrs Mack was being kept in the hospital overnight.

Kaia was up and out before the sun rose. Her two dogs, disgruntled they were not going with her, curled back up in their bed with dejected looks on their faces. Fraser on the other hand had been sitting by the front door when she came downstairs like a passenger waiting at a bus stop and, as soon as she opened the front door, had crossed to the van to get in.

She drove to the north of the island then took the narrow lane that led into the Fairy Glen, a small glen filled with a series of unusually pointed step-sided mounds. Pulling into the only car park, a lay-by at the side of the road, she set off to explore.

It was still early, and the glen's steep mounds looked particularly magical silhouetted against the pale blue dawn sky. Kaia walked among them for half an hour, whilst Fraser paced up and down like a soldier on patrol. The entire place felt full of energy, but it was a labyrinth spiral made from large boulders set into the ground, and a rock formation resembling an ancient castle turret standing at the top of one of the mounds, that drew her the most.

Kaia searched every nook and cranny of the turret but found nothing. Returning to the glen floor, she walked the length of the glen then stood under some small hazel trees looking back along it. She envisioned Druids meandering through the mounds and tried opening a portal to their time, only to find herself face to face with Fraser.

'It was worth a try,' she said in a frustrated tone. At which Fraser half wagged his tail as though sympathising with her failed effort.

The day was getting brighter. Morning dew had started to sparkle, and Kaia noticed tiny orbs dancing across the heather. *Fae.* Her healing song drifted through her mind, and she softly began to sing its strange words. The lights drew nearer until she could just make out tiny beings, that looked to be made from light, hovering within them. She stopped singing. *You're eternal. Did you see a Druid hiding a crystal?*

They vanished.

Deciding she would have one last look around, Kaia walked slowly in between the pointed mounds, stopping this time at the opening of the labyrinth. The sun was showing in the sky now, and the energy in the glen was expanding like petals of a flower unfolding. She closed her eyes to soak in the feeling. When she opened them, she saw the Fae lights hovering on the stones as though to draw her attention to the labyrinth entrance.

The spiral is significant. Jim had told her times how ancient peoples had used labyrinths to symbolise a journey. Perhaps she could use the spiral to journey to when Druids were here. Opening a portal at the entrance, she stepped through and onto the labyrinth path, then methodically began following the spiral towards its central stone. The glen around her blurred as she walked. She caught glimpses of shadowy figures, at first in modern-day clothes, then in clothes reflecting different periods of history. *I'm walking back through time.* In a trancelike state, she stopped by the central stone as the figures in the glen changed again. Now they were wearing woollen tunics like the figures she had seen in her Akashic record. *Druids.*

The Fae lights had now gathered around central stone. Kaia placed her hand on it and immediately felt a familiar energy rush through her body. *A dragon.* She drew the dragon symbol. Nothing changed, but the Fae lights rose into the air, crossed to the rock turret, and disappeared inside.

Kaia followed. The presence of the dragon felt stronger. *It's here. There's a doorway.* She drew the symbol on the rock wall, calling out in her mind for the dragon to make itself known. Almost immediately the wall took on a mirage effect, and the head of a red dragon appeared. It stared at her suspiciously through narrowed yellow eyes.

Who are you to summon me?

I seek the Dragon Heart's shard.

Indeed. The dragon tilted its head on one side and smirked. *Then come and take it.*

There was a blast of warm air as the dragon breathed its magic, and the surface of the rock rippled. Kaia stepped forward and into a misty passageway. The dragon was nowhere to be seen, but she could still hear its voice.

Pick. If you touch a crystal, you claim it. Only with the Dragon's Heart can you leave.

She turned sharply. The tunnel had disappeared and behind her now was solid rock. She was trapped. She had no choice. She had to find the shard.

Before her was as black as ink, and she had no torch having left her phone in the van. Swallowing her panic, she tentatively drew the symbol that had made the kitchen light glow. The symbol instantly appeared, floating in the air and glowing soft yellow, lighting the tunnel walls and the rock floor a few feet in front of her. Kaia held out her hand as though pushing it and took a step. The symbol moved with her. Muttering her relief, she slowly began to pick her way forward.

CHAPTER 36

AFTER WHAT HAD FELT LIKE an age, the air in the tunnel grew colder, and the sound of her footsteps changed as the tunnel opened into a cavern. Kaia couldn't gauge exactly how large the cavern was, and to keep from getting disorientated, she circled its edge, keeping the rock wall to her right visible.

Her suppressed panic exploded into shock when the light from the symbol revealed a human skeleton sitting against the wall. Swallowing revulsion, she stepped closer to investigate. It was dressed in remnants of what would have been a woollen tunic, there was a metal cuff bracelet around its wrist, and its folded arms clutched a leather pouch tightly against its ribcage. Leaning against the wall next to the skeleton was a wooden staff, that was intricately carved with symbols, one of which she recognised.

The Druid!

She tentatively tried pulling the leather pouch free from the skeleton's grasp, yet the leather was brittle with age and disintegrated, spilling its contents, a crystal shard, onto the floor. *Too easy.*

Kaia quickly retracted her hand and continued deeper into the cave, taking the Druid's staff with her.

Eventually she came to three tunnels, each marked with a symbol carved into a large rock at their entrance. She examined the carvings, recognising them from Mrs Mack's book. She had to pick a tunnel, and the symbols were a clue. They were tree symbols, the first represented yew. *Transformation and death. Maybe not.* The other symbols represented oak and willow. Willow was the tree of dreams and of protection when

238

journeying into the underworld. *It sure as hell feels like I'm doing that.* It also held energy for flexibility, protection and rebirth. She was not convinced about the rebirth part, wondering in this instance if that forewarned of a death first.

That left oak, another tree of protection, but also strength, fortitude, durability, and connection to the spirit world. It was a likely choice, but she wasn't a hundred percent convinced by the bit about connection to the spirit world. In this instance had the Druid been referring to nature spirits, dragons, and crystal energies or the spirits of ancestors and dead people. If dead people, she did not fancy taking a pathway that led to them either.

She had to decide: willow or oak? She toyed with the staff in her hand. *Oak.* The staff was made of oak; the Druid had intended it to be a clue too. Feeling more confident, she stepped past the rock containing the oak symbol into the tunnel beyond.

The air around her grew even colder and damper. Ahead she could hear the thunder of water, and when the tunnel ended, she discovered herself on a narrow rock ledge near an enormous waterfall that plunged into a black pit somewhere far below. Next to the fall, at one end of the ledge, was an arched carving. Sidestepping her way along the slippery rock, she edged towards it.

The carving was of a tree, depicted on one side with all its branches bare as in winter, and on the other all its leaves fully open as in midsummer. Its trunk was covered in symbols depicting the sacred trees, and in the very centre was a keyhole, but no key.

She stood with her back to the door and looked back along the ledge. The key must be somewhere. Edging away from the door, she passed the tunnel entrance and continued to the other end of the ledge. Her heart sank.

A very narrow staircase had been cut into the rock right at the edge of the chasm. One slip would lead to a plummet into the dark pit along with the water from the fall. *Not exactly a staircase to heaven.*

She began to climb, deliberately focussing her attention on each step and willing herself not to think about how exposed she was. She stepped higher, holding onto the steps in front of her as they became even narrower with only enough room for the balls of her feet. She suddenly realised that if she climbed up, she would have to climb back down. Her head swam, and clutching at the slippery rock, she was momentarily paralysed by dizziness.

This is do or die. It was a simple choice. Gripping the steps above, she willed her feet to move, counting the steps to focus her mind. A hundred and twenty-three steps later she reached a plateau and scrabbled onto the rock in relief.

It was short-lived.

The plateau was home to what appeared to be a cross between a dragon and an eel: a long, slender ferocious-looking creature, with huge, pointed teeth that stuck out over its lips, and grey plate like scales that crackled with electric current as it moved. It turned to regard her suspiciously.

Can you understand me?

If it did, it ignored her. Instead, it narrowed its eyes and made a low calling sound, which reminded her of pan pipes, and increased the electric charge across its body. Although it made its scales shimmer iridescent colours, it was probably not a good sign. She drew the dragon symbol, but the creature ignored that too, moving its head like a snake that was about to strike.

"*No!*"

Kaia stood as tall as she could and holding the staff in front of her, slammed it down onto the rock.

"*I am Dragon Fae!*"

Her voice sounded uncannily loud as it echoed around the plateau and had an immediate effect on the creature. Its head dropped, and its eyes widened, giving it the expression of a lost puppy. It then proceeded to slide after her as she passed it.

In the centre of the plateau was a large crystal urn filled with water, and lying at the bottom of the water was an intricately carved gold key, about four inches long.

Guessing that touching the crystal of the urn might count as touching a crystal, she edged the key up the side of the urn, using the end of the staff, and then flicked it onto the floor.

It's a key of foresight.

The dragon creature slid closer.

Want to see?

Kaia nodded.

The creature breathed across the key, and immediately the plateau began to change. Mist rose from the rocks to become rippling water around her calves. She was standing in the sea looking across to the shore.

At hell.

The water lapping onto the shore was covered in an oily substance and littered with rotting bodies of fish and seabirds. The beach was in a similar state, a garbage dump of dead sea creatures and plastic. An oil-covered seagull plucked flesh from a human corpse that had washed up on the shore, and a lone figure was walking along the beach searching for something. Seeing the corpse, he shooed the bird away before falling to his knees, distraught.

'Leidolf?'

Skinwalkers appeared at the far end of the shore walking in line, systematically scanning the ground. Leidolf ducked behind rocks, but they had seen him and continued to scan the beach, knowing they all but had him in their grasp. As they passed the corpse, one Skinwalker picked it up like a piece of rubbish and ripping it in half absorbed some of the flesh. Kaia squealed as a searing pain shot through her own body, and immediately the Skinwalkers turned to face her.

Something brushed past her calf.

Come back. Now!

She switched her focus to the dragon creature as it circled its head around her, and slowly the vision returned to mist which soaked back into the rock plateau.

The gift of foresight can weigh heavy.

What was that?

Earth. If you fail.

CHAPTER 37

・◆◆◆・

KAIA SLOWLY DESCENDED THE ROCKY steps and returned to the arched doorway where she inserted the key into the lock. There was a flare of light, and the door seemed to dissolve, revealing an entrance to yet another cave.

Stepping through, Kaia found herself in a large cave lined with crystal shards – all of them were identical – and there were thousands.

This isn't getting any easier.

She slowly made her way along the length of the cave. There had to be a way of identifying the real shard. She recollected the magnetism she had felt from the other crystal shard and how it had reacted when she was near the tower. *Maybe …*

Sitting she placed her hands on the cave floor and let her mind drift to the strange words she sang. She began to sing, imagining the vibration soaking into the cave, through the rock, and into each of the crystals. At first there was no response, then all the crystals began to glow. *Great.*

She was about to stop when a flicker of light caught her attention. She focused, and to her relief, one crystal began to shine brighter than the rest. She made her way towards it, only stopping her song when she had it firmly in her hand.

The dragon immediately acknowledged her choice. A subbase vibration rippled through the cave, and the rock at the far end became translucent, showing the inside of the turret in the glen. Without hesitation, Kaia ran towards it and dashed through.

Hurrying back to the centre of the labyrinth she retraced her steps round the spiralling path. The figures appeared again, their apparel changing as before, until finally they were dressed in modern-day clothes. Now back at the entrance, Kaia opened a portal and stepped from the labyrinth into the glen, to find herself face to face with the human looking demon.

'I'll take that.'

The demon stepped nearer. Kaia dodged and broke into a sprint, but demon wolves began to materialise in front of her. It was over. She stopped running and turned.

'It seems I have the crystal and you.' The demon grinned maliciously.

She clenched the crystal defensively, as a streak of dark grey came charging towards them. Fraser leapt, but forewarned by the expression on her face, the demon dodged the attack. Fraser turned sharply to launch again, as the demon wolves made to join the fight. The demon shrieked for the wolves to ignore Fraser and surround her as he changed into his wolf form. Yet their hesitation gave her the chance she needed and opening a portal she leapt through.

CHAPTER 38

AN HOUR LATER, KAIA WAS in the cottage kitchen frying mushrooms and whisking eggs. The morning's escapade had taken a lot out of her, and she was suddenly ravenous. Her two dogs were now on patrol in the hope that something might conveniently fall to the floor, and she smiled at the normality of the dynamic. If it were not for the crystal shard currently sitting on the kitchen table, it would be hard to believe her morning's adventure had been real.

She poured the eggs over the mushrooms, watched as they began to bubble, and then turned down the heat under the pan. Catching a movement out the window, she saw Leidolf crossing the gravel from the direction of the shore and rushed to the door.

'Fraser—'

'He's OK. I've seen him.'

'I was forced to abandon him and the van.'

'It's all good.'

Thank goodness. She indicated for Leidolf to step inside. 'Any news on Mrs Mack?'

'May has taken Wilma to pick her up.'

They walked into the kitchen where Leidolf sniffed the air over the omelette appreciatively.

'It's mushroom. You're welcome to share. Hungry?'

'Starving.'

Halving the omelette, she transferred it onto two plates as Leidolf crossed to the table. 'All for this.' He turned the shard over in his hand.

Kaia gave him an account of everything that had happened. 'Why go to all that trouble to hide the shard and then sacrifice himself?'

'He was a brave man and an honourable one. Dead, he made it almost impossible for Scathchornail to trace the crystal.' He took a forkful of omelette. 'My, this is good!'

'He pretty much made it impossible for me, too!'

Leidolf finished his omelette and was placing his plate in the sink when he suddenly froze, staring out the window. 'Kaia, we've got to leave. Now.'

The look on his face told her everything. Grabbing the crystal, she shut the kitchen door to contain the dogs and followed Leidolf as he ran for the shore.

She recognised the rowing boat instantly. The scrolled bow and stern. The polished wooden benches she used to stash her bag under. *Meg's boat.*

'They were never going to let you walk away with the shard,' Leidolf said as they pushed the rowing boat into the water. Her instinct suddenly picked up on what Leidolf had sensed. Demon wolves were coming to the cottage.

She clambered into the boat, as Leidolf gave it a final push and leapt in himself. Seizing the oars he began to row, as howling broke out in the trees.

'Here they come.'

The demon wolves streamed past the cottage and onto the beach.

'It's not just demons.' Leidolf stopped rowing and stood in the boat defensively.

Kaia recognised one of the men who had shot Fraser. 'He's a Skinwalker now.' Her voice was faint.

'Aye.'

She looked at him quizzically. 'You know about them?'

'From the myth. According to the story, there's a seed crystal in Shadow Side that holds a parasitic life form which feeds on its host, taking over their mind and body until there is nothing left but the shell, their skin.'

Rick. She visibly shuddered.

'Aye, it's grim.' Leidolf gave her a concerned look.

'The key, it showed me a vision.' She related what she had seen. 'It looked like the Skinwalkers had taken over everything. Earth was all but destroyed.'

'Foresight can show a future, but that is only one possible future based on the current trajectory. It can change.' Leidolf indicated the edge of the loch all around them. 'You can at any point choose which direction you go. It's the same with paradigms of time. You can transcend one paradigm and choose another; then what you perceive, and experience is different. It's hard to explain.'

Kaia remained silent, absent-mindedly watching the movement of the water around the boat. The true extent of the Dragon Fae's role was beginning to dawn on her. Skinwalkers weren't the only threat to humanity. *The quest isn't simply to stop Scathchornail, but to ensure humanity stays free so it can transcend into a different paradigm and ultimately save itself.*

They were now nearly at the jetty by Leidolf's house. It had looked appealing from a distance and up close was even more so, a two-storey wooden construction with a large A-frame window overlooking the waterfront. Thick oak posts held a wooden veranda next to French doors on the first floor, which she guessed led into a bedroom, and on the ground floor more oak posts supported a pitched roof over a stepped entrance.

'I don't think I'm in a rush to head back to the cottage.'

'Let's drive to the glen and collect your van,' Leidolf said with a smile, pulling in the oars and securing the boat to the wooden jetty that she had lain on in her dream. She gazed across at the shore, recognising the spot where she had seen the man, him, making the boat. This boat. She suddenly noticed the name on the stern and stared, speechless.

'It's a good name, life-giving. It means purity from the sea.'

He looked at her, his eyes aflame with light, as though he was drinking her in, and she held the gaze, similarly soaking in the energy that was emanating from him, her body alive and alert. Eventually she pulled her eyes away and began to walk down the jetty.

'Van!'

His truck was parked at the rear of the building, which had another A-frame window, this time overlooking the forest.

'This is a great place.'

'Aye. Its suits Fraser. He likes the sense of lights and space. He can be a right grumpy sod if he feels trapped.'

There was a hint of merriment in his voice, but Leidolf didn't elaborate. Minutes later they were driving along the sweeping road to the north of the island.

They chit chatted about nothing for a while. Then, after a moment's silence, Kaia brought up the subject that was burning in her mind. 'You recall being Owen, don't you? And you recognise Meg in me.'

Leidolf was clearly having to collect himself, and when he finally responded, his answer was not what she had expected. 'There's a bit more to it than that. I was waiting to find the right time to say, but since you're putting me on the spot … I *am* Owen.'

'What? … You're jesting, right?'

Leidolf shook his head.

'You mean to say you were alive in the eighteenth century … and you have been alive ever since?' *That can't be real.*

Leidolf kept his eyes on the road, but his aura and face told her he had spoken the truth. She stared out the front windscreen in a daze. How could she be sitting by a man who was over two hundred years old, and yet looked only a few years older than her? Questions exploded in her head, but she remained silent.

'It's a lot to take in, hey.'

No shit.

He grinned as though reading her thought.

Hell, he probably can.

Yeah, you might wanna watch what you think. He chuckled.

Kaia burst out laughing. Maybe it was the aftermath of tension, or maybe it was the completely nonsensical conversation, but hysteria set in and she laughed as though she had completely lost the plot.

CHAPTER 39

'J UST CALL, CRAZY LADY.' LEIDOLF held the van door whilst she got in. 'At the first sign of anything.'

'Promise,' she said for the second time.

Leidolf's expression did not alter, and he still looked concerned as he closed the van door.

'It'll be fine. I'll head straight to the café and stay late. It will mean Wilma can get off early and spend time with Mrs Mack.' She pushed the key into the ignition. 'How about we meet up afterwards? I'll cook.'

Leidolf's face instantly lit up. 'Great!'

Kaia waved from the window until the road twisted and Leidolf was out of sight. Then back at the main road, she headed south for the café.

She was fifteen minutes away when she passed a store that professed to be part bakery and decided to drop in to gain inspiration for the promised meal. The tiny gravel car park was almost full, but after managing to squeeze the van in the corner next to a wooden fence, she wove her way through the other cars and entered the quaint stone building.

The inside smelt of freshly baked bread, and in addition to baskets filled with an array of rustic looking loaves, there were shelves offering deli-styled products and a refrigerator full of cheeses and pâtés. The store was rammed with tourists seemingly set on delivering a barrage of provocation to the storekeeper, an elderly man with glasses. Kaia smiled sympathetically as she edged past the counter to the shelves at the rear of the shop. One of the tourists, a rather large red-faced man, turned and glared.

Deciding it would be prudent to wait outside until the shop was less busy, she crossed the road to a wooden bench set on a bank of grass, edged by gorse bushes. Sometime later the red-faced man came out. He was looking particularly angry. His aura buzzed with hot sparks that got more intense when another car pulled up and its passengers emptied into the store, seemingly oblivious to the fact they had blocked his exit from the car park. The man immediately marched back inside and began to shout. Guessing it could be a while until everything calmed down, and spying a track leading through the bracken away from the shop, Kaia decided to take a stroll until the dust settled.

She had no sooner had the thought when the hairs on the back of her neck began to prickle. She turned in her seat. The mature gorse bushes growing at the top of the bank were covered in bright yellow flowers and had long vicious green spikes that created a formidable barrier. Yet there was something there. *Eyes.* A pair of hard black eyes stared at her from among the flowers – above the barrel of a gun – she leapt to her feet as something whizzed past her to stick into the ground. A tranquiliser dart.

She raced into the road, not noticing the oncoming car. The car swerved to miss her, sounding its horn, but she didn't acknowledge it. Yanking the van door open, she climbed in, locked the doors, and started the engine, her hands shaking.

·+++++·

She was still shaking when she entered the café.

'What on earth has happened?' Wilma lowered her voice. 'The demons?'

Kaia explained the wolves turning up at the cottage and what had happened at the store.

Wilma pursed her lips and beckoned her into the café kitchen. 'Never mind you needing a drink. I need one … and I don't mean coffee! What a to-do.'

She stuck her head through the door as the bell rang on the front counter. 'I'll just see to this. You help yourself to whatever you need for your meal. I won't take no for an answer,' she added as Kaia opened her mouth to decline. 'I won't be long … and don't go scrimping. We've got a delivery tomorrow.'

Sometime later, Wilma came back through carrying a pile of cups and plates, which she proceeded to load into the dishwasher. 'There,' she said, closing the dishwasher door with gusto and switching it on. 'Rush over, and no abusive customers either.'

'All the abusive ones are up north.'

Wilma chuckled. 'I would say not to worry about doing your shift, but I'll be happier if you stay. I don't think you should be on your own. How about staying out the back here and just doing the washing up? I can manage out front.'

'Are you sure? You had a rough night last night too. I was going to see if you wanted to get away early.'

'It's no bother, and Marjorie will be popping in later. She's fine, thanks to you and Leidolf. Just on crutches for a few days while her leg heals.' She crossed to the fridge and showed her an exceptionally large lemon flan. 'Be sure to take this when you go, dessert is on me tonight!'

CHAPTER 40

THE CAFÉ HAD BEEN UNUSUALLY quiet. They had closed early, but in no rush to go back to the cottage, Kaia had sat talking to Wilma and Mrs Mack until a quarter to five. Leidolf would be around in less than an hour. Turning into the lane that led to the cottage she stopped the van and stared. Her two dogs were running back and forth in the ditch. When she left, they had been locked inside.

Opening the van door for them to jump in, she continued along the lane to discover the cottage door half off its hinges with large gouge marks, like those on her van, running down its length. She rang Leidolf.

'I'll be right there. Stay in the van. Lock the doors.'

She rang Bella. 'I've had a break-in.'

'What! Are you Ok?'

She filled Bella in about Mrs Mack and Wilma, about finding the crystal, and then the Skinwalker and demons showing up at the house. 'I'm guessing they were looking for it.'

'My God. D'you know if they found it?'

'No. I'd taken it with me.'

'Christ. They mean business. It's not safe for you to be on your own. As protective as your dogs are, they're not exactly Rottweilers.'

She managed a smile. 'True. I haven't gone into the cottage yet. Leidolf is coming over. There's something else, Bell. He told me earlier that he *is* Owen.'

'He was alive in the eighteenth century?'

'Apparently.'

Bella groaned. 'My ego cannot take any more! Its perception of reality is smashed to pieces.'

Kaia laughed. 'It's hard to get your head round, but then so is seeing dragons and getting locked in a cave!'

'I'd be locked in a mental asylum by now if it were me.'

Leidolf's truck pulled up next to the van and he got out. Kaia waved. 'He's here, Bell. I'll catch you later.'

'Yeah. Take care, keep me posted, and girl, if you can stand up to a dragon, you can stand up to anything!'

———— ·•✦✦✦•· ————

The cottage had been turned upside down. Everything had been emptied from the cupboards and drawers in both the kitchen and bedroom. The mattress and sofa cushions had been split, and the contents of all shelves within the cottage were strewn over its floors. Seeing Wilma's beautiful little sanctuary desecrated to such a degree was the final straw. Collapsing onto a chair, Kaia broke into tears.

'It's just things, Kaia.' Leidolf spoke softly, clearly affected by her distress. 'It'll set right. I can fix the door. Wilma will just be happy you weren't in when this happened.'

Pulling a bin bag from a roll that had been lying on the floor, Leidolf began gathering the strewn items together, stacking unspoilt ones on the table and putting broken ones into the bag.

Kaia watched him for a moment, unable to move. 'I can hold it together in the face of being trapped in a cave, climbing cliffs next to bottomless waterfalls, and charging at demons, yet this … this breaks me.'

'You are strong, brave, and sensitive. You are now, and you were then. That's what makes you special. That's why—' He broke off, tied the filled bag and pulled another from the roll. 'You're not safe here on your own. Move in with me.'

She froze.

'There's plenty of room. I've got a spare room. You can use the place as your own. You'll be safer with Fraser and me. We can keep an eye on you.'

She began crying again, this time in relief.

'It's a done deal, then. I'll finish up downstairs if you want to get your things together,' Leidolf said decisively. 'I don't think you should be on your own, not even for one night.'

CHAPTER 41

THEY HAD FINISHED TIDYING THE cottage as best they could and then left for Leidolf's house. Leidolf had let her in then had gone to his work shed to collect some more wood for the fire.

She made her way through into the lounge with its beamed vaulted ceiling. It was large and airy but still felt cosy with its enormous wood-burning stove, an ancient-looking sword mounted on the chimney breast above it, and ethnic style rugs and throws. Walking across to the large window, displaying its vista of the shore, she gazed across the water.

At that moment Leidolf entered carrying an armful of logs. She watched as he crouched by the stove and stoked the fire, bringing it back to life.

'This used to be you at Morag's. Morag liked a good fire.' The flames suddenly burst into life, and a warm glow sprang into the room. 'Got you!'

'Not before you have half-killed us with soot,' she jested, wafting her hand through the smoke drifting through the room like sea mist. She took Meg's book from one of her bags and passed it to him. 'Can you read Gaelic?'

'Aye, but dunna think that book will help you much. Most of it is Meg practicing to write. She used to copy text from Alexander's books.'

'Alexander MacDonald?'

'Aye.'

Jim is going to have a field day when he meets you. She sat on the chocolate brown faux fur covering one of the large settees.

Leidolf smiled and flicked through the pages. 'To think you found it after all this time. I gave Meg this to help with her amnesia.'

'Meg had amnesia?'

'The demon hunted her too. She was unconscious in the water and when she came round had no recollection of anything. I hold him responsible. When I get my chance, I will rip his throat out.' His eyes flashed.

'It will save me the job.'

'I'm not talking about Scathchornail. Though I would if I could. It's the demon I want. Malphas.'

'Malphas?'

'Aye. The one who can turn into a wolf or a crow.'

'If you were hunting him in the eighteenth century, you two have a lot of history. Excuse the pun.'

'His luck can't hold out forever.' Leidolf looked back at the book, read some snippets and then told her of ceilidh's and of life in the village. His words echoed. Faded images, like clips from an old film, ran across the screen of her mind. She recalled the emotion, the frustration and confusion of Meg's condition, but also the joy, the connection, and the love she had for the villagers and the life she shared with them. The more she heard, the greater her connection to Meg grew, as though part of herself buried deep inside was coming back to life.

CHAPTER 42

THEY HAD MADE AND EATEN their meal including a large proportion of Wilma's lemon tart and were now sitting back on the settee finishing a bottle of Shiraz. Kaia let her body sink into the chair. Leidolf, it had turned out, had a dry wit and a way of lightening the most threatening situations to make them seem more doable. Not only was she feeling warm to the core, but she was also feeling calmer than she had felt for days. The doorway to Shadow Side might be crumbling, and Skinwalkers and demons might be closing in, but she was determined to stay strong. She had one shard and knew where the other shard was. She just had to discover how to unite the crystal shards when she had them both in her hand.

'You told me about the clearance and Morag's suicide. What happened after?'

Leidolf took a slow sip of wine, momentarily looking haunted. He described how after they had buried Morag in the cairn on the shore they had left for Canada. 'It didn't end there though. You got taken.'

He had spoken as if she were Meg, the deep affection he had felt evident in his voice. Her unformed question was finally answered. Owen had been in love with Meg. Leidolf went on to describe how Meg had been seized by one of Sir John's men and of how she had escaped. He suddenly stopped speaking.

She knew what he wasn't saying.

'Meg died, didn't she.' *How?* She didn't need to hear the answer, she already knew. *Malphas.*

Leidolf looked lost in the memory and didn't respond.

'It answers a lot of questions,' she said eventually, breaking the silence.

'But there is still a big piece of the jigsaw missing. If Meg had amnesia, how did she recall the symbols, or did she meet someone who gave them to her?'

'It's a different lifetime for you, but not for me. I still feel the weight of not telling you.'

The realisation hit like a bolt out the blue. *Mrs Mack's story.* 'Meg was Ianna!'

Leidolf nodded. 'Ianna knew she had to get grounded, find a way she could feel at home in the surface world, as she called it. She always had an affinity with nature and wildlife. Then we met, and she started to learn to read and write. She fell in love with life on the island. When Atlantians fall in love with humans, they turn human and lose their memory. A cruel irony. Ianna forgot everything.' He sounded bitter.

'You never told Meg who she was?'

He shook his head. 'It was too dangerous. She had epileptic fits if the truth got too close. Morag knew, and we used to try and speak of it without saying the truth straight out. Meg worked it out in the end, but it was all too late.'

The dam inside her mind burst, and the room spun.

'Kaia!'

The next thing she knew, Leidolf was putting a rug round her and offering her brandy. She took a sip.

'I was hoping there might be something in the diary that could help with uniting the shards.'

'The symbols are light codes. Ianna said they were in the Atlantian shard. She thought they could be used to connect the two crystals.'

'Traditionally there are five elements. I've worked out that the symbols represent, air, fire, wood, earth and light. With a water symbol there would be six symbols which is puzzling.'

'Perhaps the wood and earth ones combine to make one symbol?'

'I hadn't thought of that.' She drained the brandy glass and, feeling more fortified, got to her feet. 'But that doesn't change the fact that the water symbol is missing. The Atlantians would know wouldn't they. I'm going to see if I can open a portal to the shore where I saw the merman again. Perhaps he can help.'

Leidolf stood. 'I'll come with you.'

CHAPTER 43

OMENTS LATER THEY STEPPED FROM a portal, only they weren't on the beach where she had met the merman but by Meg's cottage. They rushed into the trees for shelter from the wind and rain as the sound of howling broke out in the distance.

'This is when Meg died!' Leidolf said, struggling to be heard over the wind.

'Probably because we were talking about it before I opened the portal!'

There was a movement from the cottage as its door opened. Owen stepped out to disappear in the direction of the howling demons.

Leidolf clutched at her arm. 'I know Malphas is with them. This is my chance! I can take him and stop him from killing Meg.'

'Leidolf!'

The wind took her voice, and Leidolf, seemingly oblivious to the potential danger of meeting Owen, ran in the direction he had gone.

Moments later a beautiful white stallion galloped past from the direction of the shore and disappeared in the same direction. Kaia made to go after it, but then the cottage door opened again and Meg appeared, looking ashen. She looked around anxiously. Then, pulling her shawl tight around her shoulders, she raced for the beach. Kaia followed, arriving at the treeline to see that Malphas had escaped Leidolf, and was now standing in front of Meg.

Malphas extended his claws to knives and lunged as other demons began to materialise at the far end of the beach. Meg twisted away and made a dash for the shallows, but Malphas caught hold of her arm. Meg yanked free and in doing tore her flesh on the demon's bladelike claws.

Kaia clutched her own arm as a searing pain suddenly shot down it. Meg was now rushing into the water, holding on to her arm too.

The demon wolves were streaming along the shore, but Owen suddenly appeared behind them. He began fighting like a man possessed, using both a sword and a short blade. Meg stood transfixed, oblivious to the enormous wave that was racing across the loch behind her. Lifting her from her feet, the wave sent her crashing onto the shore where she lay on the ground spitting out water. Malphas pounced, and seizing Meg by the neck, pulled her to her feet.

Kaia cried out in pain. Daggers pressed against her throat, restricting her windpipe. She clutched at her neck and saw Meg do the same, yet Malphas did not let go his grip.

There was the sound of hooves as the white stallion appeared a second time. It charged for the demon and reared, lashing out with its hooves. The demon dropped Meg but not before he had slashed her stomach. Kaia felt like she had been cut in half. Pain consumed her and holding her hands to her stomach she collapsed onto the sand.

She saw Owen rush to Meg's side. They spoke, and then he kissed her. Seconds later he crouched and in the blink of an eye had transformed into a wolf.

Fraser!

Perhaps the pain was making her delusional, but the haunting howl the wolf sounded was real enough. In the next instant it was gone.

'Kaia!'

Leidolf was at her side. 'Open a portal! Quickly, for the love of God! I cannot lose you again!'

Blood was now seeping through her clothes and onto her hands. She felt too weak to speak and too weak to open a portal. She noticed that Leidolf was also wounded and yet lifted her in his arms as though the wound across his chest wasn't there.

The majestic stallion approached them.

I'll carry you.

It lowered its muzzle touching her face with its lips. A bubbling lightness instantly flooded through her, and her pain lessened.

I'll carry you both.

Pendragon?

Her body began to tremble. 'I know what we have to do,' she whispered. 'Pendragon can help. This doesn't have to be death, but rebirth.'

She was barely conscious. She was aware of Leidolf lifting her onto Pendragon's back and then of Meg's body being placed in front of her. Placing an arm round Meg, she held on to Pendragon's mane as he stepped into the sea. He waded out, sending magic into the water around them, and the water began to rise like a vortex. Energy began to build as the water rose higher, blocking everything from view. Then pale blue light began to shine within it, that deepened to the most beautiful hues of deep blue and green.

Draw the light codes.

She drew the five light codes. Each one spun into the vortex, and as she drew the final one, the vortex seemed to burst open. Bright light blinded her, and for an instant she felt nothing but euphoria as Meg's body merged with her own. Her wound healed, and then her mind opened. She recollected the faces of the villagers and conversations from when she was Meg. She remembered the cottage, making remedies, lying by the fire with Owen when he had saved her from the demons, the wolves, and seeing Owen change into the brave alpha wolf that fatal day on the beach.

The light contracted. Leaning forwards, she hugged Pendragon's neck. *Thank you.*

I have waited a long time. I couldn't save you before. Meg's body was not human enough to hold healing here.

I know.

Pendragon walked slowly back to the shore, where she slid from his back. As soon as her feet touched the ground she raced across the sand to Leidolf. He swept her from her feet. Then, holding her tight, he kissed her. For an instant the rest of the world melted away. Time, names, external events, none of it mattered. Their auras merged to shine like the sun, lighting up the beach around them.

CHAPTER 44

◆◆◆◆◆

KAIA AND LEIDOLF HAD SAT talking on the sofa in front of the fire until the early hours, sharing memories from their time as Meg and Owen. Leidolf had brought his sgian dubh back through the portal and told her it had been a gift from a Viking craftsman. He asked her of her time before coming to Skye, and she explained how Rick was now a Skinwalker. Yet Leidolf hadn't said anything about his own origin or explained how it was he could change into a wolf. He said only what he had told her when she was Meg, that he was an animi, a demon hunter.

Kaia woke on the sofa, covered by one of the faux fur throws, to the sound of excited yelping and the smell of croissants warming in the oven. She found Leidolf in the kitchen scrubbing his hands in the sink and her dogs dancing round his feet, almost tripping him over. He feigned annoyance.

'Pests. That's what they are.'

'Round one to the varnish,' Kaia sniggered, noticing the state of Leidolf's hands and shirt, which were splattered with sticky-looking liquid.

Leidolf rolled his eyes and pointed at a dog. 'I was making great progress on a new door for Wilma until *she* dropped a ball into a tin of varnish and *then* tried to dig it out.'

She could imagine the mess. 'She has got a bit of a ball fetish.'

'I should have put the lid on properly. Still, there's one advantage. The mutt is covered in varnish too.' He regarded the dog critically. 'Once it goes off, she'll be rock hard. We can attach her to the rowing boat as a figurehead.'

He dried his hands and took a tray of croissants from the oven. Kaia took one and nibbled it. 'These are divine. I still haven't met the girl who makes them.'

'Mea's a cool kid. She makes them as a hobby, and a lucrative one at that. I think you'd like her.'

He poured the coffee he had made, and once their croissants were finished, they walked to his work shed. Dawn had brought a swirling mist in from the sea, and the breaking sun made moisture shimmer on the numerous spiderwebs among the bushes.

'It must be really annoying for spiders, all their effort wasted. Every insect in the vicinity can see their webs now. Unless of course it was their intention to decorate the gorse in sparkling lace.'

'You can focus on a positive outlook and feel inspired by things. Or you can have a negative outlook and feel everything is pointless. I have come across many people who have the latter attitude to life,' Leidolf said wistfully. 'But not the villagers back then. They were some of the most courageous people I've ever known.'

'Was it hard in Canada?'

'What you'd expect. It was bloody tough at first. No rights, no dignity, yet Laylan never cracked; he was always ready with a song. And Lithe became a voice to be reckoned with, but it's no surprise after what he went through. They set us up good and proper with false promises of land. We had to fight for the right to get settled, but it worked out in the end.'

'What about Elsie, did she have another bairn?'

Leidolf shook his head. 'She didn't make the crossing. She was weakened by the demon attack and died on the ship.'

It was centuries ago, but grief washed through her as she recollected Elsie's face in the forest when they had saved her from the demon, how she had looked when they had picked blackberries, and her shock as the man had leapt from the bushes. 'Morag would have never survived, would she.'

'If Morag had been alive, I think it would have killed her had she heard what had happened to you.'

They arrived at his work shed, a large wood-clad building, weatherworn to a dark silver. As he pulled open one half of its barn door the smell of varnish billowed out.

'Oh, hell. Carnage!'

Dodging round the edge of the mess. Kaia fetched a broom from the rear of the shed and began to sweep up the sawdust Leidolf had scattered to soak up the spilt varnish.

'Thanks.'

'It's the least I can do.'

With the sawdust in a pile, she was looking for a dustpan and brush as her dog came running into the shed carrying a ball. Leidolf looked flabbergasted.

'She is a master of manifestation. The trick is not to touch the ball, and don't give her eye contact. If you do, you're doomed.'

As if to prove her point, the dog dropped the ball onto the pile of sawdust then launched for it, sending it shooting back across the floor.

'Enough to test the patience of a saint.' Leidolf suddenly froze, humour vanishing from his face. 'Run to the house. Now!'

They sprinted for the house as howling broke out in the forest nearby.

'Stay put. I'll head them off.'

Leidolf raced for the trees. Closing the door, Kaia hurried into the lounge. Should the demons come to the house she needed to be ready. She had used some of the symbols for other things aside from her own healing. She needed to discover what they all could do.

Sitting on the floor, she drew the symbol air. A pale blue hologram appeared to hover in front of her. *Air ... what would air do?* She envisioned wind whooshing through trees and then a tornado, but nothing happened. She dismissed the symbol with an impatient flick of her hand. Instantly the symbol shot across the room and hit a bookshelf. The shelf crashed to the floor, narrowly missing one of the dogs, who made a hasty retreat underneath the coffee table.

'Sorry.' She wasn't sure whether she was apologising to the dog or to Leidolf for breaking his bookcase.

She tried earth. The symbol appeared as a green hologram and like the one before hovered in the air. She moved her hands tentatively towards it, causing the symbol to tremor slightly but nothing more. She drew the wood symbol. It appeared, shimmering a brownish coloured light, but did nothing. *Yet in the forest it created the barrier.*

The earth symbol was still visible, it must be interfering with the energy of the wood one and stopping it from working. She moved her hands to try and rub the earth one out.

The earth symbol spun and overlaid the wood symbol. They did connect, to form a larger and more complicated pattern! She moved her hands instinctively to seal them together. The completed symbol changed colour and slowly rotated. *Now what?* The light code hung in the air as though waiting for her to direct it. Kaia glanced at the broken bookshelf, reluctant to move her hands.

At that moment, deciding that it was safe to come out, the dog crawled from her hiding place. In an instant the light code detected her movement, shot to the ground, hit against the dog and disappeared. Kaia anxiously checked the dog over. She had a pulse, but her body had gone rigid. *Petrified wood.*

'I think you'll be alright,' she whispered, praying the effect would eventually wear off. 'You *are* having a difficult day, but perhaps this is karma for the shed floor. Leidolf did say you would go solid.'

She laid the dog on the sofa and tucked a throw over her, wondering which symbol might help the dog recover. She glanced at the broken bookcase. *Not air!* She drew the symbol for light, and it appeared with its familiar soft glow. Kaia directed it to be around the dog and then, moving her hands, envisioned she was massaging the light into the dog's body, soothing and warming, sending energy back to every fibre and cell. The dog whined, wagged her tail, and finally sat up.

There was movement near the window, and not a demon. Kaia crouched, scooted into the kitchen, and peered out to see Rick disappearing around the side of the house.

She had to get away. Climbing onto the worktop, she opened the kitchen window and dropped to the ground. She ran for the trees, there was the sound of a gun, and a sudden pain in her leg as a dart shot through her leggings. Then everything swam.

CHAPTER 45

H E HAD BEEN CLOSE ON their tail for the last mile. Then, as he scrambled up a small bank to a clearing, the trail suddenly cut off. Fraser instantly knew that the demons had melted into the shadows, and Malphas … he scanned the sky. It had been a ploy. They had led him away on purpose.

He turned to run the way he had come, but paused, instinct telling him that someone was approaching, someone who did not want to be heard. He slunk into a thick patch of ferns at the edge of the clearing and waited.

He was not there long. After a flicker of movement among the trees, a demon wolf appeared from the shadows. Yet the demon was not what he had heard. He eyed it suspiciously as it crossed the clearing, sniffing at the ground to pick up a scent trail.

Even if it wasn't what he had heard, the demon was tracking him now, and he had to keep the element of surprise. Hackles raised, Fraser poised, ready to attack. He waited until the demon was a few feet away and then leapt, knocking the demon to the ground. It snarled in anger, turned its head, and bit, tearing fur from Fraser's shoulder as he reached for its throat. It bit at him again, tearing his ear, but its movement was fatal. Grabbing the exposed throat, Fraser tore with his teeth, and the demon fell to the ground.

There was a whizzing sound, and a sudden sharp pain hit his flank. Fraser growled in anger and turned to face the Skinwalker as he stepped into the clearing, reloading a gun.

'Not using tranquilisers this time.' His tone was mocking as he clicked the barrel shut.

Fraser roared and leapt, sending him sprawling onto the ground. The Skinwalker dropped the gun but fought back and, in a burst of effort, threw him to one side.

Fraser leapt again, tearing at the Skinwalker's throat, revealing not flesh but a thick black substance that oozed like lava from the wound as he fell. The Skinwalker did not get back up. Fraser sniffed at the lava like substance as it solidified. Stone. The Skinwalker was dead.

He ran through the trees to the house, blood draining from the bullet wound in his side. The door was ajar. The wound was preventing him from transfiguring, so he pushed it open with his muzzle and picked up the scent of another Skinwalker. Yet it hadn't gone further than the hallway. Leaving the house, he scouted the ground and picking up the trail again, followed it across the grass to Kaia's, where it stopped.

Fraser walked back and forth, his nose to the ground, trying to ascertain what had happened, but he was losing a lot of blood, his head felt dizzy, and it was hard to stay focussed.

He headed for Alex and May's, getting weaker with each step. Staggering across their drive, he barked. Then finally his strength left him, and he collapsed unconscious at their door.

CHAPTER 46

KAIA TOOK IN THE DARK metal panels on the ceiling and ran her hand along a slimy metal floor. Turning her head to the side she surveyed the grey cell-like room, lit by its one dirty-looking yellow bulb set into the ceiling. Muttering a curse, she tried to stand, but her legs crumpled beneath her. The tranquiliser had still not worn off. Not to be defeated, she crawled across the room, placed her hands on the metal wall, and used it as a support to stand.

Moments later the doorway slid open to reveal Gracilior standing in a dreary corridor. 'This way.'

She must be in the base, only it didn't look like it had before. There was no equipment, no computers, barely any light, and the air smelt rank. It had smelt pungent before, but now the stench of rotting bodies hung so thick in the air, she could barely take a breath. *It must be some sort of substation.* She followed Gracilior along a series of metal-lined tunnels, passing an entrance to a large, dimly lit hangar containing animal pens, the nearest one rammed with cattle and horses.

They turned into another dreary corridor, this one lined with metal pipes down one wall. The size and complexity of the base suddenly struck her. Finding a way through the endless network of corridors was going to be difficult.

Eventually they came to a metal door that slid open to reveal what looked to be a laboratory. Equipment lined the walls. Torturous-looking devices were attached to the ceiling and floor around an oversized dentist's chair, at the foot of which two Skinwalkers were setting a large mirror.

Gracilior pushed her onto the chair and fastened her ankles to it with metal clamps.

'The colonel wants to meet you.'

'I'll not do anything he wants.'

'You'll find he can be very persuasive.'

Grabbing one of her wrists, Gracilior clicked it into a clamp on the side of the chair as the other two Skinwalkers left the room.

Now was her only chance. 'Get away from me, you beast.'

Flicking her fingers through the air, she drew the air symbol and sent it hard at the Gracilior, praying it would work. To her relief it did. Hitting him full in the chest, the symbol knocked the unsuspecting Skinwalker from his feet and flung him against the wall. Before he had the chance to retaliate, she drew the symbols for earth and wood, and as they joined, she threw them at him.

Gracilior froze, his face set in an angry snarl. Yet the symbols might not hold indefinitely and the other Skinwalkers could come back at any moment. She had to get out fast. Reaching to her ankles she tried to free them from the clamps, but they refused to open. She looked around frantically and spying an evil-looking spike set on one of the arms attached to the ceiling, she drew the air symbol again. She whipped her hand causing the symbol to knock against the arm, lowering it within her reach. Straining against the restriction of the clamps, she pulled the spike nearer, jammed it into the opening slot of the wrist clamp, and prised it open. It fell with a clatter as she set to work on the clamps restraining her ankles. *Come on.* Gritting her teeth she opened one and then wiggled the spike in the other. There was a click, it cracked open, and after pulling her foot free she ran for the open door.

She raced back along the corridor. Moments later she heard running footsteps behind her, and a siren sounded. Guessing her escape had been discovered, she turned down a different corridor and ducked inside an open doorway.

She was in an abattoir. Crates filled with crudely cut sections of animals were stacked high along one side of the room. On the other, two Skinwalkers were hacking up what looked to be horses.

'... finish this lot, then get the rest. There's more due in later, he wants the pen empty.'

Keeping to the crates Kaia crept past, hoping the room would lead on to the animal hangar. A loud voice sounded in the doorway behind her.

'Seen a woman?'

'If we had, she would be among this lot.'

'Search the room anyway.'

Weaving her way through the crates, Kaia found what she was looking for. The abattoir did have a large garage like door that led directly into the animal pens. She scooted into the hangar and found herself ankle-deep in urine and faeces. The noise from the confined animals was chilling. Cattle bellowed, and horses screamed, as they clambered over one another in a bid to be free from their confinement.

Kaia had an idea. Sliding the metal bolt on a pen containing horses she flung its gate open. The horses charged, high on adrenaline, their eyes wild, and snorting like steam trains. She raced to another pen and released cattle. They also charged, stampeding through the hangar as she opened another pen and then another.

The Skinwalkers knew where she was but couldn't get to her for stampeding animals. Racing to the rear of the hangar, she opened a portal. Sensing a way of escape the animals began to stream through, but she didn't follow. Instead, she opened another portal to the base above.

CHAPTER 47

◆ ◆ ◆

THE VEHICLE HANGAR WAS ALSO filled with the sound of an alarm. Kaia quickly closed the portal and reaching into the back of a parked pickup truck, grabbed the jacket and cap that had been left lying on the top of some crates. She put on the jacket, twisted her hair under the cap, and pulled the peak well down over her forehead to obscure her face. Then she picked up one of the crates and crossed the hangar to the main corridor, nearly bumping into a troop of Skinwalkers as they came hurrying in response to the alarm.

'Watch it!'

She stood to the side and let them pass, nodding by way of apology. Then continued along the empty corridor to the transmission tower.

She walked slowly round the tower, cursing its height, and reached for the narrow ladder.

'You bitch!'

Gracilior was on her and looked ready to explode. Kaia raced around the bottom of the tower and ducked behind pipework, then doubled back to the ladder after he had run past.

Yet Gracilior was not so easily tricked. She had just started the climb when she felt him grab her ankle. She kicked out, but he held her fast, pulling to dislodge her. Hooking her arm over a rung, she drew the air symbol and pushed it at him.

The symbol hit Gracilior in the face, shot him across the hanger, and slammed him into equipment against the far wall. He cursed at the metal pipe now protruding through his left shoulder, glared at her with hatred, and then began pulling himself free.

Focussing on the ladder, she climbed fast and was halfway up when it began to shake. Guessing Gracilior was now on the ladder below her, she increased her pace, willing herself not to look down.

Once at the top, she crawled onto the narrow ledge circling the dome. Her knees were shaking, and her hands, damp with sweat, slipped against the glass as she sidestepped along the ledge. Coming to a tiny door, she slid it open and let her body fall through.

The dome housed an array of circuitry and a set of steps leading to a mirrored chamber that housed the crystal. It was set into a piece of apparatus that crackled and sparked with electricity. She approached a control panel and began to work various buttons and switches.

Gracilior leapt through the door.

She drew the fire symbol as he made to grab her, but this time he was prepared and dodged. The symbol hit the glass, and a section melted as Gracilior lunged again. She ducked out of reach and drew wood and earth. They merged, hit him in the chest, and he froze.

Kaia drew several fire symbols and sent them spinning at the circuitry. With a crackling and popping sound it shut down and then burst into flames. She raced up the steps and yanked the crystal free as a sudden explosion came from the control panel. The fire spread rapidly. Rushing back past Gracilior, she made for the door as the dome began to melt like wax.

She was halfway down the ladder when it juddered. Gracilior was on the ladder. Glancing up, she saw his bulky form above her and the dome crumpling inwards. She was running out of time. Leaning in and holding onto the sides of the ladder, Kaia took her feet off the rungs and let her body plummet to the floor. She raced away as the tower began to topple, and over her shoulder she saw it fall like an enormous tree, with Gracilior still hanging onto the ladder. With its integrity weakened, the weight of the Skinwalker caused the ladder to break away, and Gracilior hit the ground still holding onto it, seconds before the burning tower landed on top of him and exploded.

Immediately the fire started to spread. Kaia darted through the chamber as a fire alarm sounded and triggered sprinklers. Soon the chamber was filled with thick mist and smoke. She ran back the way she had come, dodging figures scurrying through the smoke.

Rick.

She peered through the gloom to where Rick was addressing another Skinwalker. 'We cannot afford for fracking to be compromised. The doorway is almost open. Have you checked if this blasted water has shut off the system?'

'No.'

Rick muttered his opinion of the other's incompetence and marched for a nearby corridor. Keeping close on his heels, Kaia followed him to the room containing the monolith's control. Rick typed in a password, and instantly a series of maps marked with red dots appeared.

'I know you're here, Kaia. You always have as much finesse as an elephant.'

This wasn't Rick. No matter what he said, it wasn't him. Yet despite knowing Rick was dead, a wave of old resentment washed through her as he turned to face her.

'Been having fun in that clapped-out heap of shit you drive around in, swanning around Skye like you've nothing better to do? Magazine to café, bit of a comedown, even for you.' He took a step nearer.

Rick was dead.

'Then you always were a joke. Proved it too, turning up to that fancy do as a banana. What a slap in the face to all the idiots who said you should model.'

One more step and he'd be near enough to grab her.

'Pity I couldn't get a lemon. Right colour, wrong fruit. I—'

He didn't get the chance to finish. He froze as the symbol slammed into his chest.

'Agaricus, Rick was always such an arse!'

She drew the symbol for fire. There was a pause, the computer system burst into flames, and seconds later the red dots on the map started to disappear. Certain that the monoliths could no longer function, Kaia opened a portal and leapt through.

CHAPTER 48

$\mathcal{A}$LEX'S BLUE CAR WAS PARKED outside the house. Closing the portal, Kaia raced into the kitchen, expecting to see Alex and Leidolf. Yet only Alex was there, sitting at the kitchen table with her dogs by his feet, having a heated debate with someone on the other end of the phone. Seeing her arrive at the door, he cut the person off and stood to hug her, as her two dogs leapt around them, equally delighted with her safe return.

'Kaia! Thank God! I've not been able to get any help from the authorities as it's been less than a day. Where did they take you?'

'Dartmoor.'

'Christ.' He noticed she was holding a crystal shard. 'Bloody hell!'

'Had to make the most of a free lift to their base. Where's Leidolf? He went after the demons.'

'He's in bad shape, Kaia.' Alex grabbed his jacket from the chair. 'He made it to our place. May is doing what she can. Come on, you two.' He whistled for her dogs to follow him out.

The kitchen hadn't been ransacked. Rick had no doubt been so delighted in shooting her with tranquiliser, that he hadn't searched for the crystal. She hurried into the lounge and collected the shard from its hiding place behind the wood burner, then grabbing her jacket followed Alex from the house, taking both shards with her.

Alex screamed the car to his house, bouncing through potholes as though he was driving an off-road vehicle.

'How bad is it?'

'He got shot. The vet has taken out the bullet, but it's bad. He lost a lot of blood and is fading. The vet says there's nothing more he can do.'

'Vet?'

Alex swerved to miss a particularly bad pothole, then swerved the other way to avoid an oncoming car. 'How much has Leidolf told you about animi?'

'Demon hunters. Can change form. Immortal unless killed in battle. Oh Christ!'

'Yeah. It's evident from his coat, Fraser had been fighting demons. I don't know who shot him, but the bloody shot counts as being part of a battle.'

May had made a bed for Fraser by the fire and was in the process of attaching an IV bag. 'God bless the vet, but he doesn't know what we know. We must make sure Fraser has the right balance for a human.'

It looked bad. Fraser's fur had been shaven where the bullet had been removed, his ear was shredded, and other clumps of fur had been pulled away from where he had fought a demon. His eyes were open but frozen as though he were already dead. Collapsing to her knees Kaia drew the symbols and sent them into his body. She held her breath as the bullet wound changed. The dried blood cleared, the cut shrank, and the flesh around the wound looked a healthier colour. However, as the symbols faded the effect reversed.

'No! No!'

She drew the symbols again, tears starting to stream down her face. The same thing happened. The wound started to close, only to reopen as the symbols vanished into Fraser's body.

She made to draw them again, but May caught hold of her arm. 'I think it's because he is animi,' she said softly. 'Immortal unless killed in battle. He wasn't even strong enough to change back, Kaia. He lost a lot of blood. I think you are healing the human and the wolf, but the symbols aren't powerful enough to heal his magical side.'

'Then you think he is going to die?' She whispered the words, not wanting to hear herself say them.

'We'll do what we can, but I've got to be honest. It's not looking good.'

Her tears were replaced by a surge of rage. She picked up the two crystal shards, stuffed them into a rucksack and then stormed from the house.

CHAPTER 49

K AIA STOOD AT THE TOP of the Fairy Pools and stared at the side of the mountain in dismay. The rock veneer that had covered the carved doorway had vanished, and instead an enormous arched cave entrance led into the mountain.

The doorway's open!

She scrambled across to the cave mouth and listened for any sign of Scathchornail. There was nothing. In fact, she was suddenly aware that the entire glen had gone deathly still. There were no birds, no breeze stirred, and everything was silent as though holding its breath. Drawing the light symbol, she set it hovering in front of her and then cautiously stepped forward.

The inside of the cave was normal enough, a tunnel of rock with water dripping from the walls. This did make a sound, echoing eerily through the gloom. Smaller tunnels and passageways led off from either side, but Kaia ignored these and followed the main tunnel as it twisted deeper underground.

Eventually she came to a chamber lined with some sort of fluorescent mineral that glowed in the light cast by the symbol, and here a spiral staircase had been carved into the rock. She slowly descended then followed another tunnel to where it opened out as an enormous cavern.

Stalagmites and stalactites grew from the ceiling and floor, and in places, these had joined together forming huge columns of rock, which created the impression of a cloistered walkway around the edge of the dark lake that expanded across the centre of the cavern floor.

She hurried to the edge of the lake as a dark swirling mist began to form over its surface in the shape of a small hurricane. The lake itself was as black as a night sky, and instead of reflecting the light emanating from the symbol, it absorbed it like a black hole. She tentatively reached out.

Hell.

She touched not liquid but some strange thick mist. The lake was not water at all but a dark energy, as cold as ice. *Shadow Side.*

Taking the two crystal shards from the rucksack, Kaia placed them on the ground in front of her. She had to join them together and fast. The swirling mist was gaining momentum, and in the centre of the vortex, a shadowy form wearing a Victorian suit and top hat had started to appear. *Scathchornail.*

You're too late.

Tendrils of black mist reached from the vortex towards her. She flicked her hand and sent the light symbol at them. The tendrils retracted but then re-formed and reached for her from a different direction. Focusing on the shards, Kaia drew all the symbols and sent them into the crystals. They flared with light, the tendrils retracted, but the shards did not join. She needed all the elements, and she hadn't got the symbol for water.

The vortex was getting larger, the figure within it looked clearer, and a menacing laughter filled the cave as the black tendrils stretched towards her, now thicker and darker than before.

You have failed. Again!

Scathchornail looked more solid, and behind him she could now see a large black crystal that was emitting dark energy, the same energy that had filled the transmission dome.

There will be no light. Earth will be mine. Atlantia will fall.

Atlantia. Water. Ianna had been water fae, merfolk. Ianna had become Meg. Now Meg and she had merged. *I'm the missing element!*

She was suddenly aware of the interior of the cave, the rock, the water dripping down it, the air in the cave ... *the Druid. Mrs Mack's book.* That was the answer! She knew what to do, and she needed the space in which to do it.

Turning to face the direction she intuited was north, she drew the Celtic Druid symbol that represented earth, then turned a quarter clockwise to face the rock that had been at her right. *East.* She drew the Druid symbol to represent air, then turned again to draw the one for fire facing south and finally drew the one representing water at the west. Having cast the circle around her, she drew the light symbol again and sent it to the roof of the cave where it exploded, filling the circle she had drawn with light. The tendrils immediately retracted to the outside of her boundary.

Kaia quickly drew the light symbol again, along with the other symbols, and sent them spinning into her circle. Then clutching the two shards together, she connected to who she was as a human being, as an Atlantian, and as the Dragon Fae. Then she began to sing her healing song.

The crystals flared with intense light as she closed her eyes. She focused on being at one with the sky, an expanse of blue, with sunsets and sunrises stretching across different lands. Then she was those lands, along with the rivers that criss crossed over them. She breathed, following the energy of the water cycle. She was the sea, the clouds, the rain, and the air within the sky. … She was all things. She was within all things, and she was within the crystal she was holding. She was complete, she was whole, and so was the crystal. A surge of energy flashed through her body, and looking down, she saw the shards merge in her blue webbed hands. Ignoring the transformation of her body, she closed the circle and plunged the crystal, now a burning white star, into the lake.

Stop her!

Agaricus stepped from a triangular portal behind her. She drew the wood and earth symbols to stun him and then sent energy through the Dragon's Heart to the dark crystal she could see behind Scathchornail. The dark crystal shattered as bolts of electric black showered around her.

Gritting her teeth, Kaia held her ground and turned her attention back to the lake. Scathchornail disappeared, the vortex faded, and the dark energy of the lake began to solidify. However, the energy of the light symbol present in the cave caused Agaricus to come round sooner. Taking one hand from the crystal, she drew the air symbol and sent it spinning towards him as he made to grab her. Agaricus staggered and fell into the solidifying energy. As he tried to clamber free, she created the symbol a second time, knocking him farther in, but he stood again, taking cumbersome steps towards her, as though wading through thick toffee.

Replacing both hands on the crystal, Kaia drew on all her strength. There was a final flare, and the lake turned to solid rock, trapping Agaricus within it.

She stopped sending energy. Immediately the light from the crystal retracted, with dramatic effect. The lake surface began to quiver and crack.

An earthquake!

She had no time to waste. She sprinted back along the cave and raced up the stairway. The rock walls were crumbling, and behind her the ceiling of the tunnel began to fall in. She leapt for the cave mouth and cleared the entrance just as it collapsed behind her.

She stood shaking with exertion as the dust settled. She didn't think it was enough, but she needed the crystal for something else first. She gazed down at her Atlantian body. *Needs amendment.* Envisioning her appearance as Kaia, she imagined roots at her feet, grounding her energy to earth. Her Atlantian traits instantly disappeared and opening a portal she leapt through.

+ + + ◆ + +

May and Alex didn't say a word as she raced into their lounge holding the crystal.

Kneeling by Fraser, Kaia sang as she had in the cave, causing the crystal to again flare its intense white light. She directed the light at Fraser's body, not seeing his wounds but instead envisioning him running through the forest, smelling the intense fragrance of the pine and the forest floor. Then she pictured him as Leidolf, running along the shore, healthy, whole, magical, and healed. She stopped singing, and the light from the crystal faded.

It was not Fraser lying on the floor but Leidolf, his wolf tattoo looking as though it had just been drawn. He sat up and stretched, glancing at the drip bag and May's open hospital bag that was on the floor nearby.

'That was a close call. Thanks, all of you.'

'There is one more thing I have to do.'

Leaving the croft, Kaia opened a portal back to the mountain. Thin black tendrils were now visible within the rocks from the collapsed tunnel. The vortex had closed, but the doorway was not yet sealed. Activating the Dragon's Heart for the third time, she sent its energy at the mountainside where the doorway had been. There was an enormous groan as though the mountain was waking, and she saw the ornate carved doors of Shadow Side standing firmly intact. Yet still this wasn't enough.

Pulling on all her strength she slammed the glowing crystal against the closed doors. The was an immense surge of light as the doorway absorbed the crystal, and then the rock turned smooth as it disappeared.

Rocks began to fall and rumble down the mountainside as the mountain shook as though waking from a nightmare. Moments later it fell silent, the dust settled, and there was nothing to show that there had ever been a doorway there at all.

CHAPTER 50

IT WAS SEVEN O'CLOCK THE following morning. She stood in Leidolf's kitchen looking out the window. She had called Bella early, wanting to catch her before she left for work, but despite the hour Bella was already in the office.

'I'm giving him another chance. Maybe I'm feeling so lenient because I've had such a good breakfast, and JD is now my eunuch slave!'

'Thus speaks Kali. I'm glad it's worked out.'

Bella shuffled some letters on her desk and then spoke again. 'I'd best go. Layna is on her way up, and she is on form. In fact, she has levelled up since being run down by the stampeding cattle and horses that suddenly appeared in the park.'

Kaia sniggered. There was something immensely satisfying about the image of cool, collected Layna being discombobulated by a herd of animals. 'It was the first place that popped into my mind when I opened the portal. I didn't think they would be any trouble in a park. I thought they would get rescued!'

'They did. It's Layna's karma. Like I said, Kali is in you too, girl!' With that, Bella rang off.

Putting her phone on the table, Kaia poured coffee into a mug and then went along to the work shed to find Leidolf. He was busy painting varnish on Wilma's new cottage door. She stood in the doorway watching him work, remembering how she had seen him in her visions. First as Owen in the great plaid kilt, and then as Leidolf in the same beanie hat that he was currently wearing.

'I know you're watching me, woman.' He flashed a grin, his green flecked eyes mirroring his merriment.

She met his gaze, and his expression changed. His look was that of a wolf, alert, astute, perceptive.

She smiled, set the mug of coffee down on the bench, and kissed him on the cheek. 'I'm just going for a run and swim. I'll be back for breakfast.'

She ran round the loch shore to where she knew Pendragon would be grazing. Then, discarding her clothes, she waded into the sea. Focusing on the water and her connection to it, she dove, stretching out her fingers to maximise the effect of the webbing which now connected them. She scoured the seaweed.

There, a movement among the plants gave away the form of the kelpie. Lowering herself into the kelp, she silently swam nearer. When she was near enough, she grabbed hold of the kelpie's tail.

Pendragon startled and raced for the shore as fast as lightning. Leaping from the water, he transformed into a white stallion and unceremoniously deposited her onto the sand. Kaia burst out laughing, joy exploding within her as Pendragon reared in delight.

Ianna! Let's run!

EPILOGUE

Her brain no longer seemed phased by the fantastical. It was like Bella had said, the ego's perception got smashed to pieces, but that allowed you to grow into new constructs and acceptance of things.

The End

www.ingramcontent.com/pod-product-compliance
Ingram Content Group UK Ltd.
Pitfield, Milton Keynes, MK11 3LW, UK
UKHW041618190225
455269UK00001B/16

9 781982 289591